Alfred J Bamford

Turbans and Tails

or, Sketches in the Unromantic East

Alfred J Bamford

Turbans and Tails
or, Sketches in the Unromantic East

ISBN/EAN: 9783744766586

Printed in Europe, USA, Canada, Australia, Japan

Cover: Foto ©Andreas Hilbeck / pixelio.de

More available books at **www.hansebooks.com**

TURBANS AND TAILS;

OR,

Sketches in the Unromantic East.

BY

ALFRED J. BAMFORD, B.A.

"I pity the man who can travel from Dan to Beersheba, and cry, ''Tis all barren.'" STERNE.

LONDON:

SAMPSON LOW, MARSTON, SEARLE, & RIVINGTON,

LIMITED,

St. Dunstan's House,

FETTER LANE, FLEET STREET, E.C.

1888.

PREFACE.

THE times past may suffice for the publication of entire diaries by globe-trotters and holiday makers in the East. There be many who say that its faiths have been enumerated and analysed, its races catalogued and discussed, its mountains and plains, its seas and rivers described and pictured with sufficient completeness. Yet as long as different men in looking at the same object see different things, a few chapters of selected reminiscence may find a friendly welcome even though the reminiscence be of residence in well-known cities and travel along well-beaten tracks. In this hope the writer offers these pages to the public. He has made no endeavour after the conscientious exhaustiveness of treatment which marks the work of those who write for the instruction of their fellows. He writes avowedly for their recreation. Though he deals with subjects which he has studied with some care and in which his interest is deep, he claims no authority as an exponent of them and does not venture to ask the attention of the serious student.

These pages have been penned during holidays and at long intervals—some in the early days of first and deep impressions, others in later years when scenes and customs once striking had become weary, stale, flat and unprofitable—but always *con amore.* They have been to the writer as the labour we delight in that physics pain and that is, therefore, a pleasure when less voluntary tasks would be sadly irksome. Nevertheless, the line—" Easy writing's curs'd hard reading," has been warningly and, it is hoped, profitably kept in mind. They have been written leisurely but not lazily. The writer has found pleasure in them but has spared no pains.

TETTENHALL,
January 25th, 1888.

CONTENTS.

THE MILD HINDU.

THE MAN OF HAN.

THE MILD HINDU.

"Dusk faces with white turbans wreathed."
MILTON. *Paradise Regained.*

"Mislike me not for my complexion—
The shadow'd livery of the burnish'd sun,
To whom I am a neighbour and near bred."
SHAKSPERE. *Merchant of Venice.*

"Occidental manhood springs from [self-respect] as its basis.
Oriental manhood finds the greatest satisfaction in self-abasement.
There is no use in trying to graft the tropical palm upon the
northern pine. The same Divine forces underlie the growth of
both, but leaf and flower and fruit must follow the law of race, of
soil, of climate."—O. W. HOLMES. *Poet at the Breakfast-Table.*

"He was a scholar, and a ripe and good one;
Exceeding wise, fair-spoken, and persuading."
SHAKSPERE. *Henry VIII.*

THE MILD HINDU.

CHAPTER I.

BABUDOM.

THE WESTERN VENEER.

THE Calcutta Babu is a character that ought to be well-known, if not well-understood, by Englishmen. He has been often described, nor does he shrink from self-exhibition : he is sensible of no temptation to hide his light under a bushel.

What the oriental gentleman was like before contamination by Western influences it is difficult for a resident in the Calcutta of to-day to imagine. The babu now is what the combination of hereditary instincts and European customs has made him, and, when we think how strangely incongruous a combination this is, we should be prepared to find some startling results. Oriental courtesy is associated with oriental shiftiness, insincerity and craft—with the oriental character in fact, than which nothing could be more unlike the sturdy manliness and the reckless justice which are part of the best side of the British character. The Eastern thinks the Western a barbarian —savage and unmannerly; the Western thinks the Eastern a sycophant—servile, cringing and treacherous. But the babu as he flourishes in Calcutta is a strange endeavour to combine the two, and the effect is not without a ludicrous side. If he attempts, as he not infrequently does, the frank demeanour of the Western in addressing you, he is pretty certain to be rude instead of frank, but unconsciously, this being a distinction he has not apprehended. To dispense with ceremony is, with him, to be discourteous ; for ceremony, hollow and meaningless, covering the most unblushing selfishness, is the only form of courtesy he knows anything about. What will it profit me ? is the question he asks about everything, nor is he ready to believe that any man can act from disinterested motives. It is hard to persuade him that there is such a thing as a gratitude that is as lively a sense of favours received as of favours to come, or that mutual regard may command service irrespective of considerations of advantage.

When a babu calls on you and begins to pour out all sorts of fulsome compliments, it will save much time if you interpose the question, "Babu, what is the request with which you intend to conclude these general remarks ? " He will think that you have failed in the etiquette of the occasion, which required a more circumlocutory method, but he will be in no wise disconcerted, and will at once proceed, since such is your pleasure, to ask the favour which is the object of his visit. I speak from experience, having thus saved a good deal of time.

There is an absence of disguise about the babu's selfishness which is almost charming. He sees no reason to hide it; why should he, since, as he assumes, it is universal? He is simply careful to observe a certain sequence in the expression of it. His ceremoniousness does not serve so much to cloak as to introduce it.

Then there is connected with this selfishness a wonderful sense of self-importance. Fulsome is his flattery, loud are his expressions of admiration of you and of depreciation of himself, but these formulæ are understood to represent nothing. The particular babu speaking to you at any time is always the centre of the universe, and you have been born into the world for the high honour of serving his ends. I remember how, before residence in the East had destroyed the capacity for astonishment, my servant brought up a card, and on my sending my salaam, a spruce young babu was ushered in. He told me that he had heard of me, and, from his description of my worth, it was evident that he had heard a great deal more than I should have felt at liberty to tell him. My erudition, my generosity, my philanthropy, and all kindred virtues were, I found, world-known—as was also my influence with the Director of Public Instruction. Here was a hint of the practical point, and, after some more compliments, I found that the young man was a candidate for some vacancy in the educational department, "and

I think," he proceeded, "that your honour will be good
enough to write to Mr. ——, saying that you hope I
may receive the appointment." "But, babu," I replied,
"if I write to Mr. —— I must tell the truth, and,
since I never saw you till just now, how can I con-
scientiously say that I hope anything of the kind?"
"Surely you *do* wish that I may get the appointment?"
This with an air of astonishment great enough to
astonish me. "I wish," I said, when I recovered
myself a little, "I wish that the best qualified man
among the various candidates may receive it, and, if
you should be the best qualified, I wish that you may
receive it, but not otherwise." His astonishment
seemed to increase, and that I should look him in the
face and venture to say that there might be circumstances in which I could wish another rather than him
to obtain the appointment he sought, was doubtless
recorded in his memory as another instance—perhaps a
flagrant one—of the want of manners of the "savage
Englishman."

Such interviews as these were frequent, and the calm
expectation that, apart from their qualifications or your
knowledge of them, you would interest yourself to get
your visitors coveted appointments, remained interesting for a time even after the marvel wore off, till at
last the interest was also lost and it became tire-
some.

Similar applications were often made by letter. The
following is the copy of a letter received by a friend of
mine on his obtaining an appointment as registrar of a

government department that had been for a time merged in the Home Department, but was now "resurrected," as my friend's correspondents put it. I give the letter as a sample rather than an exception.

"Calcutta, — ——, 18—.

" *To* —— —— Esq.,

" *Registrar of the Department* —— *and* ——, *Simla.*

" HIGHLY HONOURED SIR,

"We your most obedient and humble slaves hasten with hurried feet to congratulate Your Honour on his exaltation to the Head of the New Department of Government. This auspicious event your petitioners always expected and daily prayed for, and Providence has at length fulfilled our earnest desires. For why did we so desire? Because we were fully persuaded of your Honour's kind heart, and consideration for such lowly but not undeserving creatures as your poor petitioners.

"We solicit that out of your bountiful nature you will be kind enough to grant each of your abject slaves a situation as Chuprassie in the Department under your Honour's feet.

"Your Highness is intimately acquainted with our good character and our expertness and zeal in the Home Department, as well as in the late lamented but now resurrected R. A. and C. Department ('O, Abolishment! where is thy victory!')

"We beg your Honour will grant the boon we solicit as if we begged for it personally and not through this petition-writer, who cannot give Quite expression to our feelings.

> " Your most humble servants,
>> " BISESSUR PAPREE-Durwan, H.D.,
>> " HUR PAUL Chaprassie,
>>> " Home Department."

" P.S.—The petition-writer begs for a post of 25 Rs. a month.

>> " SHIREH MITTER.
>> " (Bisessur knows.)"

It would be easy to multiply specimens of this kind of thing. I content myself, however, with these two instances.

A great desire after things English possesses these babus. This is not out of any sense of their superiority, but in the hope of one day being able to turn them to good account. In their hearts they think far more highly of themselves than of us, but, for the profit of those said selves, they will make considerable efforts to acquire the English language, to become acquainted with English customs, and to obtain familiar intercourse with English people. The eagerness with which they take the University of Calcutta by force is remarkable, and the rage for degrees is such that I have heard it jokingly said that every shopkeeper in Old China Bazar is a graduate of the university. The perseverance exhibited by candidates in presenting themselves year after year at an examination, which successive attempts have already proved to be too severe for them, is most praiseworthy. Less praiseworthy are the methods sometimes adopted. The Bengali is allowed by all to have a certain smartness, and this is too often seen in the skill with which he will reap that whereon he has bestowed no labour. Some years ago the questions for the various examinations were lithographed in the city and innumerable were the tricks of fertile brains by which the candidates obtained illicit knowledge of them. One of the examiners in the Arts course told me of an ingenious youth who, by some means having gained access to the room where the lithographing was going on, seized a favourable opportunity of sitting down upon the stone, and walked home in the happy consciousness that on his own person he bore a private printing-press with which he might print off the secrets of the dread examiners. The university now attempts to secure itself against such tricks by obtaining the questions from the examiners in time to permit of their being sent to England to be printed, the printed copies returning by post direct to the hands of the authorities. As an additional security the examiners are requested not to keep duplicate copies of their questions in India, and it is felt now, with a degree of confidence, that there is little chance of any candidate seeing them till he meets them fairly in the examination-room.

This thirst for academic distinction shows itself in yet another way. Familiar as I was with the abbreviations adopted at home to represent university standing, I found myself puzzled when I read in the papers advertisements in which babus sought for educational appointments, or tutorial engagements, and signed themselves R. C. Ghose, F.A., or Chandra Nath Mukerji, F.A. "What is this degree of F.A.? Is it Father of Arts?" So I questioned, and it was explained to me that the Calcutta students are required to pass, first, an entrance examination, then an intermediate examination, which, in the Arts Faculty, is commonly known as the First Arts, after which comes the graduating examination, success in which gives the degree of Bachelor. Having passed the intermediate, or First Arts examination, a man has not yet graduated, and is not entitled to append letters to his name implying that he has a degree, and undergraduates of corresponding standing in our home universities would not dream of such a thing. But here *nous avons changé tout cela;* if a man has passed this intermediate examination it is considered far too great an accomplishment for the world to be left in ignorance of it, and he proudly wears the letters, F.A., behind his name.

But I soon met with a stranger phenomenon still. For some Siva Nath Chatterjea, failed-F.A., or Kali Charan Mittra, failed-B.A., would be asking for a post as master of a school—or for any other equally lucrative employment. To have been "up for an exam.," even if the result has not justified the attempt, is counted something, and many a babu did I find rejoicing thus in the honours of failure. He had at least got a handle to his name, and if he could write himself "Failed-F.A.," it was at least a proof that he had passed the entrance examination, while, if he could write " Failed-B.A.," it was a proof that he had succeeded at the F.A.

There was indeed even more in it than this. The eagerness with which students rush to the university makes some sort of sifting process necessary, and no student is allowed to present himself who does not come accredited from one or other of the affiliated colleges. The professors of the colleges hold preliminary examinations of their own students, and are only supposed to give the certificates, on which they are admitted to the examinations at the university, to those who may be supposed to stand a chance of passing. So that to have failed at the B.A. or F.A. examination at the university, implies having passed at the preliminary and corresponding examinations at the college. But it need hardly be said that the professors are apt to exercise a lenient judgment in this matter, and, appealed to by their students, as I have myself seen, in the most beseeching manner, they often do not find it in their heart to debar a man from going into the examination-room though morally certain that his highest success will be a " Failed-B.A.," or " Failed-F.A.," as the case may be.

In illustration of the practices which these men will adopt for the sake of perfecting themselves in the English language, I may instance the following :—A middle-aged babu called one day and said that he was a tutor in one of the government colleges, but he would much like to come and study the Bible with me. He was not a Christian, he said, but was deeply interested in the Christian Scriptures and would like to know more about them. Having a prejudice against being imposed upon and being a little suspicious of my visitor's motive, I kept him in talk for a little while and found that he expected me to give him an hour a day regularly, himself fixing the hour—one not very convenient to me. Suspecting his real motive to be to get out of me six hours a week gratuitous instruction in English language, literature, and conversation, I proposed to him that, as I could not devote so large a proportion of my time as he proposed to mission work which was outside my sphere, he should go to a friend of mine. I then mentioned the name of a missionary of ripe experience, who had, of course, command of the living Bengali tongue, and who had also given special attention to the study of the Vedas, and was indeed in every way qualified to help a sincere Hindu inquirer. But there was one small matter that made my proposal serve as a test of my visitor's sincerity. This missionary came from the northern part of the island of Great Britain, and, notwithstanding long residence in India, talked broad Scotch. The babu knew enough of my friend to lead him to detect my motive. He admitted that, after all, he did not care very much about the contents of the Bible, that he wanted to improve his English pronunciation, and that he was afraid Mr. —— would not be of much service to him.

Of course it may be said that I ought, as a Christian man, even on detecting the babu's insincerity, to have given him the time he wanted, and so have given myself the opportunity of influencing him towards Christianity. Now this is precisely what most of the missionary societies which are represented in Bengal are doing in their colleges, which some ardent supporters of missions feel to be outside the legitimate province of the missionary. The babus wish an English education ; the offer is made to them, " Come and study the Bible among other books, and we will give it you." There is I imagine a considerable diversity of opinion among the missionaries themselves as to the relative worth of education and bazar preaching as a means of evangel-ising, and the advocates of neither can bring crushing evidence against the other in the form of apparent results. On the one hand, men have been spending a lifetime in preaching in the bazars and have nothing to show for it. On the other, students pass through a full college course and leave the institution with as little apparent evidence of change of heart as when they entered. But it is a noteworthy fact that most of the converts to Christianity of late years have been men who have previously passed through one or other of the various missionary colleges. They may not seek baptism till years afterwards, and then at a different place, and at the hands of missionaries of another society ; but I believe I am right in saying that nearly all recent additions to the native church from without have been by the accession of those who have passed under the influence of missionary professors.

Objection is urged against these colleges sometimes
on the ground that so many of the tutors in them are
heathen, or, at least, non-Christian. I once met a good
lady who was a strong advocate of mission-work, but
who had been greatly scandalised on paying a visit to a
missionary college in Northern India, where she had
seen men at the teachers' desks with the sectarian
marks on their foreheads, proclaiming the sect of the
Saivas or of the Vaishnavas to which they belonged.
But this would seem to be inevitable. The bargain
with the student is, If you will put yourself under our
Christian influence and give up so much time a day or
a week to Biblical study, we will provide you with
teachers, lectures and classes, by which you may be
prepared for the university examination you wish to
pass. It will hardly be denied that the college
authorities may teach their students geography and
mathematics, through Hindu teachers of these subjects,
and, to many of us, insisting on a man's receiving his
Euclid through a Christian teacher would seem to be
parallel to insisting on his buying his rice of a Christian
dealer. Be this as it may, enough qualified Christian
tutors have not hitherto been forthcoming. In fact, so
great is the demand for Christian natives of sufficient
teaching qualification, that some fear may well be felt
lest a premium be set on hypocrisy. Since the head-
ships of branch schools in the mofussil, where there are
no Europeans, are never given to heathen teachers,
there is always a demand for Christian scholars, and on
this account, a Christian graduate can command a higher

salary than a Hindu graduate of the same standing. This fact contains a reason which many a native would consider sufficient for becoming a " Christian."

The missionary colleges, where religious instruction is part of the curriculum, are able to compete with the government colleges, from which it is strictly excluded, by the simple method of charging lower fees. It is not unlikely that some of the non-success of the former, as Christianising agents, is due to the influence of the latter. The British government, with a justice more severe than the Hindu can appreciate, forbids Christian teaching in its colleges, and to insure the carrying out of this principle of religious impartiality and abstinence it may even happen that in filling those college-chairs preference is sometimes given to men of agnostic or positivist views. Now this neutrality of the state in religious matters cannot but meet with the approval of British free-churchmen. But there are two facts in the light of which this attitude has been very puzzling to the Hindu. The first fact is that the sovereign of Great Britain is the head of the established church. The attitude of professed neutrality assumed in India by that sovereign's government in relation to a faith of which she is the acknowledged head and defender is difficult to the Hindu understanding and suggests a suspicion that the government must be in reality adverse to be professedly neutral. The second fact is that those trained in the traditions of state-establishments of religion are inclined to regard a country which supports a form of Christian faith as a Christian country, and to teach accordingly that Christianity is the religion of England. The Hindu who has been thus instructed, and then sees men approved by the British government, and honoured with professorial responsibility in spite of, and it may even seem to him in some measure because of, non-Christian convictions, knows not what to think, and complains, " I have been deceived. I was told that Christianity is the religion of the English, and I find it is the religion of a section only. It is not the religion of the scholars of England, but of the uncultured only." This charge of deception may be just as against those who claim that their country is Christian because it supports with the wealth and prestige of the whole the church of a part, but it is unjust against the free-churchmen who have not taught that Christianity is the religion of England, but that it is the religion of all who believe in Christ independently of nationality, and that they only are Christians who are disciples of Christ.*

Just or unjust, however, the effect is to make agnostics and positivists of the native students. As with much readiness they once accepted the opinion that all the English were Christians, they now seem

---

* The same criticism applies to the statement occasionally heard that the work of the missionary is oftentimes sorely hindered by the immoral lives of his fellow-countrymen, which are so many proofs that Christian morality is not universally accepted in the land from which he has come. This would be found to be a less hindrance if the missionary could make it clear that he is not preaching the religion of England or of America, but the Gospel of the Son of Man.

equally ready to suppose that, at least, most English scholars are agnostics. This surely is a state of things making educational work an essential department of a Missionary Society's labours. In the missionary colleges the students have the advantage—no mean one in some cases — of familiar intercourse with Englishmen who are as scholarly as Christian. Doubtless they too often judge their professors by themselves, and assume that their Christianity is the result of their salaries, that they teach what they are paid to teach, and that they would as fervently teach the direct contrary if they saw an opportunity of doubling their income by so doing. That this is not always the case we would fain believe. In not a few instances the students are capable of recognising and honouring the sterling qualities of our Christian missionaries, and every such capacity is at once an evidence and a means of grace. If we might judge by their words, indeed, it would be understating the case to speak of this as occurring in not a few instances, for one will hear language of the most unqualified and extravagant eulogy spoken of missionaries in general and missionaries in particular on all occasions that afford the slightest excuse for it. Whenever young Bengal has an opportunity of speaking of missionaries in their presence there lacks nothing of laudatory rhetoric. The words of his mouth are smoother than butter.

"Truly your freest utterances are not by any means always the best. . . . Nay, of all animals, the freest of utterance I should judge is the genus *Simia*."—CARLYLE. *Past and Present.*

"Jocelin is weak and garrulous, but he is human."—*Ibid.*

"He draweth out the thread of his verbosity finer than the staple of his argument."—SHAKSPERE. *Love's Labour Lost.*

"Gratiano speaks an infinite deal of nothing, more than any man in all Venice."—SHAKSPERE. *Merchant of Venice.*

> "To carry out an enterprise in words
> Is easy; to accomplish it by acts
> Is the sole test of man's capacity."
>
> *The Ramayan.*

CHAPTER II.

BABUDOM—*continued.*

VAPOUR AND GAS.

I STATED at the close of the last chapter that, judging the babus by their words, their appreciation of honesty is not rare. But we must not always judge them by their words. At any rate, we must not suppose that they mean what Englishmen would mean by the same words. They are too gifted in exaggeration. It is said that when Bishop Heber first came into contact with the natives of India, he was overwhelmed by the cordiality with which he was everywhere received. Wherever he went. he was welcomed by the graceful salaam and the "Mabap," "My father and mother." One is not long in the country however without discovering that he is always everybody's father and mother; and especially is this the case when he has occasion to find fault. The Indian *Punch* once pictured an amusing scene founded on this fact. A young Sahib was giving his servant a somewhat severe rating, closing with the outburst—"You son of a jackal —you!" The servant mildly, deprecatingly bows: "My father and mother."

There is nothing that delights a Bengali more than the opportunity of speaking. Provided he can sit down with the consciousness of having been fluent and of having got his superlatives well placed, he requires nothing further. To mean anything is no part of his purpose; to put his professions into practice no part of his dream. Consistency between word and act does not strike him as necessary. I remember well, for instance, how, at an address delivered by a favourite orator at an annual meeting of the Bengal branch of the National Indian Association, some eight hundred students who had crowded into the theatre of the Hindu College applauded rapturously his glowing periods. He was speaking of some of the blots of the Hindu social system, and in the most unmeasured terms condemned child-marriage, zenana seclusion, and widow persecution. But I felt sure then, as I remain sure to this day, that of those applauding students—nearly one thousand in number—there would scarcely be half-a-dozen who would seriously face the questions:—Is there anything I can do to bring about a reform in these matters? Shall I personally refuse to yield to these customs?

This same gentleman is a very typical Bengali, not a type of all, but a type of a very large class. Formerly in government service, he retired from it after some act of which the government did not approve, and has ever since figured more or less as a martyr. At the time of the excitement aroused in India by Mr. Ilbert's Bill, I believe his name was figuring in the home papers as that of a man imprisoned for writing against the High Court Judge in connection with it, and the honours of martyrdom were falling even thicker upon him. My own impression of the man, confirmed by the opinion of those who knew him much better, though I myself saw not a little of him, was that he was a mere talking machine, of whose high-flown words it was scarcely worth while to take much notice.

There was a monthly lecture founded at the City College, an institution originated by the Sadharan Brahmos, and soon after the appearance of Sir Edwin Arnold's *Light of Asia*, the late Dr. Krishna Mohun Banerjea was announced to give a lecture upon it, while this gentleman was advertised as his chairman. The Rev. Doctor's lecture was not a very great success. It was dull, confused, and unappreciative. At its conclusion the chairman rose and spoke of it in the conventional words of exaggerated eulogy, passing on gradually, however, with altered tone, to a lengthened criticism of it which was not only severe but contemptuous and ill-mannered, after which he sat down with the satisfied smile of a man whose dearest wish had been realised. He neither saw the absurdity of the contradictions in what he had been saying, nor the bad taste and ungraciousness of treating thus one of the most venerable members of his race on the occasion when he was acting as his chairman. He simply knew that he had had an opportunity of being eloquent, that he had spoken for three quarters of an hour, and that

the audience had been borne along on the torrent of
his oratory. What could it matter what it had all been
about? It was thus apparently that the lecturer
judged. To see him criticised thus with a lofty air of
superiority was irritating to me, but the good doctor
knew his young compatriot better than I; he listened
placidly to his remarks, and when the opportunity was
afforded him of speaking again, he did not pay them
the compliment of a single reference. They were taken
for what they were worth, and received, as far as he
was concerned, with imperturbable silence. The man
had spoken vehemently enough, but it was understood
that he had meant nothing.

This appetite for rhetoric and strong language is
perhaps but insufficiently taken into account by persons
who, from what they hear in speeches or find in the
vernacular press, would argue that there is a general
discontent seething in native society, and constantly
threatening danger to the British government. This
discontent is largely simulated, and where it is not, is
little more than the fractiousness of ill-trained children.
From what has been said, it may be gathered that the
English-speaking babu is a conceited believer in himself and his claims on the world's consideration. He
expects some one to provide him with a post to which
is attached an income suitable to so great a gentleman.
He scorns manual labour of any sort, and has too much
regard for his skin to enter the army. I understand
that it is true still, as when Macaulay wrote his essay
on Warren Hastings, that there is not a single Bengali

in the so-called Bengal regiments. He cannot dig though he is not ashamed to beg. Therefore, after over-crowding the legal profession and the desks of the mercantile offices, he must either take to speechifying, newspaper writing, or idling. If the last, he will from the nature of the case be dissatisfied, and if either the first or the second, he will find it so much easier to be fluent with than without a grievance, that it will be strange indeed if he cannot always enlist one in his service. While I was living in Shanghai, our morning daily culled for our delectation a cutting which the *Pioneer* had taken from one of the vernaculars affording a striking instance of the avidity with which the Bengali will seize on a grievance, and illustrating incidentally how instinctively he feels that the legal profession—whether on account of the opportunities it affords of revelling in intricacies and quibbles I dare not say—is the native atmosphere of the Oriental. At Woosung, where the Huangpu, the little river on which Shanghai stands, falls into the Yangtsze, there is a deposit of mud, usually spoken of as the Woosung bar. During the Franco-Chinese war, the Chinese announced their intention, on the ground of real or professed appre-hensions that the French fleet would come up the Huangpu, of sinking a number of junks on this bar of mud. The Shanghai Chamber of Commerce, seeing the harm that would be done to the trade of Shanghai, and believing that such an expedient either was or could be rendered unnecessary, called a meeting to devise steps by which it might be prevented. A

Bengali editor got hold of the fact that Europeans were attempting to "prevent the blocking of the Woosung bar by the Chinese," and became righteously indignant at this new example of oppression and high-handed dealing. "Woosung, we suppose," said the Bengali editor, "is a Chinese town ; and to prevent the overcrowding of the local bar by Chinese lawyers is a monstrous proposal."

There is one other matter which must not be over-looked in estimating the value of native utterances in India, though of course specially relevant to the task of estimating native evidence in the Courts of Law. It must be remembered that what we stigmatise as bribery is a virtue in the East, one of the civilities of life, one of the safeguards of respect, and, therefore, as universal as good manners. We are careful not to omit the conventional courtesies of our race, and the Bengali will not omit those of his. And notwithstanding that it is laid down in the Laws of Manu that—

> " Headlong in utter darkness shall the wretch
> Fall into hell who, in a court of justice,
> Answers a single question falsely; he
> Shall be tormented through a hundred births,"

I have been assured by friends belonging to the learned profession which has its habitation in the Halls of Justice, that at Calcutta, in the streets outside the various courts, there wait for hire any number of persons who get their living as professional witnesses and are not without skill in their profession. You can among

them obtain the services of men prepared to swear
to anything you wish. Would it be just to allow such
merit to pass unrewarded ?

A man had a cow and an enemy. The cow died
under most suspicious circumstances. Speaking among
his friends, the owner of the defunct beast found himself in possession of clear evidence that his enemy had
poisoned his cow. Collecting witnesses, he started off
with them for the nearest town at which he could lodge
his complaint. It happened that, living in an out-
of-the-way place, they had some distance to travel, in-
volving a night's encampment. Unfortunately for the
complainant, he had some little differences during this
night with his witnesses on the subject of compensation,
and when they arrived before the magistrate, they all
swore the cow had died a natural death, and that the
accused man had no hand in it whatever. The result
was that the accuser lost his cow and got hardly dealt
with by the magistrate for bringing an unnecessary,
vexatious, and unjust case into court. I had this from
a European friend who knew the persons concerned.
For the following I have no such external authority,
but the internal evidence is good.

A man was charged by another with having received
from him a loan which had not been repaid. Knowing that his charge was a false one, the plaintiff took
the precaution of bringing forward as many as five
witnesses to prove the transaction : they had seen the
money change hands. The defendant, though he knew
he had never received a pice, knew also how little he

must depend on that fact; so finding out that the other was going to bring five witnesses into court to prove that he had borrowed the money, he admitted that he had received it, but brought ten witnesses to swear to his having repaid it. This unexpected defence saved him.

Such example will indicate what " evidence " is worth in India, and may well suggest the question how far the machinery of British courts is best for such a people. Probably there was as much real justice done by men having irresponsible power, who were at liberty to seek the truth of the cases that came before them according to the suggestions of their mother wit, educated by a life-long knowledge of the people, as is done now. Solomon might not have astonished his subjects by the justice of his famous decision if he had been hampered by a system of trial by jury.

The consideration of these characteristics has its bearing on the questions that are sometimes raised, under the cry of " Justice to India." This cry is often heard at home; but, were all the things clamoured for granted, it might be a hard day for many a poor Indian.

The aim of the British government should doubtless be to educate the people for self-rule, and to keep that in view as an ultimate goal. But for the present the masses of that country would be far better off under a just-hearted British despotism than they would be under the most constitutionally-conceived government administered by their own people. It sounds like justice to say, " Put no difference between native and

European; admit to privilege and responsibility independently of colour." But this may mean the putting of one native in power to the doing of injustice to a hundred. If the facts given in the foregoing pages prove anything, they prove that, though of the same Aryan stock, the Hindu and the Englishman are divided by a pretty deep gulf. It is not an impassable one, but the passage is at present effected by but few, and I do not think it an extravagant thing to say, that, speaking generally, the native of India is not yet qualified to be put in charge of machinery which the British people have only learned to use in the course of centuries and at the cost of untold bloodshed.

There was doubtless fearful oppression in the old days before the British conquest, but a rough justice was possible then, owing to the comparative weakness of the petty states into which the country was divided. When the oppression became intolerable, the oppressor was overthrown in the uprising of the oppressed. He always knew that there was a limit to his oppressions fixed by the limit of the endurance of the people. But a native official, with the power of the empire at his back, or a native usurer able to appeal to British law to enforce his iniquitous claims, may be an oppression such as the former times knew nothing of.

And if it be felt that the putting of increased power in the hands of natives might be to the injury of their own countrymen, it is not surprising that there should be a strong feeling against placing Europeans under the power of natives. An educated babu and a European were speaking of the Ilbert Bill, the babu cordially approving of its provisions and condemning the outcry that had been raised in opposition to it. The European replied, "Babu, the other day was the Jagannath Festival. You pretended that Jagannath had been bathed and had caught a cold, and must needs go on a visit to a friend for change of air. So you dragged his car a short distance and professed to believe that he had gone to his friend. Then, a few days after, you put the whole population on the car ropes again, and pretended that he had returned home cured. How can you expect us to wish ourselves in the hands of men who profess to believe in such superstitions?" "But, sir," said the babu, "you know perfectly well that we educated Bengalis do not believe in any such nonsense." "I know it, babu; but you were present with your educated friends on those occasions, and not as spectators but as sharing in the ceremony. You tell me that you have not made up your mind about Christianity, and so excuse yourself for not avowing yourself a Christian. But you tell me you have made up your mind about the folly of Hinduism. You can call it nonsense to me, and yet you and your friends dare not acknowledge publicly your real position in regard to it. Does not this show that you natives lack moral courage?" "Yes," answered the babu, "I admit that we have neither the moral courage of Europeans nor their independence." "This is true of those who mean well among you," pursued the European; "what about those of whom even so much could not be said?"

It will need time for those changes to take place in the native character which will be necessary before Europeans who know India can be expected to regard with favour a bill such as that which Mr. Ilbert brought forward.

"Men's thoughts are much according to their inclination; their discourse and speeches according to their learning and infused opinions; but their deeds are after as they have been accustomed."

BACON. *Essay on Custom and Education.*

"No fact is more firmly established than that lying is a necessity of our circumstances—the deduction that it is then a virtue goes without saying. No virtue can reach its highest usefulness without careful and diligent cultivation; therefore it goes without saying, that this one ought to be taught in the public schools—at the fire-side—even in the newspapers. What chance has an ignorant, uncultivated liar against an educated expert? What chance have I against Mr. Per—— against a lawyer? *Judicious* lying is what the world needs. I sometimes think it were even better and safer not to lie at all than to lie injudiciously. An awkward, unscientific lie is often as ineffectual as the truth."

MARK TWAIN.

"An honest man's the noblest work of God."—POPE.

'You yourself are much condemned to have an itching palm."

SHAKSPERE. *Julius Cæsar.*

CHAPTER III.

"WHAT'S BRED IN THE BONE WILL NOT OUT OF THE FLESH."

IN the conclusions arrived at from the facts already given, I would not be thought to speak disparagingly of our brothers in Bengal. The fact is that both friend and foe are often unreasonable in their expectations. The one would give too much to them, and the other exact too much from them. People here at home cry out for what they call justice and equal treatment on abstract grounds of human brotherhood, making no allowance for the necessary differences that grow out of different national histories. And people who live among them, and who recognise these differences when met by native claims, are not always more reasonable when the case is reversed. This is especially seen in the views held by many Anglo-Indians in regard to native Christians. Of course there are many hypocrites among those who call themselves Christians in Bengal, as there are among those who call themselves Christians in England. In addition to those who imagine that they are Christians without being such, there are those

who are professing to be earnest inquirers after truth,
while they know themselves to be the most thorough-
going liars. One such "anxious inquirer," a Kulin
Brahman, once came to me, and professed to be dissatisfied with Hinduism, and wanted me to instruct him
in the Christian faith. I appointed a time for him to
call again. Before that time had come he returned,
saying his father had heard of his coming to see me, and
had turned him out of his home. This of course ought
to have touched my heart and prompted me to offer
him free quarters in my house. Instead of that, however, it being about midday, I suggested that he should
have tiffin with me ; and then I would drive him down
to the London Mission compound, where he would
doubtless be received in the catechumens' quarters.
He did not seem to jump at the proposal, but agreed.

> "So down they sat,
> And to their viands fell ; nor seemingly
> The angel, nor in mist, the common gloss
> Of theologians, but with keen dispatch
> Of real hunger and concoctive heat
> To transubstantiate."

I was surprised at the freedom of my "angel
unaware" in dealing with a European tiffin. There
was a more thorough absence of awkwardness than
would have been anticipated in a man up to that hour
in caste who had never before partaken of any meal
save of Hindu food, prepared and eaten in Hindu
fashion. After tiffin, while the gari was being got ready,
he seized an opportunity of decamping, taking with

him the serviette he had been using, which was
probably the only thing he could conveniently secrete,
as the khitmatgar had been constantly going in and
out of the dining-room where I had left him. That
was the last I saw of my guest; but some time after
his name caught my eye in the newspaper, and I was
curious to see to what he owed the publicity. On
reading I found that he had been attending regularly
at the house of Mr. ——, the minister of a Wesleyan
Church, who had eventually baptized him, but had
now been compelled to prosecute him for thefts
committed. In the examination before the magistrate,
it further transpired that he had similarly victimised
another minister who was preparing him for confirmation. But such men are not native Christians,
they are native hypocrites; and the existence of
hypocrites does not prove the non-existence of honest
and truthful men, though I fear that some are inclined
to assume this non-existence in cases where they have
not seen the real thing and have seen the counterfeit.
In the saloon of a mail steamer between England
and India some one mentioned the words, Native
Christians. "Native Christians! There are none.
I've been in India for many years and I never saw a
native Christian the whole time." So spoke a military
officer among the company. Some days afterwards the
same officer was telling of his sporting experience, and
said that at one time and another thirty tigers had
fallen to his rifle. "Did I understand you to say,
thirty, colonel?" asked a missionary of the Church

Missionary Society, who was at the table. "Yes, sir, thirty," replied the officer. "Because," pursued the missionary explanatorily, "I thought that perhaps you meant three." "No, sir, thirty"—this time with emphasis. "Well, now, that is very strange," said the missionary, "for I have been in India some five-and-twenty years, and I have never seen a wild tiger in all that time." "Very likely not, sir," responded the colonel; "but it is not at all strange, it is simply because you never went where they are; you did not go to look for them." "Perhaps it is so," said the missionary after a moment or two of apparent reflection, "and may not that be also the reason why you never saw a native convert, as you affirmed at this table the other evening?"

It is true both that there are native Christians and that some of them are of a type of Christianity which will compare not unfavourably with that of their European co-religionists. The Dr. Banerjea to whose lecture on Arnold's *Light of Asia* I have referred above might have been taken as an example of a scholar and a Christian justly commanding respect anywhere. His manner was invariably courteous, and his bearing—owing, it may be, partly to his years—by its combined dignity and urbanity, always compelled admiration. But justice will not be done to the native Christians till it be more clearly understood that they are not Europeans. It takes a good deal of honest thinking to dissociate in our minds what we owe directly to our Christian conviction and what we owe to Christianity indirectly as it has influenced the European atmosphere in which we have been nurtured.

A man brought up in England, where he has seen no Christians except as associated with his own nationality, goes to India, and sees native Christians in whom he finds that something is lacking which he had always hitherto seen in a Christian. It is as likely as not that what is lacking is simply the Western temper. He would cordially agree with the principle, Let us make these men Christians without denationalising them, without attempting to make them Europeans; at the same time, when they are made Christians and left Bengalis, he is not satisfied. The fact seems to be, as I have just pointed out, that Christianity has a double influence on us. We are influenced directly by it in our personal conviction, and we are influenced indirectly by it in the hereditary instincts which it has during many generations been creating in our race. The Bengali necessarily lacks this latter, and is not to be put down as a hypocrite because his Christian convictions have a constant struggle against hereditary instincts which are in his case as antagonistic to his Christianity as in ours they are helpful to it. I do not say that the result in the native Christian is so satisfactory as in the best specimens of English Christianity. I say rather that it is unreasonable on our part to expect so satisfactory a result. You may get a Hindu to accept the doctrines of Christianity, you may get him to associate himself with a Christian church, and, in so doing, to cut himself off from all association with idolatry, and this even at considerable cost to himself; he may be perfectly sincere in his determination to make Christ his example, and to serve Him as his Master, but he does not thereby receive the moral tone which is one of the slowly-wrought effects of an Englishman's upbringing. He still retains his own national characteristics, in some of which he may have an advantage we do not realise, though in others a disadvantage which we can clearly see. From which we may judge that the same outward moral conduct indicates a greater Christian triumph in a Bengali than in an Englishman. We ought to be prepared to find in a Bengali Christian, indications of the self-centred thought, the love of vapouring and the inability to see contradictions, incongruities, and absurdities that appear to be part of the heritage of the race. A member of one of the native churches, a graduate in both the Arts and Law faculties in the Calcutta University, and a pleader by profession, was advertised to deliver one of a course of lectures being given in English at the London Mission College to educated natives. He announced his subject:—"The Monistic Theory of Darwinian Evolution," and asked a lady to "select a hymn appropriate to the subject" out of Sankey's *Songs and Solos!*

Nor indeed ought we to feel very much surprised to find evidence of some of the worst faults of the native character remaining in them even after the acceptance of so purifying a faith as the Christian. When we remember, for instance, that from their earliest infancy they have been taught to lie, that their characters have been formed, and their lives moulded by heathen influences, by worship of gods of whom their legends relate the most shameless untruthfulness and impurity, we may accept their own testimony that we can have no conception how hard it is for even converted members of their race to tell the truth. It is something they have to acquire; they have to think carefully and constantly if they would do it.

With two or three others, I was once asked to investigate some rather unpleasant matters that were causing disturbance in one of the native churches, and was therefore brought a good deal into contact with the members of it. The result was that, while my faith in their Christianity suffered no abatement, my respect for their national instincts did not increase. One babu, a man of years and large experience, and of some prominence in the native Christian community, assured me, in connection with this inquiry, that I was not to suppose I could understand the natives of Bengal. A European without being a Christian could nevertheless be a gentleman and know how to behave himself, could exercise self-control and even be an honest man. But, he continued, of many natives you could not say as much even though they were Christians. A meeting of native Christians in council without a European president was to be imagined with difficulty. Moreover, my informant further assured me that on any point a vote could be obtained as wanted, since " undue and improper influence "—he carefully avoided the word "bribery" was a marked characteristic of native proceedings.

If it be true that the old leaven of the native character still works in those who have so far broken with the past as to avow themselves Christians, it may well be expected to remain in the members of the several samajes. The natural modesty of the race revealed itself strikingly in the annual addresses of Babu Keshub Chandra Sen, the most prominent and well-known, if not the most worthy of the samaj leaders. One utterance which I heard fall from his lips would have sounded blasphemous to me had I not already learnt to believe that a Bengali's eloquence did not mean anything, even though the Bengali were a Brahmo. Speaking on the development of the Divine purpose, he said that Moses had made Jesus a necessity, and Jesus had made Paul a necessity, and Paul had made him—the speaker—a necessity!

In concluding this sketch of the Calcutta babu, in which, without, as I trust, being altogether unappreciative, I fear that I have dwelt more on his weaknesses than on his virtues, from the unfortunate fact of having been more impressed by them, I feel I ought to refer to one matter in which we must humble ourselves before our brown-skinned brother of Bengal. He is a sober man as compared with us. Nor is he blind to the failing of Englishmen, or to his danger from our influence and example. As long ago as 1848, among the native community in Calcutta a society was formed to stay if possible the spread of the drunken habits

introduced by the Christians—for so they put it. We
are little justified in finding fault with their type of
Christianity, when they find so serious a flaw in ours.
" Of what caste are you ? " asked an Englishman of a
native. " Oh, I'm a Christian. I take brandy-shrab
and get drunk like you," was the reply. That the
natives of India are learning at least one bad habit
from the Europeans is an undoubted fact. It is a fact
to give us pause where we should otherwise without
hesitancy endeavour to increase the social intercourse
of the races. There is a readiness on the part of a
large proportion of the educated natives of the larger
cities to throw off the thraldom of the social customs
of their fathers, and to seek acquaintance with the
home life and social customs of the English. I have,
by private invitation, attended amateur theatricals in
the Calcutta house of a zemindar, in which, even his
wife and the ladies of his household took their part
upon the stage, though when they are on their zemin-
dary in the mofussil under the rule of the dread
mother-in-law, the said wife has to be content with
the imprisonment and 'occupations of the zenana. I
have frequently met men at dinner who, a few years
before, would not have looked upon a European dinner-
table. But the question has, time after time, forced
itself upon me, Will it be for the benefit of the
Hindus to be initiated into our social customs ?
Would that the social life of our fellow-countrymen in
India were healthy enough to justify an unqualified
and unhesitating affirmative answer.

"Beauty and anguish walking hand in hand
  The downward slope to death."
      LORD TENNYSON. "*A Dream of Fair Women.*"

"As unto the bow the cord is,
  So unto the man is woman;
  Though she bends him, she obeys him;
  Though she draws him, yet she follows.
  Useless each without the other."
      LONGFELLOW. *The Song of Hiawatha.*

"A perfect woman, nobly planned
  To warn, to comfort, and command."
      WORDSWORTH. *Poems of the Imagination.*

"Even follow your own inventions; you men will be masters, and we poor women are born to bear the clog of obedience, though our husbands have no more sense than a cuckoo."
      CERVANTES. *Don Quixote.*

"Infidelity, violence, deceit, envy, extreme avariciousness, a total want of good qualities, with impurity, are the innate faults of womankind."—*The Hitopadesa.*

CHAPTER IV.

THE BABU'S WOMANKIND.

" OUR lawgivers being men have painted themselves pure and noble, and have laid every conceivable sin and impurity at our door. If these worthies are to be trusted we are a set of unclean animals, created by God for the special service and gratification of man, who, by right divine, can treat or maltreat us at his sweet will." This, and more, wrote a Hindu lady some little time since to the *Times of India*, and there is only too abundant evidence that she in no way overstated the case. The Gentoo Law, which was compiled for Warren Hastings by qualified natives from the ancient law books of the land, out-Popes Pope in his line that "every woman is at heart a rake," and lays down in the calmest and most unblushing manner the abysmal and inherent depravity of the female nature. According to it, the imagination of a woman's heart is only evil continually and the decencies of a woman's life determined solely by the restrictions placed upon her. For this reason she is never to be entrusted with the control of herself, never to be mistress of her own actions; in her early life she must be ruled by her father, in her youth by her husband, and in her widowed age by her son. Mr. Shib Chunder Bose, in his account of his own people, describes women, speaking generally of course, as having no other idea of themselves and their destiny than that which raised the indignation of the lady as quoted above, which is not surprising, since they have been taught this and this only from their infancy; and his pen, when it touches on the subject of their vitiated thought and conduct, hesitates—and fails. The source of much of the severity of the Gentoo Code is found in the Law Book of Manu, which Sir William Jones held to have been drawn up before, and Mr. Elphinstone soon after 1000 B.C., though Sir Monier Williams can find no place for it earlier than the fifth century. This ancient code says that day and night women must be made to feel their dependence on their liege lords, though it seems also to draw a distinction between women and women, for, while of some it speaks hopelessly, saying that all watchfulness over them will be unavailing—"even if confined at home by faithful guardians, they are not really guarded,"— it adds concerning others—"but those women who guard themselves by their own will are well guarded." A virtuous and faithful wife is thus recognised as a possibility; yet even she, with all her virtue, must regard herself as inferior to her husband, be he ever so empty-headed a noodle, besotted a debauchee or un-controllable a savage.

> "A faithful wife who wishes to attain
> The heaven of her lord must serve him here

> As if he were a god, and ne'er do aught
> To pain him, whatsoever be his state,
> And even though devoid of every virtue."

These are cheerful and hopeful lines of instruction for a woman who is not "devoid of every virtue." But what shall we say of these, taken from a later page?

> "Whatever be the character and mind
> Of him to whom a woman weds herself,"

which, by-the-bye she now-a-days does not have the opportunity of doing; it is done for her—

> "Such qualities her nature must imbibe,
> E'en as a river blending with the sea."

Whereto serves virtue, if the virtuous woman not only has to regard an unvirtuous husband as a god but must herself imbibe his unvirtuous character?

It has not indeed been always thus. In the far-off Vedic days woman is seen to participate in her husband's freedom, to share the festivities and occupations of his life, even to study and teach the Vedas. And in the great epics, to whose earliest and pre-brahmanical composition Sir Monier Williams gives about the same date as to Manu's Law Book, we have brighter pictures of woman's life.

The *Ramayana* tells us of Sita, the furrow-born princess, wife of Rama and worthy of him, though he stands out in all the mythology of the Hindus as a hero *sans peur et sans reproche*, a Sir Galahad of the ancient world. Strong in heart, pure in soul, Sita is a type of a faithful wife. Not unworthy of the throne, she unrepiningly shares her husband's exile ; carried off by Ravana, the ten-faced demon king of Lanka, she is proof against his blandishments and his threats, untempted by the wealth and grandeur of his kingdom, and unaffrighted by the horrible rakshasas with cannibalistic propensities to whose tender mercies he, in despairing rage, had savagely committed her ; and when at last Rama discovers where she is concealed, invades Lanka, and overcomes Ravana, she proves her purity in the flame, is vindicated by fire, Agni himself placing her in the arms of Rama, unhurt.

In what strange contrast also to the modern opinion of women in India is this passage, from the *Mahabharata*—

> " A wife is half the man, his truest friend—
> A loving wife is a perpetual spring
> Of virtue, pleasure, wealth ; a faithful wife
> Is his best aid in seeking heavenly bliss ;
> A sweetly-speaking wife is a companion
> In solitude, a father in advice,
> A mother in all seasons of distress,
> A rest in passing through life's wilderness."

In the *Mahabharata* again, figures " Draupadi, with her dark skin and lotus-eyes—the faithful Draupadi, loveliest of women, best of noble wives ; " and here too, occurs the pathetic story of Savitri and Satyavan. The Princess Savitri not only makes her own choice of a husband, but abides by it against the wish of her father, king Asvapati, and the advice of the old sage Narada. After her marriage she lives a free, open-air life, and, by accompanying her husband into the forest on the fateful night of his doom, is able to win him back from Yama, the terrible god of the dead.

The Hindus are accustomed to date their present system from the Mohammedan conquest, but the seeds from which it has grown were germinating long before that date. In the *Bhagavad-Gita*, a poem incorporated in the *Mahabharata*, Krishna, "the Holy One," * pours shame upon women by associating them with the lowest castes. "For even those," he says, "that are born in sin—even women, Vaishyas and Sudras—take the highest path, if they have recourse to me;" and we have already seen that in the Laws of Manu,

---

* Owing to the similarity in the sound of the names, this god is often spoken of by the babus as corresponding to Christ—"You have Christ and we have Krishna"—but never to any one who is supposed to know anything about the legends relating to this "holy one." Calling once on a native gentleman, not a Christian, I saw in the corner of the room a small image of this deity under a glass case. Wondering what sort of an account he would give me of him, I asked if that were not Krishna. Yes, that was Krishna. "And he is one of the Hindu gods, is he not?" I pursued further. My native friend looked at me a little uncertainly, and then— "Yes. . . ." (a meditative pause)—"Yes. . . . Yes, I suppose he was a god; he had genius; yes, he had genius; he must have been a god. . . . but" (another pause, and then, with a sad shake of the head)—"but he was a most debauched character." Mrs. Weitbrecht, in her *Women of India*, tells how "when a missionary on a preaching tour once noticed a Brahmin with a circle of village women round him, to whom he was relating stories of this god's profligate life, the Brahmin was so distressed by the missionary's presence, that, after coughing and hesitating, he actually could not proceed in his polluting discourse, and twice begged the missionary to leave the place."

while women were allowed more freedom than would have been allowed them after the Mohammedan invasion, they were unhesitatingly declared unfit for independence. Without any aid from the Koran such teaching would easily develop into the severer doctrine and practice of later days, though doubtless the faithful Moslems accelerated the development.

The modern degradation and misery of woman in India is probably incapable of being exaggerated. The members of the lower castes indeed have freedom. They, where a large body of earth has to be removed, may enjoy the privilege of carrying it away in huge basket-loads upon their heads, their husbands and brothers amusing themselves with filling the baskets, or, where a house has to be built, they may carry aloft all the bricks and mortar, their husbands and brothers, as before, loading and unloading them. But these are the coolie's not the babu's womenfolk. The latter have not even the privilege of being beasts of burden; they are the wild and beautiful, sometimes perhaps fierce inmates of the menagerie. They are not trusted to look upon any men save their husbands, fathers and brothers. Even in times of sickness no skilled physician is allowed to attend them. My medical adviser and friend was once asked by a babu to come and prescribe for his wife. The doctor was astonished by the request but gladly consented and went at once, marvelling if the night of seclusion was coming to an end and the day of emancipation dawning. Arrived at the house he asked to see his patient, thereby exciting horror and conster-

nation among the male members of the family to whom
alone the demand was made. "See his patient"! Of
course not! Why the doctor-sahib knew that such a
thing had never been heard of and could not possibly
be. But they would explain everything, they could take
his questions and bring back her answers, they could
describe her symptoms and tell him anything he needed
to know. The doctor, judging that the applying to
him at all in such a case indicated something like a
breach in the walls of the citadel of zenana seclusion,
determined to see how far he would be able to push the
advantage that science and humanity had thus gained
in their conflict with custom. He was therefore ob-
durate, absolutely refusing to prescribe for an invisible
woman or to take the risk of dealing with her at second-
hand. At last the anxious husband devised a compromise. A large sheet was fixed up as for a magic-
lantern exhibition, and the doctor was stationed on one
side while the woman was brought to the other. Her
hand was then cautiously brought round its edge and
he was allowed to feel her pulse. So far so good. But
now the doctor declared that he must see her tongue.
She could put her hand and wrist round to the other
side of the intervening screen, but scarcely her tongue.
However, where there's a will there's a way, and the
problem was happily solved by the simple expedient of
slitting a small hole in the sheet, through which the
tongue was protruded for investigation without danger
of exposing more.

Children are married in infancy to save their morals,

on the assumption that they have none, and that maturity and maidenhood are incompatible. It would be strange indeed if such a custom, founded avowedly on such a reason, did not do much to induce the condition from which its necessity is supposed to have arisen. That the women of India are capable of something better than has yet been expected from them is amply shown in the brightness of the girls in the schools which they are allowed to attend for the few years before their removal to a father-in-law's establishment, and in the ability of those women in whose case exceptional opportunity has been afforded of proving the gift that is in them. Indeed it is shown whenever they are visited and taught in their seclusion by the zenana missionary. But notwithstanding natural capacity, the custom of caging them for life in apartments from which not even a view of the outside world may be obtained, and of taking them from one cage to another through the still unseen outside world in a closely shrouded palanquin, is calculated to make the passion fierce and the mind dull. So much is this the case that the younger men are beginning to wish that they had wives otherwise trained. For woman may be debased but cannot be dethroned. That she held the sovereign power in the earlier days of freedom may be shrewdly guessed from the lines in the *Mahabharata* which describe a model king, of whom is required, among other virtues hard of attainment, that

> "His spouse he well will guard and school,
> And ne'er succumb to female rule."

And she wields the power still, even though in the present day she dare not come before the purdah. The young babus may count women vastly inferior to themselves, but the women rule them nevertheless ; and just in proportion as the man has a larger culture, the rod of the uncultured mother and wife will be heavy on his back. Here is the testimony of a native newspaper, a little less pronounced in its babu-English than is sometimes the case, though its "thorough-going Cockney" as the ideal of the British character is very delightful : "The educated native is nowhere so miserable and crest-fallen as in his home, and by none is he so much embarrassed as by his female relations. His private life may be said to be at antipodes with his public career. A Demosthenes at Debating Societies, whose words tell as peals of thunder, a Luther in his public protestations against prevailing corruptions, a thorough-going Cockney in ideas and tastes, he is but a timid, crouching Hindu in his home, yielding unquestioning submission to the requisitions of a superstitious family." The writer explains that there can be no sympathy and no real companionship between the husband and wife. "The only way of patching up a temporary and nominal reconciliation is for the husband to forget his scholarship, and lay down his crotchets of reform, and assume the attitude of complete orthodoxy and foolish ignorance. Surely an educated husband and an illiterate wife cannot possibly agree, and so long as the latter governs the household according to her orthodox prejudices, the nation cannot make any real advancement."

E

The babus have considerable hope from the work of the zenana missionaries—hope in regard to evils all of which perhaps are not special to Bengal. "I want you," said a young man to a lady who was arranging to visit and teach his wife, "I want you to teach my wife how to behave her husband (*sic*), and also the advantages we all derive from the practice of cleanliness." And to the same lady said another: "I do not wish you to teach my wife reading and writing, but to change her nature." Happy, hopeful youth!

On the condition of Hindu widows I dare not write. The story has been often told, and yet it may be doubted if its woe has ever been fathomed. The British government abolished sati in 1829, but so fearful is the fate of the widow that she may well regard the action of the government much as the lad Andres regarded the well-meant meddling of Don Quixote between him and his master. In the Journal of the National Indian Association for November, 1881, appeared a paper written by a young widow than which I think I never read anything more pitiful. She wrote unhesitatingly, "I would rather choose the sati!" The customs in the different provinces vary somewhat, and all the details of her description might not hold good everywhere, some would not hold good in Bengal, but even where the hardships are least heavy, they are far from light.

The ground on which widows are treated with such cruelty must appear absurd to the younger generation trained largely after a Western fashion. But, as our newspaper editor has told us, the babu who is an en-

lightened reformer in the debating society is powerless to effect or even to advocate reform in the home
where it is most needed.   He lacks courage there,
and the real public opinion of the land is under the
power of the women whose long years of seclusion
and degradation unfit them to direct it wisely.   The
conservatism naturally growing out of ignorance, fears
the untried freedom and clings to the chains.   Woman
is woman's worst enemy and will be until her husband
and brother find the courage to deliver her against her
will.   England has passed a law making the re-marriage
of the widow legal, and many a young orator is ready
to air his rhetoric on the propriety of the widow's
availing herself of so beneficial an enactment, but—
that is all.   The widows, many of them, are still
children who scarcely ever saw the boys by whose
death they are accounted widows.   Their youth, their
beauty, their griefs are tender and touching subjects for
impassioned eloquence in the public meeting, and the
eloquence is not wanting.   Some years ago a widow
sent a letter to the *Madras Mail* which she had got a
friend to put into English for her, and in that letter
she very forcibly challenged the sincerity of all this
talk.· Knowing how such a marriage in real life would
be regarded, she wrote, " Now I beg to ask the gentlemen who take such great interest in young widows, who
argue in favour of widow marriage with such great enthusiasm, whether they will help me in my re-marriage.
I do not want any pecuniary aid.   I only want those
gentlemen to come to my house with their wives and

daughters to witness the marriage and dine with me
and my future husband ; and then invite both of us to
their houses and dine with us in their company at my
cost." With a caution that is not perhaps without
reason, she requested that those who undertook to do
so much would give "this assurance through a duly
registered document; because my neighbour Seetaboy,
the widow of the famous Ajodhyanath Row, tells me
that all these meetings and resolutions are nothing but
sham," and that the speakers "forget all that they say
in meetings soon after they leave the hall," being
"careful not to mention a word of their acts to their
wives, or to their young widowed daughters and
sisters."

What response this challenge met with in Madras I
do not know. A native gentleman wrote to one of the
Calcutta papers in regard to it, and said that he would
be happy to dine with the widow and her husband, "if
distance permitted." He then moralised on caste and
infanticide, suggesting the establishment of a secret department of government for the detection of the latter,
such as formerly existed for the suppression of thuggee,
throwing cold water however on his suggestion by
adding: "But as long as the zenana system reigns, it
would be almost impossible for any government to find
out the facts of all the horrible crimes traceable to the
two customs of child-marriage and widow compulsory
celibacy."

"Lo, the poor Indian!"—POPE.

"I have not patience with the groans of half the world, and declare there is more happiness among these miserable blacks, who have not a meal from day to day, than among our own middle classes. The blacks are glad of a little handful of maize, and live in the greatest discomfort. They have not a strip to cover them; but you do not see them grunting and groaning all day long, as you see scores and scores in England, with their wretched dinner-parties and attempts at gaiety, where all is hollow and miserable."

C. G. GORDON.

"Thou shalt not steal; an empty feat,
    When it's so lucrative to cheat."

A. H. CLOUGH.

"If you have a worthless servant, keep him lest you get a worse."—*Egyptian Proverb.*

CHAPTER V.

THE SUB-BABU.

An Indian house, or, more strictly, an Englishman's house in India, swarms, not only with ants and mosquitoes, but also with servants, and the friends of servants—natives of a class beneath those to whom is given the title of Babu. The good folks at home, when they hear how many servants are kept by their friends in India, are apt to think that they live in an unnecessarily luxurious style. But the good folks at home do not realise the necessities of the country. It is all very well for them to imagine themselves twice as hot as they are as a means of getting an idea of what living in India is like. The intention is more praiseworthy than the result is reliable. Thinking one is hot for ten minutes is a different thing from enduring heat for ten months. But the heat is not all. If men could live in India with no other consequence than getting hot it would be well. The heat is a prince of a legion of evils that follow in his train, and under the Indian sun one feels not only hot but helpless. The lack of a bracing climate makes itself felt in everything, and a very little doing of what servants can do for him will unfit a man for the doing of those things which the servants cannot do. Moreover, having a large staff of servants is not necessarily 'equivalent to being well served and living at ease. It is quite as likely to involve worry as luxury. But, apart from this, the number of servants a man engages is not altogether a matter of his own choice. The great god Caste has its word to say on this subject. The servants are so thoroughly under its tyranny that this man can only do things of this kind, and that man of that kind, and the sahib must, therefore, have about him men of almost as many castes as the duties he expects done. The whole of the modern development of the caste system is probably being elaborated and complicated by those whose interests it is to do so. The ancient castes were fewer in number than those of to-day and their rules apparently far less strict. The bewildering catalogue of the castes and sub-castes which now exist has been growing up by inter-marriages and trade-associations, and it may be suspected that no inclination to check it has been aroused because it was seen to be producing a state of things which made the not too-well-loved foreigner dependent on an increased number of natives. It was an Asiatic re-conquest of the conquerors.

But now, especially in regard to the servants, there is the inevitable Nemesis. The sahib of to-day is not the Crœsus of the earlier years of the British occupancy and the more servants he has to keep the less he can afford to pay to each. That, however, is not all. It is chiefly in the increased power that the complication of the system gives the priests over the common people that the servants are now paying the full price for all the advantage they originally obtained over their employers. The preservation of caste is among the Hindus the one test of orthodoxy. A man may think what he likes and believe what he likes, but he must obey the rules of caste.* Now the ordinary Hindu knows practically nothing about these rules beyond the fact that if he break them he will be turned out of caste and the priest will "squeeze" him, as a China-man would say, of every pice he can, as the price of re-admission. He does not know what things are, and what things are not infractions of these rules, and he is therefore most anxious to err, if he err at all, on the safe side. He would be little moved by fear of doing anything not belonging to the legitimate occupation of his caste, if it were not for fear of the priest getting to know of it and fleecing him. Rather than fall into the hands of that avaricious tyrant, he will refuse lucrative employment, he will be guilty of the greatest inhu-manity in withholding his hand from help, excelling priest and Levite in passing by on the other side, even where the voice of necessity is loud and urgent. Take as an example the following:

* "It is a remarkable fact that the jails in India often contain hardened criminals who have fallen, in our estimation, to the lowest depths of infamy, but who, priding themselves on the punctilious observance of caste, have not lost one iota of their own self-respect,. and would resent with indignation any attempt to force them to eat food prepared by the most virtuous person if inferior to themselves in the social scale."—Sir Monier Williams. *Indian Wisdom.*

My mali, or gardener, climbed up one day into a champa-tree overhanging the road to cut off a dead branch for the double purpose of removing an unsightly object and of adding to his store of fire-wood. He foolishly allowed himself to get upon the dead branch, which, not being equal to sustaining his weight, broke, and the mali fell heavily upon the footpath of the road. I was absent at the time, but my neighbour saw the accident from his house and ran out to the man's assistance, sending for a palki in which to have him taken to the hospital. When the palki-wallas, who were Ooriyas, came, they refused to take him. He also was an Ooriya, and, as my bearer afterwards told me, of a caste a trifle above theirs, but he was reported to have done something contrary to caste rules, and until he had been back to Orissa, and drunk a solution of sacred cow-dung and observed certain other ceremonies, and, above all, paid his fees to the priest, they could not take him into their palki without defilement to themselves, so they left him there in his agony, refusing to touch him. My neighbour then had a charpai, or native bedstead, brought, and got some men of caste too low for defilement to carry him to the nearest hospital, where all that could be done for the poor fellow was done, but his injuries were serious, and he died the next day. Two other of my servants, also from Orissa, poured scorn on the idea of treating the case surgically ; they judged it to be a case for exorcism. "You see," they said, "the devil was on that rotten bough, and was offended at the mali's getting upon it, so he threw him down, and threw the bough after him. and now the devil is in the mali "—the poor fellow was delirious enough to give some colour to this statement —" and if the doctors would only let us drive the devil out, the mali would get all right again." Presumably his sin against caste had made him especially susceptible to diabolic possession. I rather sympathised with the feeling that associated the devil with rottenness and death.

But the Hindu is not naturally unsympathetic, he has a fair share of human feeling, and, during the period of his service, a servant generally identifies himself with his master to the extent of considering himself a member of his master's household and its credit as his own. Against an outsider, he will champion his master's cause and advocate his rights. One of my friends when out on a holiday was told by some natives of a panther they had entrapped, and was invited to come to shoot it. He went with them and found the creature in a strong bamboo trap; getting on to the top of which, he bade them open the door and let him out. The poor beast having probably been in confinement the greater part of the night, and having been disturbed and not a little worried by visitors since early morning, was so nervous and scared that it required a good deal of prodding and a little exaggeration of the noise that natives are accustomed to make about everything they do before it could be induced to make a run. When it did bolt my friend unfortunately missed it. Presently he overheard a villager saying something in a disparaging tone about his missing it. "Missing it," rejoined one of his servants indignantly, "why, how could the sahib shoot a brute that sneaked off in this cowardly fashion?" and the man dropped on to all-fours and mimicked the skulk of the panther so absurdly as to call forth a general laugh which in a measure restored the sportsman's credit.

All native servants are rascals. *Cela va sans dire.* They are Asiatics. That is enough. So runs the common verdict, and he would certainly have a hard task who undertook to whitewash them. The most I would venture to say is that this rule is not without exceptions. There are servants even in Calcutta who are conscientious, servants whose fidelity and anxiety to serve their master's interest is such that they will compare favourably with servants elsewhere. Of course they take their commission on all transactions to which they are in the most remote degree parties. If for instance you pay your bearer to pay the gari-walla you have hired, he takes his anna or annas in the rupee, and if you pay the gari-walla yourself with the hope that he will thus obtain full payment, he will have to pay your bearer what he would have deducted had the payment been made through him, or the said bearer will see to it that the said gari-walla has no further opportunity of driving his horses in at your gate. This is so thoroughly and ineradicably a custom that one cannot be sure it is not regarded as among the rules of caste the infraction of which is at all costs to be guarded against. Anyway it is business, not dishonesty. And where there is a servant—and I had at least one such—who would not dream of doing what is dishonest according to his standard of honesty, though I may wish to teach him a new standard, for the time being, I count him honest. Notwithstanding all that is heard of the untrustworthiness of the servants, it is surprising to see the confidence that is reposed in them. Furnished houses are left in the charge of men whose names and native village are unknown, while the owners go away for days and weeks. Sums of money are sent by them which would be a fortune, on which they could live all their lives in their distant villages in what to them would be luxury. Even men who are known to pilfer in small things, men who have something approaching genius in petty larceny, may be trusted with large amounts, though whether this is because of a certain littleness of spirit which cannot rise to the occasion of a greater crime, or whether it results from a moral training which determines the bounds of honesty by material measurements, so that to appropriate one rupee is within, and to appropriate a hundred is without the line, I cannot tell.

It must be admitted that the servants as a class are not noted for probity, and some find it rather a trial to have a number of people on the premises engaged in different capacities but united in their purpose of getting as much as possible out of their employer. Nor are they accustomed to betray each other. After a servant has been detected and dismissed, his former

associates will be emphatic in their condemnation
of his iniquities, and communicative as to his sad
peculations, but as long as he is on the staff, they
have usually no word to say.   Occasionally, however,
a quarrel in the servants' quarters will lead to loud
and vehement mutual recriminations, and, since both
parties will be very much stronger in attack than in
defence, to dismiss all concerned will probably be as
just a judgment as any, and the simplest solution of
the difficulty.

The native *penchant* for lying is a fundamental
vice.   It shows itself in everything.   It is far more
natural to a native than the truth; there is more
freedom in it.   It is a natural effect of years of
oppression, the outcome of a history of conquests and
tyrannies.   You ask a native a question.   Before
answering that question, he wants to see why you
asked it.   He wants to know for what purpose you
seek the information.   A hereditary suspicion sees in
every inquiry·a purpose to do harm, and so the habit
of misleading with false information wherever possible
has become a second nature.   A rabbit has no particular fox or weasel in his mind when he makes his
burrow, but he judges as a general thing that it is well
to have a dark hole, and to put a twist or two into it
so that the outside world of foes may not know just
where the other entrance comes out.   The native has
learnt to put a few turns into the dark workings of his
mind.   He has no special reason perhaps for any particular lie, but he has a general instinct which leads

him to hide his intentions. Your servant who wants a holiday to attend some festive occasion among his friends will come to you with the sad intelligence that his mother, or grandmother, or some near relative is dead and that the responsibility of ordering the funeral rites devolves on him, for which reason he prays for leave of absence. It is quite astonishing how many mothers a man can lose in a year. I was one day sitting with a missionary in his verandah when a servant came in and asked to be allowed to go and attend the funeral obsequies of his mother. It was before I understood the matter and I was not a little shocked at the, as it seemed to me under the circumstances, unsympathetic way in which the missionary calmly said, "Yes, you can go this time, but you must see to it that this does not happen again."

Servants leaving employment are accustomed to ask for a short note or chit to serve as a recommendation to a fresh place. There has arisen quite a trade in chits so that it is never worth while to place much reliance on them. In addition to the fact that persons getting rid of servants too often think that it is only fair to give the rascals a chance somewhere else, as they put it, and so give them a good word which they are never likely to deserve, there are many chances against the presented chit belonging to the man who presents it. Some, however, offer their services without chits. They assure you that their chits with all their other belongings were consumed in the great fire. Some years ago—it must now be quite a long while, before the folks were born who profess to have lost their chits in its ravages—there was an extensive fire in Calcutta among the native huts. It was this which led to the regulation that all huts within the municipal boundaries should be roofed with tiles. Before that time thatch had been allowed, and seeing the Calcutta babu is extremely fond of letting off sky-rockets, the sticks of which are to be seen dropping down upon the house roofs all night long, fires were of constant occurrence. The substitution of tiles for thatch has wrought a marked diminution of their number. Outside the municipal rule, thatch still prevails as the cheaper material. In a native hut no extravagance is allowed nor any unnecessary expense incurred. It is picturesque to the passer-by, but lamentally lacking in comfort for the inmates. A roof overhead, a few posts on which the roof is supported and to which the mats are attached that constitute the walls when they are put up, and the earth for a floor, do not promise very largely in the way of accommodation. During a large part of the year one may see the footpaths covered at night with men rolled up in their chudders asleep, with neither pillow nor mattress. This may be taken as an index of the comforts of inside which they have forsaken for those of this long footpath-bed across which they lie side by side.

Fortunately for the poor Hindu, he has not been spoilt by the previous enjoyment of luxury. His life is destitute of comforts but he does not miss what he has never known. From the days of his toyless childhood, when he stands about listlessly, "clothed in the horizon," as it is euphemistically expressed, to the day when he attains the honour of headship in his family, owning a wife, a charpai, a lota and a hubble-bubble, and having to keep perhaps, a score of relatives—aunts and uncles, brothers and cousins—besides his own family, as we use the term, he has, I fear, never conceived the idea which the word "enjoyment" conveys to our mind. His life is hard, but uncomplaining. He does not often touch the question of the rights and wrongs of it. If he should be tempted to ask why he has not what he sees others possessing, the explanation is ready and unanswerable: He is reaping now the inevitable harvest of the deeds of a previous life. So he has been taught and it is certainly out of his power to disprove it.

It may be that in this is part of the explanation of the callousness with which an average native will inflict suffering on animals. He takes his fate without murmuring, why should not they? There is scarcely a draught ox in the city that has not got its tail broken in two or three places, since the hakri-wallas have discovered that twisting the tail is more effective than using the goad. But have not the gods twisted the tail of the hakri-walla's destiny as pitilessly? The cruelty of the Hindu does not seem akin to the savage delight in suffering of which one occasionally hears among the barbarians of civilised lands. It is rather indifference, callousness, growing out of a community of wretchedness. But the torture endured by its

F

victims is none the less horrible. For the sake of the most trifling profits, poor brutes will be subjected to suffering that cannot be calculated. There was much need for the institution in Calcutta of a branch of the Royal Society for the Prevention of Cruelty to Animals, and all honour is due to Colesworthy Grant, the man who was the means of starting one, and who was, up to his death, the mainspring of its beneficent activity. If they only knew their benefactor, what a chorus of gratitude would the "dumb creatures" of Calcutta raise! In the excitement of such knowledge, at the vision of such an angel in the way of less forbidding aspect than his, the sight of whom opened the mouth of Balaam's ass, might we not expect "a man's voice" —or some even more competent organ of thanksgiving —to be given to the cow in the milk-shed, to the ox in the hakri, to the poor tat in the overloaded ticca-gari, to the dhobi's donkey, staggering under the load of his master's entire trade, and even to the fowl which the bawarchi is carrying from the market, doomed to curry?

"Lo! Juggernaut's stupendous car;
So high and menacing its size,
The tower of Babel seems to rise;

    *   *   *   *   *

Satan himself would scorn to ape
Divinity in such a shape.

    *   *   *   *   *

The unwieldy wain compels its course,
Crushing resistance down by force;
It creaks, and groans, and grinds along
'Midst shrieks and prayers,—'midst dance and song."

JAS. MONTGOMERY.

"Pure religion and undefiled softens the manners by enlightening the mind, while superstition, by making it blind, inspires every kind of madness."—VOLTAIRE.

CHAPTER VI.

THE CAR OF JAGANNATH.

A SIGHT of Jagannath, the Lord of the World, is a lesson in the sin, or at least the folly, of curiosity. The legend tells that a pious king, being inspired to form an image in which to deposit the bones of Krishna, called to his aid Visvakarma—the Vulcan among the Hindu gods. The divine "author of a thousand arts, mechanist of the gods, fabricator of all ornaments, chief of artists," as Visvakarma is called in the *Vishnu-Purana*, was gracious and undertook to make an image worthy of his skill and reputation, on the condition that no one was to look upon him or in any way disturb him while engaged upon his task. Should such an interruption occur, the divine handicraftsman assured his royal highness it would put an end to his labours, and the image would remain in whatsoever state it might be at the moment of the interruption. The king consented to so simple a condition, and Visvakarma set to work. In one night he reared a temple for his image's abode, which was meanwhile to serve as his workshop. Fifteen days he wrought within it and had almost completed his task when the king, who had with difficulty restrained his curiosity so long, could restrain it no longer. He peeped. And Jagannath is to this day handless, footless, and with a face sadly lacking the finishing touches of the artist's hand.

A similarly disastrous result of the evil of curiosity meets us among the legends of China. A certain district was suffering from want of rain, owing to the anger of the gods. The people in their distress went to the chief guardian of one of the local temples and besought help. He, it would seem, was in a position to grant the needed help, but, not wishing to incur the displeasure of the gods by opposition to them, he referred the suppliants to the Rain Dragon, who, being more pitiful or less cautious, heard the people's prayer, and nightly caused a heavy dew which led to a more than usually fruitful season. The gods, evidently not in a humour to be trifled with, sought for an explanation of these luxuriant crops in the fields of men on whom they had laid their curse, and discovered what the Rain Dragon had been doing. In fury the divine sword fell upon the hapless Dragon, and his works of mercy were at an end. The temple guardian's heart was grieved as he thought that he had been the cause of the gracious creature's death. Reverently he took a jar and, like the fish in the story of Cock Robin's decease, caught the blood of the Dragon as it fell to the earth. This blood, duly sealed in the jar, was stowed away in the temple in the confident faith that at the end of forty-nine days an infant would be found in its place. But so wondrous a transformation going on in their very midst exercised mightily the minds of the temple attendants, and one of them on the forty-eighth day could no longer resist the temptation to satisfy his curiosity and looked within. Truly enough there was the infant, but the change was not quite complete, his face was still of a deep blood red colour. And Kwan-ti, the god of war, has had occasion ever since to regret that unlucky curiosity. He has grown from an infant in a jar to monstrous proportions, but through all his stages he has borne a red and truculent countenance.

Yet neither Kwan-ti nor Jagannath has suffered in the esteem of the people. Kwan-ti is the god specially worshipped by soldiers, barbers, thieves, and the like, while all sorts and conditions of men have reason to take more or less notice of him, since good harvests and years of immunity from severe sickness depend on his not forgetting to grind his sword on his birthday, the thirteenth day of the fifth moon. The evidence which satisfies the people that he has not been forgetful is the falling in rain of the water with which he wets his grindstone. Should no rain fall on that anniversary the people are filled with forebodings, whereas the slightest shower comforts their hearts. Kwan-ti, there-fore, gets on pretty well, notwithstanding his rubicund face, and is, indeed, far more likely to make red faces the fashion with others than to be despised for his own.

As for Jagannath, he too has overcome all personal disadvantages and is an exceedingly popular deity. So far from shrinking from the public gaze on the ground of deformity, he comes before his worshippers more openly than any other god in India. While more presentable deities are content with the dim sanctities of their shrines, the disfigured, or rather unfigured, Jagannath three times in every year leaves his temple and visits common ground. The first of these is the Bathing Festival. His godship is publicly "tubbed" by the priests on a brick-built stage, raised about seven feet from the ground, in sight of crowds who gather to see, shouting madly and long as the water of the sacred Ganges descends on the head of the god. Notwithstanding the annual recurrence of this performance, the priests never seem to become expert. They are so clumsy that every year, as regularly as the bathing takes place, they manage to give their deity a severe cold. This calls for sympathy, and, after bearing with his infirmity for almost a week, Jagannath finds it necessary to go for a change of air and to visit a friend. So much is sure ; but it is not easy to find out with any certainty who this friend is. Though Jagannath is said to have been made to hold within himself the bones of the deceased Krishna, there are those who tell that Krishna is the friend he goes to see. Others suggest that it is his grandmother—a far more probable suggestion, both in view of the above difficulty and of the fact that a grandmother may be expected to be a far better nurse than so wild a character as Krishna. Yet others again suggest Radha and various other acquaintances and relatives. But about the going there is no uncertainty. He goes out for a change some-where to get cured of a cold. This is his second annual appearance and the most notable. The third is his return home cured.

It was at the second, the great Rath Jattra, or Car Festival, that I first looked on Jagannath as an old friend of many years' standing. For he had ever been to me a representative of the Hindu gods. Of the older Indra, Agni, and Surya, and of the later favourites—Krishna, Siva, Durga—I had heard, but they all stood in the dim background of the picture in which the Lord of the World was the prominent figure. When a child in happy England, never dreaming of the possibility of ever treading the soil of India, I had seen portrayals of his face and read accounts which had vividly impressed me of his car and of the long line of mangled corpses stretching far away behind. Of one portrait I retain a distinct remembrance. It made me feel that, if by any chance I should meet this god, it would be more agreeable to me for the interview to be by daylight. But portraits are not always either exact or flattering, and, notwithstanding the misfortune that befel him through the undue curiosity of king Indra-dhumna, this was a portrait of which even Jagannath had a right to complain.

Considering this so long indirect acquaintance, I was not likely to let slip an opportunity of personal intro-duction. When, therefore, soon after my arrival in India, I received an invitation to spend the day of the Rath Jattra with some friends at Serampore, I accepted gladly, since Serampore possesses a temple of Jagannath, only less sacred and renowned than the parent shrine at Puri.

To escape the heat as far as possible, for it was midsummer, I went up by an early train. But the summer sun in India does not need to reach the zenith to make things unpleasant, and we—I had met with fellow visitors in the train—were right glad to reach our journey's end and to get a refreshing bath, after which breakfast became a possibility. That meal despatched, we retired into darkened rooms to chat and doze while the sun was spending his fierce anger in intolerable light and heat. Later on, but before the time for the car-drawing, we ventured out, for Serampore is of note also in the annals of Christian missions, and we were anxious to look over the noble college founded by the pioneer missionaries—Carey, Marshman, and Ward. In the cool seclusion of this fine building we lingered looking reverently at the very chairs on which " the immortal three" had sat, and at a pair of crutches, more useful than ornamental, from which one of them had derived assistance.

It is not surprising, considering the attractions of the place, that we presently looked at our watches and found the time for Jagannath to set out had already passed.

" Well," said we, " let us go and see the car, at any rate." So we went. Many were the beggars with outstretched arms along the way, most of them lying down as though they had fallen over from sheer exhaustion, but still clamorous. They, poor creatures, had been loudly appealing for alms all through the day under the burning sun from which we had taken refuge, and had hardly earned all they had got. Great was the crowd of people, and busy were the dealers in the booths erected on either side of the road, and, if their wares were individually of ridiculously trifling value, there was hope of profit in the multitude of their transactions. Though the crowd was dense there was none of the horse-play and violence that may be expected in a crowd of English roughs, and we were able to work our way through it with ease. Happily for us in this particular instance—on other occasions a source of more irritation than happiness—the Bengalis are not good time-keepers, and though, when we arrived at the scene of the ceremony, it was past the time when Jagannath should have reached his friend's house, he had not yet left his own. We had therefore ample opportunity of inspecting his car. He is apparently on amicable terms with all the other powers, for he admits on to his car representations of scenes and persons which must include nearly the whole of the Hindu pantheon. The car is indeed a kind of picture gallery in its way. Its predecessor, which was destroyed by a colony of white ants, more enterprising than reverent, is said to have been covered with figures of the most grossly indecent character. The illustrations that adorn the present car are not the work of a prude, but, in deference I believe to European sentiment, are in this respect a great improvement on those which the white ants were partly instrumental in abolishing. It is something to the credit of these much-abused insects if they have helped to improve the morals of one of the native deities.

Of course greater than the car and greater than its ornamentation is Jagannath himself, who sits with his brother and sister at the top, the most airy but not probably the place of wisest selection for one suffering from a severe cold. In the hoisting him up from story to story on the many-storied vehicle the assembled multitude takes an interest that finds loud expression, in which however there is not the least suspicion of the element of solemnity. It recalled to my mind an incident on the voyage out. We had had bad weather which had carried the hurdles of the sheep-pen overboard, and the sheep were running about the deck. Our lascar sailors were set to work to fix up a pen on the top of some deck-houses and to hoist the sheep on to this safer elevation. I remember how heartily they seemed to enjoy it—I judged that the sheep did not—and the way in which they hoisted up those animals came back irresistibly to my mind as I saw the brahmans hoisting up Jagannath.

In regard to his appearance, it could only be by the most gross self-deception that he could lay claim to being unusually handsome. For reasons already given, he is somewhat deficient in the personal advantages of feature and expression, yet there is a frankness and openness in his dusky face that are re-assuring. The pictures I had seen at home were slightly libellous. No one could look at him and for a moment think him capable of the sly tricks and rascally pranks of Krishna. If you felt you could not place much reliance on his intelligence, you would feel that there were many you could trust less willingly. For my own part, I should have been glad to have been invited to a vacant seat beside him had there been one.

By the courtesy of the magistrate, who from his responsibility for the safety of the people, was in a manner compelled to act as master of the ceremonies, our party was placed close alongside of the rope-pullers—between them and the men who were ranged on either side of the car and its ropes, bearing bamboo ladders longways to ward off the general crowd. It speaks not a little for the good humour and self-control of this crowd, that when the signal was given to start, amidst all the excitement, so slight a barrier proved sufficient for the purpose.

Now that the car had started, we thought we should surely discover who it was that our invalid deity was going to see. But no. The car was pulled, amidst deafening shouts, a comparatively short distance and then—it was left. All was over, we were told. Jagannath had reached his destination, from which it seemed that the friend he was visiting dwelt invisible in the middle of the road; was a kind of Sairey Gamp's "Mrs. Harris," in fact. Having seen him safely to his journey's end, we extricated ourselves from the crowd and made our way back.

The sight of this same festival was the occasion of deep soul-stirrings to the early missionaries. Some of my companions were their successors, but I could not perceive that they, more than I, were moved with the holy horror and indignation which many might think necessary in Christian witnesses of so idolatrous a scene. We indeed with one mind, as I believe, regarded it much as in other days we had regarded the Easter Monday excitements of Hampstead Heath and the like places of holiday resort. Doubtless the missionary of to-day has moved somewhat from the position of his predecessors, but in all probability the nature of this festival has changed still more. The outward observances are the same; that is all. To the English eye it is marvellously like an English fair with its merry-go-rounds and swings, and, while Jagannath is doubtless the supreme attraction for some half hour or hour, these swings are doing a thriving trade throughout the whole day. To a large proportion of the natives the festival is losing its religious significance. Probably the owners of the car are the least convinced of the divinity of their black idol, but considerations of profit and loss forbid any decrease of honour being shown; and, in view of the immense crowds which pour in by the extra trains from Calcutta during the day, the same considerations must weigh pretty strongly with every petty tradesman in Serampore. The festival is not likely to become less popular—the profits of the day forbid that. In fact, not many years ago, a second car, of size and proportions similar to the old one, was built, and the combined attractions of the orthodox and heretical rivals are doubtless being utilised by the persons concerned to bring grist to both mills. But it is becoming, I imagine, more and more a big social fair, and less and less a religious convocation.* To think of poor deluded wretches bowing in worship before such a wooden-headed idol is indeed sad enough; but to see a multitude enjoying a holiday in as harmless a way probably as is compatible with any large concourse, is, on the contrary, rather a pleasant sight.

Then, again, in earlier days were witnessed suicides and accidents which are now happily impossible. A trifling disappointment is enough to make a Hindu destroy himself, and to all crossed with adversity, the rolling of these ponderous wheels presented a fascinating opportunity. Especially was this the case since by throwing themselves beneath them they could deceive the god in the top window into thinking that what they were doing, prompted by a sense of misery, was intended as an act of homage to him. Thus by one act they expected to gain release from present trouble and a divine favour beyond. But in addition to this, after seeing the drawing of the car, one cannot conceive how it was possible in former days for such a ceremony to take place without numerous unintentional sacrifices of life to prevent which to-day calls for much precaution and the personal superintendence of the

* We have of late even heard rumours that the brahmans are being forced to hire coolies to drag the cars.

magistrate. Everything is under his control, and the car moves along escorted by armed police and fenced round by the ladders carried on either side. In former years, when the natives were left to their own devices, no such care was taken, every one who could seize the rope had a right to do it, a special blessing being supposed to attach even to the touching of it while the car was in motion. This means that while the car was being dragged along, there was a steady pressure of the crowd into the space immediately before it. In this crush the weak would inevitably go down, and it was woe even to the strong who should once lose their footing. As we walked alongside of the rope-pullers, though we were not crushed, we had to keep a sharp look-out lest the car should overtake us, especially through the uncertainty of the pace, every now and then the most frantic spurt being made amid deafening and exultant outcries. After noticing how clearly freedom from accident was the result of the magistrate's presence and precautions, we were prepared to credit statements about the annual loss of life at the Jagannath Festivals which at one time we had suspected to be exaggerations.

"No kind of beast is there on earth, nor fowl that flieth with its wings, but is a folk like you: nothing have we passed over in the book: then unto their Lord shall they be gathered."—*The Koran.*

"A wailful gnat." —Keats. *Endymion.*

"[Naturalists] call a mosquito by a difficult name, and know how its stomach looks under a microscope; but this view, though intrinsically valuable, scarcely rises to the subject. There is no feeling, no poetry in such treatment of a mosquito, and the knowledge is of a lower kind than seems required."

Phil Robinson. *In My Indian Garden.*

"Earth in her rich attire
Consummate lovely smiled; air, water, earth,
By fowl, fish, beast, was flown, was swum, was walk'd
Frequent."—Milton. *Paradise Lost.*

"I understand animals better than any other class of human creatures."—Artemus Ward.

CHAPTER VII.

"THE CURIOUS HUMANITY OF BEASTS AND BIRDS AND LITTLE INSECTS."

EVERY man who has been in India is supposed to have snake-stories and tiger-stories to tell. In the imagination of some people the country is made up of these creatures. That there are indeed plenty of them is a fact, but in a large centre of population like Calcutta one sees comparatively few snakes, and no tigers outside the zoological gardens.

But what are tigers to mosquitoes? A tiger loose in the city would arouse to aggression a populace which against mosquitoes can do no more than stand feebly on its defence. This conscienceless fly is destitute alike of fear and shame. He, or more accurately she, sails calmly in front of you within half an inch of your nose, and sings her teasing metallic song in your ear close enough to tickle your creeping flesh by the touch of her wings. She is perfectly aware that your clumsy hand will sweep her harmlessly out of its own reach on the rush of air made by itself. Seldom is she to be overtaken unless laden with spoil. Even under the punkahs, which might be expected to clear the air

G 2

of such a gossamer creature, she will carry on her iniquity; and when the punkah-walla wakes up to fitful periods of exceptional vigour, she adjourns to the under side of the table to test the thickness of the hose on one's ankles.

Man's only refuge is to retire behind the mosquito-curtain. And even so strong a hint as that is scarcely sufficient, for granted a hole in the netting or a little carelessness in the fixing of it, and the man will presently find it out indirectly through the insect's previous discovery. It seems impossible that she should accidentally fly just exactly to the weak point. There is no explanation satisfactory except that she looks for it. Whence this instinct of research it would be difficult to tell. The number of mosquitoes in the world which are tempted by human blood must be but an infinitesimal proportion of the mosquitoes in their native swamps who know not what a man is. Yet where man dwells, their skill in strategy as against him is such that the conclusion appears irresistible that the proper study of mosquitoes is man, and that in their youthful days they attend schools of the science and art of circumventing their human victim, and perhaps take lessons in the construction of mosquito-nets. How else does it happen that they hit at once on the weak and likely places without wasting time over an expanse of continuous net-work?

The helplessness which one feels in regard to these almost invisible tormentors, these nearly spiritual wickednesses, finds expression in a story, which some

of my readers may have heard, though I have never
seen it in print. A ship was lying in the Hughli.
On board were two sailors terribly worried by mosquitoes, and as night approached they found things
getting worse rather than better. From one corner to
another they went, and the insects followed. At last
they seemed to have found a retreat, and, after a little
yarning, were dropping off to sleep, when a fire-fly
came sailing through the air. One of them saw it
and exclaimed, " Jack, I give up; it's of no use, here
they've been and fetched a lantern to look for us."

I resist the obvious temptation to moralise concerning
being frighted with false fire, and merely give the story
in illustration of the helplessness which the Anglo-
Indian feels in presence of some of the minor evils of
India, or rather of the evils that take a minor form.

This mention of the fire-fly leads the thoughts from
one of the most irritating to one of the most beautiful
of insects. With its soft green light floating gently on
the evening air, associated necessarily with the coolest,
and therefore, the most pleasant part of the twenty-four
hours, it deserves the kindly feeling with which it is
universally regarded. Even in the centre of the city a
large number might be seen flying about the gardens ;
but on the outskirts, bushes and trees would appear
literally covered by them. And since their light has a
pulse, and the light of thousands would ebb and flow
synchronously, the effect was marvellous. Mindful of
the bush at Horeb, one was tempted to imagine that he
had found a revelation of a possible pantheism, and that

the presence of Deity was the pulsating life-blood of the trees and shrubs around him. The grace of an Indian night is not trifling to one who can select that which is gracious, and of this the fire-flies are no small part.

But the night has horrors as well as charms. Out from their thousand holes in the garden in which during the day they have been hiding from the fierceness of the sun, creep forth at evening the jewel-eyed toads, and signal to their cousin frogs in all the tanks within a mile. Musical emulation strains the throats in tank and garden as pæans of triumph are sung over the discomfited god of day.

But pour not out your vials of bitterest wrath upon these batrachians. It will not be long ere you hear what by comparison will make you consider their music sweet and low. Kind friends had warned us ere we retired to sleep the first night in Calcutta, not to suppose that there was anything the matter if we should hear the cry of the jackals. But for that warning I do not know what our feelings would have been, when, awakened from our first sleep by them, we heard a pack pass close to the house. It seemed to us as though the conscience of the whole city had unbarred the portals of hell and put a trumpet in the hand of every liberated fiend. I had presumptuously imagined that familiarity with the concerts of London cats would enable me to sleep through the jackals' efforts. But though the cat has undeniable power, he can never hope to reach the top-notes of the jackal. This latter indeed lacks the conversational variety of the more domestic animal. He confines himself mainly to one tune, which begins in a semi-apologetic, low note; then ascends a little, still with a suspicion of apology and explanation that he did not mean to make quite so much noise but could not help it; and then the flood-gates are open, and seeming to say that he does not care, he yells with an ecstatic *abandon.*

Sometimes a solitary brute will be found sitting on his haunches under your bedroom window. An object of pity—sad-hearted as sad-coated. What private griefs he has, alas! you know not. He may be a creature of tender conscience, unable to connive at or participate in the villanies of his fellows, vexed with the filthy conversation of the wicked, and self-banished from the pack. But more probably he is a sinner who has been ostracised for bad behaviour, and is thinking sadly of his lot. If he would think quietly he might win a measure of sympathy. But the picture of his woe is probably too vivid and he will lift up his voice and weep. When you hear the first low note it will be worth while to seize any handy article of not too great value and sacrifice it ruthlessly ere the baby wakes, for it is not easy in a hot climate to get the baby to sleep again when he has been aroused by a nightmare.

Terrible as "a wandering voice" of the night, the jackal appears a poor creature should he be come upon in his own proper person by day. True, his teeth are to be respected, but that is because, like all carrion feeders, his bite is more or less poisonous. He is himself a sneaking coward. Useful, however, beyond description. No system of drainage will enable Calcutta to dispense with its natural scavengers, and of these the jackal is among the most efficient. Peering into dark corners and with a nose keen to scent out what has escaped even the crow's bright eye—little as that seems to miss—he fills a special place in the sanitary economy of the City of Palaces.

In places too strait for him his duties are deputed to the rats. There be land-rats and water-rats, as Shylock says, though he and the popular nomenclature have here joined together what the naturalist would put asunder. Of all rats, *pace* the naturalist, the musk-rat is the most notable. It is a creature to smell and to be smelt, the active verb being indicated by the length of its nose, and the passive proved by experience. A noisy little quadruped, he scuttles along after dusk with rapid ejaculations of the schoolboy's please-sir-it-was-n't-me type. No one supposes that its "chit-chittering," as Mr. Robinson happily calls it, is a cry of exultation or a happy, much less a defiant, announcement of its presence—such were unnecessary : it can be detected by its odour—it is rather the apology which that odour renders obligatory. Indeed the creature seems to live a life of eager explanations.

A beast with so little self-respect is not likely to command respect from others. Nor does he. He is among the most abject and contemptible of vermin, and yet he is by no means to be left out of account. The scent seems strong enough to infect his voice, and the man who, walking on the roof, hears the creature on

the ground below him forthwith smells, or thinks he
smells, as well as hears. It is commonly believed that
the crawling of a musk-rat over a well-corked glass bottle
will taint its contents, and Bass's ale has often been
sent from the table on this account. Being an abstainer
from the various forms of alcohol, I cannot vouch for
the necessity of this : I have never had to reject, as
musk-rat flavoured, any temperance beverages ; perhaps
they are healthier in their constitution and more
capable of resisting evil influences. But, alas! for
the hand that touches the creature. Here's the smell
of musk-rat still ; all the perfumes of Arabia will not
sweeten this little hand.

Belonging properly to the scavenging department, but
always attempting to shirk their legitimate responsibility, are the ants. " Of this sort are they that creep
into houses," and if they can forage in a store cupboard
among things that would otherwise keep, they care not
to pay attention to matters outside that would decay.
The necessity of setting all four of the feet of food
almirahs in saucers of water, in fact the manufacture
of saucers of a peculiar form especially adapted for this
purpose, is a standing commentary on their maurauding
instincts. In defeating these precautions and in getting
at the sugar they exhibit a perseverance and firmness of
purpose that are remarkable. In all legitimate occupations proper to them they manifest an apparent aimless-
ness equal to their undoubted industry. Like Mr. Will
Carleton, in regard to the circling gnats, I've " wondered
if they thought sometimes they'd maybe get somewhere."

It is perhaps due to them, as to others, to suppose that they ought to know their own business best, but what is gained by an ant's rushing madly a yard and a half in an easterly direction, and then retracing his steps westwards before starting out again in a southerly direction from the original starting-point, has not been revealed to me.

I once witnessed a furious battle between two bodies of ants. The armies came up from opposite sides. There was no strategy, no fencing. It was warfare in its simplest form. Every ant rushed at its enemy with open jaws, and seized him in that middle segment where already he was refined by nature to almost nothing—and bit through. And, since his enemy had simultaneously seized him in the same manner, where there had been two ants there were now four half ants. The battle over, neither victorious nor conquered army was to be seen—only a heap. But what they killed each other for I could not well make out. At the same time it must be admitted that conduct analogous to this and as inscrutable is found elsewhere. Is it not Carlyle who pictures for us thirty sons of the British village of Dumdrudge meeting on the plains of the Peninsula thirty from the French Dumdrudge whom they had never before seen, and at the word of command killing and being killed so that sixty corpses lay where two bands of thirty men had stood ?

The birds which share in the quotation serving as the title of this chapter must be reserved for the next.

"Circles and sails aloft, on pinions majestic, the vulture
　Like the implacable soul of a chieftain slaughtered in battle,
　By invisible stairs ascending and scaling the heavens."
LONGFELLOW. Evangeline.

"Third Servant.　Where dwellest thou ?
　Coriolanus.　　　Under the canopy.
　Third Serv.　　Under the canopy !
　Cor.　　　　　Ay.
　Third Serv.　　Where's that ?
　Cor.　　　　　I' the city of kites and crows.
　Third Serv.　　I' the city of kites and crows !　What an ass
　　　　　　　　　it is !　Then thou dwellest with daws too ? "
SHAKSPERE. Coriolanus.

"Thou buoyant minion of the tropic air."
WORDSWORTH.

CHAPTER VIII.

"THE WING'D PEOPLE OF THE SKIE."

WE pass from night to day, from fur to feathers. Among the inspectors of nuisances whose duties fall in the daytime are some of whom it becomes us to speak respectfully. For among them are included the adjutant, the vulture and the kite.

The adjutant holds military rank, and mounts guard on Government House. He stands between three and four feet high when his head is buried, as it usually is, in his shoulders; when he raises it at the length of his neck, he can return one's gaze with a disadvantage the most trifling. His face is wrinkled, and his head bald with a few straggling hairs scattered upon it. Altogether, except in his early youth, he has a care-worn expression. But there is a dignity in the stride of the long legs, and withal a wicked look in the eye that indicates a self-possessed soul, conscious of relative superiority, if not of absolute perfection. One can imagine indeed a certain feeling of shame in an adjutant detected sitting down, for there is something approaching the ludicrous in the figure he cuts in that attitude; but, on the other hand, if the sitting lowers him beneath the dignity of his standing, his flying proportionately exalts him. Far above the lowlier wings, he wheels in majestic circles, high enough for the legs to be lost to sight entirely and the large feet to appear like nebulous satellites. His outspread wings appear motionless, and the white on their under sides and on his breast, which, it must be confessed, looks rather dirty on close inspection, is purified in the sunlight. The bird that may be seen sweeping through the heavens under the bright Indian sun on a tireless wing hour after hour must be accounted worthy of the roof of Government House by day and of the highest pipal trees by night.

Early in the morning he and his friends are accustomed to take a constitutional over the dewy grass of the maidân, on the trees round which they have been roosting. One day, as I was driving across to Hastings, I saw what struck me as a particularly comic sight. About a dozen adjutants were standing in a straight line and at regular intervals as though they were being drilled. The distance between them just allowed the stretching out of their wings till the tips met. There they stood, as solemn and still as statues facing the rising sun, whose level rays were drying the inside feathers of their outstretched wings after the damps of the night-dews, which in Calcutta are very heavy. There was reason in the act, but the picture was irresistibly ludicrous.

One of these birds was once attached to the Chandney Hospital. His appointment on the hospital staff happened in this wise: Kite-flying in Bengal is an

amusement that excites great interest among all ages—
an interest one would think greatly disproportionate to
the unexciting nature of the occupation. There is not
the skill displayed in the variety and workmanship of
the kite itself which is seen in China, where during
the kite-season the air teems with mammoth centipedes,
gigantic beetles and butterflies, besides aerial men and
women, and is filled with the sound of music as though
the morning stars were rehearsing. The Bengali pretty
uniformly makes his kite of a square piece of very thin
tissue paper, stretched on a cross of very thin bamboo,
which, being exceedingly light, can be held by a very
fine thread. It is in manipulation rather than in construction, that he displays his skill, and a common trick
of the kite-fliers is to get their thin strings across each
other and so to add to their pleasure in manœuvring
their own kites the excitement of cutting each other's
adrift. Now a native flying a kite found that an
adjutant was circling in a stratum of air below that in
which his kite was sailing. It occurred to him at once
to try his skill, which he did only too successfully.
He got his fine thread across the bird's path—surely
that bird was asleep though his pinions were spread—
and, with the wing muscle cut through, the bird
descended earthwards. The man who had achieved this
probably unexpected success felt some compunctious
pity for the bird exiled from the realms of air, and took
him to the Chandney Hospital. There his severed
flesh was stitched together, and in time healed, but that
muscle could never again bear the strain of his weight,

and he became henceforth an inmate of the hospital compound, making himself thoroughly at home, not even evincing uneasiness at the close of the rains when his kind forsake Calcutta for the swamps of the Sunderbunds. On the arrival of a patient in palki or gari he would stalk up to the conveyance and make a preliminary examination of the case to satisfy himself as to the likelihood of recovery.

The vulture and the kite have been spoken of from time immemorial with aversion and contempt. But it is the aversion and contempt of conventionalism. Doubtless the vulture is not a clean feeder, and to see him gorging himself on the municipal rubbish-heaps at Sealdah, is not an edifying spectacle. But, as with the adjutant who shares his orgies, let him rise into the air, and he compels respect not only from the impartial, but even from those whose prejudices have been excited against him as they have seen him revelling in carrion. A line of these birds will come into sight on the horizon, will pass directly over your head, and be lost to sight in the horizon opposite, one following in another's wake, like the war-ships of the gods, and from the time you first distinguish them as specks in the sky, till they are lost again in the distance, you will not have seen the movement of a wing. We can deny of neither the adjutant nor the vulture what may be called " corrupt practices," we must admit in both cases, a baldness of head that would hint at—though we trust, for personal reasons, without being conclusive proof of—uncleanness of habits, but, in spite of this, no

man who has seen either on the wing will venture to
speak other than respectfully of him.

As for the kite, he neither reaches the heights nor
sinks to the depths of the vulture. His flight may be
esteemed noble where the vulture is majestic. When
the latter is in the air, from the tip of one wing to the
tip of the other, a strong, straight line will run along
the margin of both. With the kite the outline of the
wings is a broken line, a sort of collapsed M. But he
is not bald-headed. One species, the brahmany kite,
as he is familiarly called, has the head and shoulders
covered with white feathers, giving him the venerable
and patriarchal look of age, but his eye is not dim, nor
his natural force abated. A scavenger is the kite, with
no preference, however, for putridity. Nay, there is
something of the falcon instinct in him, for a friend
who owned some tumbler-pigeons, told me that he saw
a kite strike one of his pets on the wing, and afterwards another's place in the dove-cote was vacant, as
he suspected, from the same cause. As I have seen
ordinary pigeons fly fearlessly among a whole assembly
of kites, it is possible that it was the accomplishment
of tumbling, that sealed the fate of my friend's birds,
the kite regarding it as a sign of disease or sickness,
bringing them legitimately within his province. If so,
it is a warning to those who spend labour in acquiring
accomplishments, which to the untaught in such
matters, are undistinguishable from unnatural defects.

The kite has the virtue of self-knowledge. He
knows his weak points, and has confidence in his strong

H

ones. It is usual to speak of him as cowardly. A judgment at once more accurate and more generous would pronounce him cautious. He recognises that the shortness of his legs forbids ease of movement on the ground, and that not having the power of doubling quickly, it would be unwise to allow himself to be tempted into corners. But where there is wing-room for the mighty rush of his pinions, his confidence touches the limits of audacity. For example, if opposite doors of a ship's galley be open so that he can dash clean through, he will do it—taking with him the cook's proudest triumph. He will do it too, with such dexterity and lightning-like speed, that not unlikely the true marauder may be lost in the cook's astonishment, and the blame attached to the crows that are hanging about the rigging.

Picnickers know his boldness, and while some of the servants wait upon their masters, others have to be told off to the duty of guarding the cloth with long bamboos. On one such occasion a kite, sweeping down between my neighbour and me, tore a tempting slice of beef from his plate while both knife and fork were busy upon it. Perhaps the boldest thing I ever saw in this bird was in the Wellesley Street, a large thoroughfare, full of traffic. A native woman was walking on the path holding something with both hands in front of her under her chudder. One of these unmannerly creatures swooped down over her shoulder and seized it with his talons. For some seconds the woman and the bird wrestled for it, but, to the credit of the woman be it recorded, the bird had to go without it. As a rule, he will attempt nothing that involves hindrance in his flight, and on this occasion I am inclined to believe that he had calculated on feminine nervousness prompting the dropping of the coveted prize at the moment his wings flashed past the woman's ear; in which case he would have caught it ere it reached the ground, and with unimpeded flight, have pursued his way triumphant. That he, disappointed in this natural expectation, should have ventured to attempt to tear it through the chudder in which it was wrapped, from the hands of a woman proved not to be nervous, speaks loudly for the courage of this maligned bird. Though a crow may venture to creep behind him on the terrace of a house and pull his tail, this speaks rather of the nimbleness and humour of the crow, than of the cowardice of the kite. The crow's attack when both are in the air, is a very make-believe effort, exciting an irritation in the larger bird which always has in it a large proportion of lordly disdain.

As for the Indian crow, one scarcely knows what to say. We have it on the authority of the 'Law Book' of Manu, that in a previous birth he stole milk, and by our own observation we know that the pilfering instinct has not been altogether eradicated by the punitive transmigration. That he has wrung from the naturalists the name of *Corvus splendens* we are aware, though the fact is one of ever fresh astonishment to his best friends, for what there is splendid about him, except his impudence, it were hard to discover. That, indeed, may

give some propriety to the term, for there is an assurance
in his manner which compels something like admiration and an instinctive acknowledgment of his right
and proprietorship in the land where human beings
. dwell on sufferance and so long only as in carrying out
their own purposes they further his.   At the first point
at which our vessel touched India, when we were still
about three miles from shore, several crows were seen
making direct for us.   We had doubtless been noticed
as soon as we showed the tops of our masts above the
horizon, and these were the deputation appointed by
the crow parliament to wait on us, and arrange about
our landing, which act, in its recognition of the requirements of courtesy, asserted the claim to the possession
and the authority which rendered that courtesy obligatory.

I incurred a crow's displeasure once, and do not wish
to do it again.   It happened after this manner :   There
was a pandanus near my verandah, which was one of
my favourite trees.   Four or five crows' nests were
already located in various parts of the garden, with the
occupants of which I was on the best of terms, but one
pair of the crows determined to build in this pandanus.
At first I offered no objection, but when the nest was
finished, the cock bird found his energies—aroused by
the task of building—suddenly deprived of direction.
He therefore occupied his leisure moments, therein
satisfying his conscience that with true marital devotion he was dancing attendance on his wife, by
digging with his strong beak at the heads of the

pandanus shoots. It was a piece of the most wanton mischief. Now as the pandanus is an endogen, this procedure threatened its life. I expostulated with the bird; he would desist from his work and listen with mock gravity, and the moment I had finished, would dig out a fresh piece of the plant and throw it down to me as I stood beneath him. When I found that he was not to be reasoned with, I felt it necessary to give the mali orders to remove the nest from the tree altogether. This was done, and as far as I could see, the mali remained in favour, but I was visited with the most serious displeasure. Whenever I ventured into the garden that crow would signal to his friends, and, in an instant, from twenty to fifty crows, according as the exigencies of the hour might allow, would flock around me and make the most unpleasant remarks. If I even showed myself on the upper verandah, that offended bird would at once fly on to the balustrade of it, and stretching out his neck, would accuse me of every conceivable enormity in such deep and sepulchral tones, as went far towards making life miserable. This deep-seated ill-will, this rancorous hatred was maintained for quite a long while, till, prompted to try another tree, in which he found he was not molested, his wrath became appeased, and, his thoughts being diverted by household cares, I was at liberty once more to walk in the garden.

Mischief is the crow's occupation. He delights to torment the kites, for whose claws, however, he has an evident respect. He will most wantonly pull a sparrow's nest to pieces if it be not far enough up the water-spout to be out of his reach. When he walks, he has a side-long gait, and jerks his wings with a motion irresistibly suggesting both the wink of a person intending to attempt some practical joke, and the rubbing together of the hands of the person who has succeeded. And, indeed, this is just his position ; he has always just done some trick, and is always about to do another. But not without an air of solemnity. As Mr. Phil. Robinson says, his step is grave and he ever seems on the point of quoting Scripture, while his eyes are wandering on carnal matters.

Howbeit, he is friendly and willing to fit himself into the arrangements of your household. You never have to wait for him at meal times. He knows and observes your hours from chota-hazri till dinner, and is as ready to join you at the meals prepared, as he has been in the intervals to assist the cook in preparing them.

He has an admirable self-possession, and a most perfect control over his countenance. I have only once seen a crow—to use a familiar phrase—taken aback, forced to own himself discomfited. It was one morning before breakfast, and I was speeding across the maidân on my bicycle. A crow, to whom the machine was perhaps a novelty, for at that time there were not many in use in Calcutta, came flying towards me to satisfy his curiosity. The bright steel spokes were, of course, invisible to human eyes, and, as it proved, to his. In the spirit of impudence and frolic, exhilarated by the early morning freshness, he made a dash to go through what seemed to him to be simply a hoop on which my saddle rested. It need hardly be said that he did not get through. I looked back, there he lay on the ground hopelessly surprised—there was not the slightest use in his attempting to disguise it. His caw expressed perplexity mingled with disgust. His head was sore, his feathers ruffled, and when he got up and went away to think about it, he looked more like a crow ashamed of himself than I had ever before seen.

Like many other persons who seem to have genius in some departments, this bird appears to lack even common-sense in others. By some youthful indiscretion a crow too young to fly had got out of one of the nests. My attention was called to the fact by the terrible hubbub that his relatives were making. The young bird was on the grass under the mango-tree in which was the nest which he had left. He was attended by a dozen or more of his friends who were eagerly vying with each other for the honour of most loudly lecturing him for leaving home against his parents' wishes. I went out and examined him, and since there was no hurt on his body that I could detect, I left him to his friends, thinking that, as it was then early morning, he would before evening become sufficiently practised in hopping and fluttering to get into the tree for the night. I knew moreover that, as at present attended, he was perfectly safe from harm during the day. But, by evening, he seemed to have acquired a liking for his terrestrial exercises and to be quite happy in hopping about the ground, nor in any way disposed to climb into a safer roosting-place, though the elder birds were renewing their vociferous advice.

Knowing that such a helpless thing could not hope to escape the prowling jackals, I put him up in the tree myself, but after he had tumbled out, and been replaced two or three times, I left him. The old birds continued to give advice for some time longer, but ultimately they too left him to the darkening shadows, and next morning no trace of him was to be found.

I cannot help feeling that if a half of the ability and genius which those crows had on occasions exhibited in playing tricks on their neighbours had been devoted to the getting of that young relative into the tree of his birth and keeping him there, he might have become a valuable member of the race and a leading spirit in their commonwealth.

Counting himself not unworthy to rank with kite or crow, notwithstanding disparity in size, is the republican myna—a serious bird, very quiet in dress and in manner, yet, withal, having an air of as complete self-possession as has his corvine neighbour, and of just so much self-assertion as necessitates a general recognition of his claims. He is not quarrelsome, nor is he mischievous; but he is both able and prepared to defend his own, and neither the kite, depending on his strength, nor the crow on his versatility may offer him insult with impunity. His assemblies parade the maidân or deliberate on the terraces with a mien of self-respect and responsibility becoming an important people. Sometimes, it must be admitted, a specially burning question produces an

unwonted excitement, and the meeting is disgraced by
unseemly and noisy wrangling, vituperation taking the
place of argument, and personalities being freely indulged in—an evil incident to communities trained in
democratic traditions.   But this is the exception.   The
rule is that the myna should bear himself with a grave
and becoming dignity in his private walk, and that in
public assembly he should observe the strictest decorum.

"The nautch-girls in their spangled skirts and bells,
  That chime light laughter round their restless feet."
SIR E. ARNOLD. Light of Asia.

"The Reverend McPherson believed that a nautch
  Was a very diabolical kind of debauch,
  He thought that that dance's voluptuous mazes
  Would turn a man's brain, and allure him to blazes.

    *   *   *   *   *

  Then suddenly sounded a loud-clanging gong,
  And there burst on the eyes of the wondering throng
        A bevy of girls
        Dressed in bangles and pearls
        And other rich jims,
        With fat podgy limbs,
        And bright yellow streaks
        All over their cheeks,
        Enormous gold rings
        And other queer things
        In the ears and the nose,
        On the ankles and toes,
        Which shuffled and beat
        A strange time with the feet,
        And sang a wild air
        Which affected your hair,
  While behind them a circle of men and of boys
  With tom-toms and pipes made a terrible noise,
  And retainers stood by waving censer and torch ;
  And—the Reverend McPherson was in for a nautch!

    *   *   *   *   *

        The minister took
        A pretty close look,
        And the minister said,
        With a shake of the head,
 'If with lassies lik' thae, dear, Gehenna is graced,
  I don't think the de'il has got muckle gude taste.'"
"ALIPH CHEEM." Lays of Ind.

"Were you with these, my prince, you'd soon forget
  The pale, unripen'd beauties of the North."
ADDISON. Cato.

CHAPTER IX.

THE NAUTCH.

I HAD been in India for two years, and had never seen the Indian dance. When, therefore, Mr. —— accosted me with the inquiry, " Do you care to go to a nautch ? " I had no answer but a ready acquiescence. I would go, and for ever roll away the disgrace of not having seen India, the true India, the India of pre-European taint.

At the hour for starting, we were joined by a mutual friend, Captain ——, who was to accompany us. He was skipper of a fine steamer trading between London and Calcutta, and during his stay in the latter port always hired a buggy, which he drove himself. The vacant seat in this was at my disposal; but I preferred to share the accommodation of Mr. ——'s gari, for I had had from Captain ——'s own lips some accounts of his driving experiences which had a little shaken my faith in his skill as a Jehu. Thus he had only a day or two before assisted in a small collision that left him aground, as he expressed it, in the middle of the road. He explained that it was not his fault. " —— was with me in the buggy, and he knows far more about navigating these things than I do, and he said that what I did was perfectly right." I concluded to watch that buggy's fortunes rather than share them; and, indeed, got some considerable amount of amusement from so doing, especially at the corners of the streets. Nevertheless, we all reached our destination safely. It was the house of a wealthy Hindu. Entering by a gateway into the quadrangle, we found it full of people of all sorts walking round the open court and standing on the steps of the puja-dalan, or worship-hall, facing the gateway, in which—for it was during the Durga Puja holidays—was a very elaborate image of Durga with her ten arms, her satellite gods and goddesses, animals and demons.

Enclosing a space in the centre of the courtyard were two or three rows of chairs reserved for the more important guests, among whom we presently had the honour of finding ourselves. It was in this space, as we understood, that the nautch would presently be executed; but we were rather disgusted to find that meanwhile our attention was invited to the tricks of a certain European conjuror, styling himself Professor Dashwood, and very indifferently maintaining the credit of his profession. Perhaps our native fellow-guests enjoyed this performance, but, as Laurence Sterne said, " An Englishman does not travel to see Englishmen," and our Western craving for oriental sights was hardly satisfied by it. We schooled our impatience, as on similar occasions, by the consideration that purely oriental sights of any sort are not to be expected in Calcutta.

Consciously, or unconsciously, the European element is admitted into everything. Thus one sees pictures drawn by natives illustrating legends of their gods supposed to refer to times anterior to the creation of Europeans, in which the gods are protected by body-guards dressed in the uniform, and armed with the weapons, of the private in the British army of to-day. And even in what we might expect to find *par excellence* an oriental scene—a torchlight wedding procession—it is becoming customary to introduce horsemen dressed in this same uniform, minus the boots, and with the addition of a cocked hat. We therefore accepted Professor Dashwood, groaning secretly at the length to which his proceedings threatened to drag themselves out. But time is no object to a native of India, and we, being in a native's house, had to submit to native ways, hoping that in the end patience would be rewarded.

Our patience was not doomed to so severe a test as we feared, for presently a babu informed us that in a room upstairs there would be a nautch almost immediately. We hailed the welcome news, and at once followed our informant's kindly guidance to a long apartment down either side of which was arranged a row of chairs. Here we found ourselves part of a somewhat promiscuous gathering, for, though our host and the majority of the guests were Hindus, there were a goodly sprinkling of Mohammedans, some Marwaris, a few Parsis, with probably specimens of other races whose specialities I was not at that time skilled to detect, in addition of course to the Europeans among whom we were numbered.

About midnight a nautch girl entered, followed by three men and a boy. It was an imposing spectacle. The men varied much in personal appearance, but they had this in common, that each was the ugliest man any of us had ever seen; i.e., each was ugliest when you looked at him. Look at number one, and a more ill-favoured man could not be found. But turn to number two, and he was more ill-favoured in direct view than number one in memory, so we gazed and marvelled. As for the boy, he gave promise, if time for growth were allowed, of qualifying for the place of any of the three who might become unfit for duty.

The girl was pretty without qualification. She had good features, a pleasant expression, a graceful figure, and scarcely needed the foil afforded by her companions. Her dress was of a light flimsy muslin, as far as my uninitiated discrimination could judge, of a general red tone, and the style of dress gave the impression that she had begun to dress at the top with great care, proceeding downward and becoming tired and negligent. The jewellery that almost muffled up the head and arms was tastefully arranged, the drapery of the body and shoulders hung in graceful folds. Then came a skirt reaching about to the knees destitute of a single line of beauty, and then we passed from the negative to the positive, for below this was a pair of what may be best described as tinsel-treated water-hose of small diameter, but, judging by their horizontal folds, of enormous length, which were prevented from coming over the feet by two exceedingly clumsy anklets with bells, which we hoped would by their melody make some amends to the ear for the offence they were to the eye.

Two of the men carried stringed instruments, the boy a pair of cymbals, and the third man, when he entered, appeared to be carrying a large baby. The bundle which so appeared when lowered into position, was found to contain two tom-toms and a pockethand-kerchief of the size of a shawl or table-cloth. This pertained to the *danseuse* though from its size and weight there was an obvious advantage to her in letting her attendant take charge of it with his tom-toms.

And now the performance began. At first the girl stood perfectly still while the music indulged in some preliminary flourishes. After a while—it seemed to us a long while—she showed signs of movement, slowly, as an awakening serpent unfolds itself, both arms were extended—very gracefully; and then a few steps were taken forward very ungracefully, the feet being strooched along the ground, and then the heel brought down heavily to bring out the music of the ankle bells. A half dozen of these awkward steps and she uncere-moniously turned round and walked back, making straight for the handkerchief. We thought that she had beaten a retreat in consciousness of failure, and pitied her, admiring her courage as she almost imme-diately faced round with as smiling an expression as the sternest necessities of her profession could demand.

Presently she started again and got a few steps farther
with the same stiff and heavy gait, and again turned
sharp round, walking back to her original position.
This happened repeatedly enough to convince us that
our thought of failure was a mistake and our pity
misapplied. The ignominious failure had been a con-
spicuous success. For some time the nautch consisted
in a succession of these advances followed by abrupt
cessations of all rhythmic movement and quiet non-
chalant walks back. In each advance the attendant
musicians followed closely on the dancer, retreating
backwards still playing when she retreated.

After some considerable amount of this she broke
out into singing, repeated the former movements to the
same musical accompaniment, but with her own vocal
efforts added. When we were almost satiated with
this, a welcome change took place—welcome partly
because it was a change—; Singling out one of the
European ladies among the guests, she settled herself
on the floor in front of her. Her exercises were now
confined to the swaying of the body, the movements
of the head, neck, and arms, and since all that was
graceful in movement as in costume pertained to these
parts of the body, we lost nothing by this change, but
what could well be spared.

This kind of thing continued much longer than our
enjoyment in it, and we began to want to see if another
girl would do as this one did. Eventually our curiosity
on this point was gratified. A new group appeared in
the doorway—as before in the matter of number and

relative attractions. The second girl had not quite so good features as the first, but she made up for this in the possession of an exceedingly happy expression and an intensely mischievous twinkle in her eye. She was apparently a wayward, spoiled child, and if the men who accompanied her had ever tried to manage her they had doubtless given up the endeavour some time ago. The two girls met with a loving kind of smile, exchanged a few words in an undertone, during which eyes were flashing and facial muscles active enough to give us the impression that we guests were the subject of the hurried conversation, and that the subject was not being treated with the severe gravity that it demanded. This second damsel was dressed much as the other, except that the general colour of her costume was green instead of red, and that being younger, and probably a shorter time in the profession, she had not had as long an opportunity of loading herself with jewellery. She went through a set of promenadings and singings similar to that of her predecessor, and we went through the same successive stages of interest, indifference, and weariness, probably reaching the third stage sooner in this second case. The only added interest was that derived from occasional contretemps between the fair performer and the gentlemen who were acting as her guides, philosophers, and friends. Now and then we saw one of them, indiscreetly as we judged, bending a little forward and whispering some suggestions. Immediately the little vixen's face would catch fire, and she would turn a look on him as though

I

it would be rather a pleasure to consume him. Generally the periodic appeal to the handkerchief gave her the private opportunity she needed of telling her friends what she thought of them, but once or twice, to the amusement of the spectators, she broke off in the middle of the song and dance and compressed into a pithy word or two a good proportion of her mind. We never supposed that what she did just after one of these little episodes was what had been advised, but it might have been.

To her succeeded a woman of mature years, dressed in more matronly style, the sight of whom gave us quite a different feeling from that excited by these two girls. With regard to them, though we knew both that they were thus earning their living, and that it would not be pleasant to follow out in thought what, by a figure of speech, may be called their home-life, yet when we looked at their merry faces we could cheat ourselves out of serious thought, and could think of them as enjoying the dance more than many of the spectators of it. It seemed in them play rather than work, the exercise of surplus youthful vigour like the games of school children in their holiday hour. But this woman was past playing, she was obviously working, and with the full responsibility of womanhood on her. The way she went about her dancing, not with the vivacity of the others, but with a sense of duty sternly lined on her face, dispelled the previous happy delusion that it was all recreation ; and enjoyment in the dance was no longer possible. Here the relation between the woman and the attendants was confessedly reversed. They made no attempt to control or guide her, but humbly listened for any hints she might quietly throw back to them under cover of resorting to the handkerchief, which, for her, as for the others, occupied a large part of the tom-tom performer's luggage. This woman, at the request of one of the native guests, perhaps partly out of regard to her age and presumed infirmities, very soon seated herself with her musicians before one of the European ladies, so that we saw but little of her dancing and were not sorry.

By this time we were tired of a performance presenting so little of variety, which had already stretched out till after two o'clock and which showed every sign of prolonging itself to daylight. So we took a stroll into the gallery running round the open courtyard where we had left Professor Dashwood, looking down into which we saw that the guests there also were now being entertained with nautch dancing. Then we went along the gallery where the girls were accommodated—kennelled would almost seem the suitable term. The ground was partitioned off into squares by fences of pillows, cloths were spread, and there, on the ground, each party in its own square, sat or lay the unoccupied performers. Most of the men were availing themselves of the chance of a sleep, notwithstanding the noise of people coming and going, while most of the girls were sitting up, wide awake, and on the look-out for a chance of a flirtation with any of the guests who might indulge them. As

we were not of this number, we made our way back
again, found our host, made our salaams and departed
home.

We were glad to have seen a nautch, but our
appetite in the matter was abundantly satisfied. As
Capt. —— put it, " I would not go the length of my
foot to see another." Our visit had however given us
an opportunity of increasing our knowledge of native
life and we saw much that evening that was of more
interest to us than the nautch itself. The well-to-do
natives in their own homes are different people
altogether from the native servants and clerks that do
their best to distract a man in his house and office.
The profuse politeness and the overflowing ceremony of
the native gentleman who is not straining after English
manners or seeking English employments, but is simply
showing hospitality and courtesy in obedience to the
demands of his own national customs, seem to have
become a second nature, free from all artificiality, and
are a pleasant study.

But, with all their graceful courtesy, they do not
seem to allow any infringement of rule to pass from
fear of hurting the feelings of the infractors. It is a
little dangerous to generalise ; but, from what I have
seen, I should be inclined to say that where a European
would overlook a fault with the remark, " It's very
unfortunate, but we must accept it, and make the best
of it ; " and so let it pass with as little notice as
possible, the Hindu would correct it without fear or
favour. One or two little incidents occurred during this

evening illustrating this. One of them recalled the words of our Saviour about the danger of a more honourable man coming when the highest seats were taken, and the less honourable, though invited, guests being compelled with shame to take the lower places. Two natives of evident respectability entered and took two vacant chairs. But these chairs had been reserved for possible " more honourable " comers. The host went up to them, saluted them, and with the utmost politeness spoke a few words to them, then with a parting salute left them. They at once rose and took their places in the doorway—literally, the lowest room—where they stood, seatless. The utmost courtesy and apparent cordiality were maintained, no irritation was expressed, the placid surface of friendliness was unruffled, but the chairs were vacated. We could not but admire the firmness with which the host's arrangements were carried out, each guest being kept in his own place and rank, and the courtesy and blandness with which the host did this himself, instead of deputing it, as a disagreeable business, to some dependent or subordinate who might have done it more offensively.

Another thing that struck us was the delicacy manifested in the showing of special attentions. Thus once or twice a Mohammedan gentleman who was very much at home in the house and gave orders pretty freely to the servants, wished the nautch girl to pay special attention to one or other guest. In these cases he managed it by calling one of the servants, bidding him tell the girl's attendants, but, lest this should seem to rob the attention of its spontaneity, the servant was instructed when he received his order to hurry out of the room as though the order was concerning some matter outside ; taking care however to pass close by the performers and to whisper his instructions as quietly as possible in passing. So well was this done that we should not have detected it but for the accident of the performers on one such occasion being so close to us that the order was executed within our hearing. After this we could of course understand the act when repeated out of ear-shot.

> "... The soft delicious air,
> To heal the scar of these corrosive fires
> Shall breathe her balm."—MILTON. *Paradise Lost.*

> " The solid mountains shone, bright as the clouds,
> Grain-tinctured, drenched in empyrean light."
>
> WORDSWORTH. *The Prelude.*

"The dry land appeared, not in level sands forsaken by the surges, which those surges might again claim for their own; but in range beyond range of swelling hill and iron rock, for ever to claim kindred with the firmament, and to be companioned by the clouds of heaven."—RUSKIN.

> " Northwards soared
> The stainless ramps of huge Himâla's wall,
> Ranged in white ranks against the blue—untrod,
> Infinite, wonderful—whose uplands vast,
> And lifted universe of crest and crag,
> Shoulder and shelf, green slope and icy horn,
> Riven ravine, and splintered precipice
> Led climbing thought higher and higher, until
> It seemed to stand in heaven and speak with gods.
> Beneath the snows dark forests spread, sharp-laced
> With leaping cataracts and veiled with clouds:
> Lower grew rose-oaks, and the great fir groves
> Where echoed pheasant's call and panther's cry,
> Clatter of wild sheep on the stones, and scream
> Of circling eagles; under these, the plain
> Gleamed like a praying-carpet at the foot
> Of those divinest altars."—SIR E. ARNOLD. *Light of Asia.*

> "Earth's crammed with heaven,
> And every common bush a-fire with God;
> But only he who sees takes off his shoes,
> The rest sit round it and pluck blackberries,
> And daub their natural faces unaware
> More and more from the first similitude."
>
> E. B. BROWNING. *Aurora Leigh.*

CHAPTER X.

"THE MOUNTAINS SHALL BRING PEACE TO
THE PEOPLE."

RUSKIN says that the spirit of the hills is action, and
that that of the lowlands is repose. It may be so. But
if the lowlands sleep they dream uneasily. Who that
has been compelled to live on "the plains"—on the
wide stretching alluvial delta of the Ganges—during the
rainy season, has not felt that the lowland repose has
been quick with the activities of life? Its palms and
pipals, its bamboos and tamarinds that stand all the year
are lost in a new, exuberant, luscious growth holding
high revel, intoxicated, mad with a summer frenzy, delirious. Even one's personal effects within the house
are overrun. A grey forest waves triumphantly over
the books, defying brush and duster; and, while men
sleep, an enemy sows spores on their shoes which ere
morning are transformed into horticultural gardens. In
a night, with the rapidity of Jonah's gourd, and with as
ill an effect on the human temper as had that luckless
vegetable, grow the lively and unlovely fungi. Not that
any one becomes as vigorously angry in regard to the
flourishing mould as was the prophet in the matter of

the withered gourd; there is too complete a sense of
helplessness for that. Vigour, even in wrath, is out
of the question—has not one's whole nature grown
mouldy? Are not the faculties of abuse and complaint
sodden? There is no crispness left in one's invective.
Struggling with fate is hopeless; objurgation, unsatis-
factory. These are the rains. You welcomed them
when the monsoon first broke upon you, and envied the
crows and sparrows as they came out from the dark
places of the trees, where they had been hiding with
beaks agape, and settled themselves on the tops of the
branches, loosening their feathers that the acceptable
drops might penetrate the more easily to the skin. You
welcomed them, for, after the scorching, merciless sun-
shine of May and early June, their waters seemed cool
and refreshing, and it was an undeniable relief to have
a cloud veil over the face of the sun.

But those waters have become heated now, the earth
no longer thirstily absorbs them as they fall, the air is
charged with steam, and nothing but the hopelessness
and the lassitude born of the rains themselves prevents
your as eagerly desiring their departure as a little
while ago you looked forward to their advent. You
wish them gone but it is languidly.

From the hills cometh your help. And the hills are
nearer than they once were. What of ease and comfort
there may be in the journey in these days I know not,
but even before I left India—some years ago now—there
was a line of rails not only to the foot of the Himalaya,
but up to the sanatorium itself, and I had the pleasure

of an early trip on the Darjiling Steam Tramway
Company—a name since superseded, I believe—in a
little experimental toy train that timorously bore six
first-class passengers on a small seated platform, and of
unclassed natives as many as could sprawl on the top of
the luggage, along a line of parallel rails laid down on
the old road to the much disconcertment of various
ponies and bullocks which had not yet got accustomed
to the innovation, and ran before the train for long
distances until happily shunted by some wayfarer into
one or other of the occasional open spaces or more
practicable slopes on which they could be passed.

No one can tell the relief of the mountain air to a
limp visitant from the plains. And the charm of the
scenery, ever changing but always glorious, is an almost
unsafe excitement, like too stimulating a diet for one
returning from the dead. Even the ride in the train was
exhilarating as we climbed upwards and ever upwards,
from the heavy atmosphere of the terai, up through the
leafy lower slopes, and now and then crept out on to a
bolder ridge, looking back on the way already travelled
and seeing short sections of the line appearing below
and behind us, and looking forward to where we could
see occasional indications of our course marked out on
higher levels and, as it seemed sometimes, on such un-
connected hills that we wondered however we could get
there. Oftentimes the rails were laid quite on the edge
of the road affording us the opportunity of looking
directly down steep precipices and wishing that the constructing engineers had seen fit to give an inch or two

more of margin. At one place, where the old road had been led round the shoulder of a hill rather too sharply to allow the rails to follow it, a supplementary hill-side had been built out and the rails led out on to it and then, in a loop, brought back and carried by a bridge over themselves and so up again on to the old road, thus giving a greater length through which to divide the rise to the easing of the gradient. The glittering micaceous rocks through which the road was cut, the trickling of the water-courses down the faces of them—of which water-courses we availed ourselves to water our little engine through a split bamboo—the beauty and delicacy of the mountain flowers by the wayside increasing proportionately with the grandeur of the general scenery as we were ever reaching higher altitudes, combined to form a varying panorama of unflagging interest and charm which no number of journeyings to and fro upon the road would be able to dissipate.

But if the ride up was exhilarating, the excursions on foot or in the saddle from Darjiling itself were even more so. One ride that I took to a friend's plantation some fifteen miles distant, I remember not so much for the loveliness of the scenery or the elasticity of the air or the joyousness of the exercise, as because it gave me, as I thought at the time, a less inadequate symbol of eternity than I had so far met with. It is easy to speak of a fifteen mile ride. You think of the starting out, you mention the paltry fifteen miles, and at once you think of the arrival at the end. But when one is on a diminutive mountain pony that is without ambitions and not without much ease-regarding philosophy, travelling along a path that is narrow, in many places rotten and unreliable and in some broken away altogether, so that it craves wary walking, the ears vexed with the sizzling conversation of the cicadas as of a minor species of forest imps slightly given to sarcasm, and the route buried mile after mile in innumerable trees, useless as landmarks, since they are all alike on the right hand and on the left, before and behind, giving no clue themselves and shutting out from sight any other possible clue to the knowledge of how much of the way has been traversed and is behind and how much is yet before, one comes to believe that the way has no end, and that, compared with this, the snake with its tail in its mouth constitutes but a poor symbol of eternity. You turn your snake round, and once in every complete revolution you come to where the extremes meet and start again. But in such a journey as this the circle seems to start again at every cicada-blessed tree, and they stand as close together as circumstances will permit.

And yet the way though so apparently interminable was not monotonous. It was full of natural delight and irresistible fascination, not unmingled with more doubtfully pleasing influences. Occasionally a certain unpleasant taint in the air would most unambiguously indicate a small settlement of the natives. These people have put on their garments once for all in unremembered days. They cannot tell when they put them on for it was long ago. They never take them off.

When a garment becomes too thin to keep out the cold, or shows signs of wearing out, they get another and place it over the old one, which is then at liberty to seek its kindred dust, gradually and unseen. Then some-times the pony would express his displeasure at the state of the road. We would come to a steep place where perhaps running water had washed away the earth and left the rocks bare, slippery and of uncertain stability, and he would stop short and contemplate the scene. Being remonstrated with and urged onwards, he would pretend a readiness to climb the steep rock-face on the one side, or to plunge headlong down the khud or slope on the other side, by way of intimating his estimate of the path on which he was required to go. Being checked from illustrating his irony in these side directions, he would again contemplate the position in front for a few moments, and then wisely and sorrowfully shake his head as he thought of the degene-racy of modern road makers. Such incidents sometimes resulted in compromise, I getting off and dragging him where he declined to carry me. Every now and then I caught glimpses of my guide, the syce, who was mostly taking short cuts through the jungle, turning up at intervals however, and indeed not failing me often where there was any special difficulty in the road or any likelihood of a mistake in the direction. Once and again I gave him the pony to lead where the road made walking more pleasant than riding, and I took the responsibility of a fat and podgy puppy which he was carrying to a friend.

The journey did come to an end at last, and in the midst of cordial welcomes and hearty greetings there arose a loud and bitter cry. It was Master Fred. He had seen the syce's pup, and refused to be comforted, because it was not for him.

During my stay among the mountains, I enjoyed the hospitality of friends in three different places at some distance apart, and from each house had glorious views of the snowy range. How the chest expands and the lungs swell in sympathy with the eyes as they are drawn from forest to forest, from ridge to ridge, on and on, through softening shades of colour until it seems as though the verge of the earthly is passed, and, in the glory of those luminous peaks bathed in the early sunlight, the first glimpses of the heavenly are revealed. While standing with a friend one morning, looking across the intervening forest-clad summits to where Kanchinjinga shone resplendent, enthroned amid the " Abode of Snow," and where, to the right, the crown of the lesser, but still mighty, Tchumalari towered solitarily over the nearer mountains, I was led to ask about the national boundaries. My friend explained, showed where this boundary line ran and where that, told me that Tchumalari was in Tibet, and, then, turning towards Kanchinjinga, he indicated the limit of British territory on the side of it, and added, pointing to the eternal and untrodden snows of the majestic peaks, " These belong to the Rajah of Sikkim." It was simply a way of stating a fact in political geography, but the phrase grated on my ear. Nothing of the sort was meant, but it seemed a profanation and a sacrilege. To speak of those sublime snow-clad mountains that appeared nothing less than the battlements of heaven, or the pearly gates of the celestial city, as belonging to a man—a dusky little rajah—it was as though the seer of Patmos, when he saw the Great White Throne and Him that sat on it, from Whose face the earth and the heaven fled away, had had his eye caught by an inscription on the base of that throne, " John Smith, sculpsit."

Doubtless men can live constantly in the presence of such glory till the sense of it is lost. Nay, many of the native inhabitants have probably never been awakened to a sense of it at all, and pursue their various callings as unaffected by the sublimity of their surroundings as the snakes and eagles. These hill-tribes work among the tea-gardens of their hills with about as much and as little interest as the inhabitants of the plains work in the rice-fields. They see the eagle strike the pigeon and the lizard seize the cricket, and hear the great sand wasp humming contentedly as she buries green grass-hoppers in the hole with her egg, and these lessons are more obvious to them than would be those that a Wordsworth or a Ruskin might draw from the rocks and the flowers, the mountains and the clouds that crown them.

K

"He dared not mock the dervish whirl,
The Brahmin's rite, the Lama's spell;
God knew the heart; Devotion's pearl
Might sanctify the shell."

J. G. WHITTIER. *My Namesake.*

"The prayer of the infidels is only in error."—*The Koran.*

"Much of the apparently harmful influence of the hills on the religion of the world is nothing else than their general gift of exciting the poetical and inventive faculties, in peculiarly solemn tones of mind. . . Strictly speaking, we ought to consider the superstitions of the hills, universally, as a form of poetry; regretting only that men have not yet learned how to distinguish poetry from well-founded faith."—RUSKIN.

"In silence, in the Eternal Temple let him worship, if there be no fit word."—CARLYLE. *Past and Present.*

"The dew is on the lotus!—rise, great sun!
And lift my leaf and mix me with the wave.
Om mani padme hum, the sunrise comes!
The dewdrop slips into the shining sea!

SIR E. ARNOLD. *Light of Asia.*

CHAPTER XI.

PRAYER-FLAGS, OR THE TREES OF THE LAW.

TRAVELLING on the Himalayas, one will frequently see lifted up high above the little squat huts of the people, objects which at a distance look like the blades of immense carving knives, the handles of which are planted firmly in the ground. These are tall bamboos with narrow strips of silk running up the entire height, tapering off to a point at the top and inscribed with prayers which the wind is supposed to repeat every time it flaps the flag. In these same districts one finds also prayer-wheels, turned some by hand and some by water, with other precatory devices of Lamaism.

The people who pray thus do not bear very high characters. Buddhism, as reflected in Arnold's *Light of Asia*, is lovely, but its modern developments are not, and it is a problem of some interest that is before us when we place side by side the facts that the teaching of Gautama is pure enough to command the admiration of Christendom, and that Buddhism in its living idolatrous forms is vile enough to earn the contempt of heathendom. It presents itself in different aspects under different conditions. But however widely the Buddhists of Bhotan, Ceylon, Burmah,

Siam, Japan and China, may differ in other things they seem to agree in being as unlike their founder as they can possibly be. Here, in China, for instance, where I write these lines, no word of deeper opprobrium can be found wherewith to brand a man than the term "Buddhist Priest.". When you have called him that you have exhausted your repertory of insult.

At the time I first saw these liturgical appliances, however, I knew less of the Buddhists than I do now, and when I beheld their devotions my spirit was stirred in me more favourably than would perhaps be the case were I to revisit those mountain slopes.

It is easy to laugh at the superstition involved in such things, but it is scarcely wise. Superstition in prayer does not depend on the form but on the spirit. Amid the grandeur of that scenery, where everything is calculated to suggest a pantheistic creed, those flags seem to bear witness to man's seeking after the living God, and to lift up his petitions before Him, nay more, they force the very winds of heaven to become his intercessors. It is true that the words inscribed are not in the form of direct supplication. They contain the magic phrase: "Om mani padme hum"—"The dew is on the lotus"—with which Sir E. Arnold has made us familiar in his poem, and to which Professor Rhys Davids attaches the meaning, The Self-Creative Force is in the Kosmos. But what form of prayer could more suitably present a helpless man before the mighty God with Whom he instinctively felt kinship, and from Whom he sought for blessing, but blessing according to

the Divine wisdom rather than according to human
ignorance?   Have we not read with sympathy of
the boy who was found on his knees in a meadow
repeating the alphabet, and who, on being questioned
as to what he was doing, said that he was praying.   He
knew he needed to receive, he knew God was able to
give, but for what he ought to ask he knew not, and so
bending before God he presented the alphabet, trusting
that from those letters God would frame for him right
petitions.   Is not this an illustration of the words:
"The Spirit also helpeth our infirmity; for we know not
how to pray as we ought"?   Is it not in accord with
the highest form of prayer ever heard: "Thy will be
done"?   And are not these flags—these "trees of the
law,"—raised heavenwards as signs of human need with
the sacred words that speak of the Divine control of the
universe, possible expressions of the same feeling?

If it be said that the flags are flapping on their bamboos all the day long while the men who placed them
there are otherwise occupied, and all night long while
they are unconscious, is that necessarily a condemnation
of the method?   Have we not a parallel to the planting
of these flag-staffs in the admittedly pious prayer of the
Roundhead captain on the eve of battle, " O Lord, there
is hot work before me and I may perchance forget
Thee; but however much I forget Thee, do not Thou, O
Lord, forget me"?   Was not that a prayer-flag, bravely
planted that morning to flutter its petition all the day
in the ear of God?   What is defective in these prayers
is not special to these mountain slopes, it is nothing more
or less than what is defective in too many prayers else-

where. The superstitious character must be admitted, but it is a superstitious character which they share with —perhaps our own petitions. Because this "form of prayer" is not usual in European countries, Europeans are able to judge it in a dispassionate way, and they condemn it, as they suppose, on the ground of its mechanical nature. But there is nothing really more mechanical in turning a phrase round on a wheel or inscribing it on a fold of silk than there is in sounding it through the mechanical apparatus formed by the human larynx, vocal chords, teeth, tongue and lips. This charge of being mechanical may as easily be brought against prayers in European lands—whether liturgical or extemporaneous—as against these vexillic or rotary prayers. All expressed prayer must be mechanical, and is in danger of becoming formal. Yet the spirit that feels after God calls for expression. It is when the form takes the place of the spirit which it should express that we have superstition. The pharisees of old were condemned because they thought to be heard for their much speaking with their vocal organs; the Buddhists of to-day lie under the identical condemnation because they think they shall be heard for their much turning of wheels and fluttering of silk. But just as that much speaking of the pharisee—the mechanism of which can be described in physiological terms—might have been made the reverent expression of continuous, sincere and acceptable prayer, his repetitions not being "vain," so these inscriptions on flags and wheels in Tibet, Nipal and Bhotan may be, and in some cases perhaps are, the outward expression of a

piety sincere and deep, of a prayer in the heart as un-
ceasing as the day-long fluttering of the silk in the
breeze. As long as the heart is in the act, whatever the
agent may be—wind, water, or the human hand—there
is real prayer, and no more can be said for the worship
of the most decorous of congregations with the stateliest
liturgy; or for the extemporaneous utterances of the
most demonstrative in our " Christian lands."

But this is the theoretically possible. The fact remains
—Buddhists are not the holy and devout saints that we
could wish. One thing that may perhaps help to explain their debased character, though perhaps as largely
the effect as the cause of it, is this: Their worship at its
best, that is, when most sincere, is not a worship of love
or hope, but of dread. They have no such conception
of the love of God as the Christian has in the reve-
lations of Jesus Christ; they have no conception of the
capacity of God to satisfy the affections of the heart;
they have only a conception of His ability to hurt.
Their religious acts, therefore, are rather with a view to
ward off evil than in the hope of receiving good, and
the much fluttering of their flags is the expression of
their sense of the need of constant watchfulness imposed
on them by the supposed unfriendly attitude of spiritual
powers. Such an idea paralyses the faculty of worship
and renders impossible the development of the perfected
humanity that grows out of a true conception of God.

But in this again, we who have had Christian training
may far more profitably correct our own faults than
condemn theirs, for not all among us have yet reached
the stage in which perfect love has cast out fear.

"Confusion now hath made his masterpiece!"

SHAKSPERE. *Macbeth.*

"Let not my weak tongue falter
In telling of this goodly company,
Of their old piety, and of their glee."

KEATS. *Endymion.*

"O, 'twas a din to fright a monster's ear,
To make an earthquake! Sure, it was the roar
Of a whole herd of lions!"—SHAKSPERE. *Tempest.*

"Rout on rout,
Confusion worse confounded."

MILTON. *Paradise Lost.*

"Mercy o' me, what a multitude are here!
They grow still too; from all parts they are coming,
As if we kept a fair here!"—SHAKSPERE. *Henry VIII.*

". . . raptures cheer
On some high festival of once a year,
In wild excess the vulgar breast takes fire."

GOLDSMITH. *The Traveller.*

CHAPTER XII.

THE MOHARREM.

WHEN Hamlet charged his father's ghost with making night hideous, he was hardly fair to the ghost. Strange as was the apparition, there was nothing hideous about it; it came in "that fair and warlike form in which the majesty of buried Denmark did sometimes march." Hamlet should have witnessed a Moharrem, and then he might have coined his expressive phrase with a clear conscience.

This Mohammedan festival occupies some nine or ten days, the earlier of which pass without attracting much attention, but on the concluding night the fun rages fast and furious to the confusing of all one's ideas of funeral propriety, for be it remembered that what is then witnessed is the obsequies of two deceased heroes, "mirth in funeral" with a vengeance. These heroes were brothers, grandsons of Mohammed, named respectively Hasan and Hosein, who both—a not uncommon fate with ancient heroes—suffered violent deaths and laid thereby the foundation of eternal funeral rites.

Although it was the rival claims of their family, and

of the house of Ommiyah to the kaliphate, that split the Mohammedan world into the two main sects of Shiites and Sonnites, both are prepared to do them honour. But in this the union ends. Both sects are represented in Calcutta, the one by the Arabs and kindred immigrants, the other by the natives of India whose conversion from Hinduism dates from the sword of the Mohammedan conquest. Both celebrate the Moharrem, but not together, and not with identical rites. Each party holds the observances of the other in contempt.

> "You know our Sonnites, hateful dogs!
> Whom every pious Shiite flogs
> Or longs to flog—'tis true they pray
> To God, but in an ill-bred way,
> With neither arms, nor legs, nor faces
> Stuck in their right canonic places."

By a simple reversing of the names these words would as accurately express the feeling of the other party.

It was on a Saturday that I saw something of the ceremonies of the Arabs in their quarter in Chitpore Road, but the following night revealed the scene that I would have liked to commend to the Danish prince. I had been spending an hour or two with a friend after church service and was returning home about eleven o'clock. As I walked along Chowringhee, all was still and dark. There was a threatening in the sky of a possible storm, but for the present it was nursing its wrath and calm prevailed. Stillness was overhead, and quiet in the street. When I reached Dharmatola corner "the scene was changed," as one of our own poets has said. This street looked like a furnace-scene in the Black Country, flanked on either side by the whitewashed dwellings of the City of Palaces.

An annual sight this, yet ever fresh in attraction ; verandahs, tops of godowns, and roofs of houses exhibited crowded and picturesque groups of spectators, while the street itself was thronged. Down the centre of the roadway, adding temporarily to the architectural beauties of the city, was a long procession of innumerable tazeas, as they were called. I say innumerable advisedly, for I tried to number them and gave up in despair. These tazeas were, I was led to understand, the tombstones of Hasan and Hosein. They certainly offered every kind of accommodation that could be desiderated for the corpses of these heroes. All were of one material—bamboo frames covered with coloured, silvered, and gilded paper, and adorned with little glass lamps. These lamps, with true Bengali economy of labour, were mostly left unlighted, "because," as was remarked to me, " the wind may begin to blow presently and they would then go out ; what, then, would be the use of lighting them ? " Under this unity of material there was the greatest diversity of design. The architect of each mausoleum seemed to have got his instructions from a different ghost. Some few were quite imposing structures, built on the general outline of a candle extinguisher, but with that outline broken by storied tiers and ornithological projections consisting usually of golden peacocks of aldermanic proportions, whose slender necks terminated in human heads with feminine features, each surmounted by a Chinese mandarin's hat. The tops of many of these " extinguishers " towered up to the level of the windows in the upper rooms of the houses. Adorned with lamp-glasses, if not with lamps, silvered or gilded with the sparkling tinsel so dear to the native heart, glorious in the blazing torchlight, it was no wonder that their appearance called forth the most exuberant expressions of delight. Mingled with these in the same stately procession were other structures reminding one forcibly of the juvenile efforts to reproduce on one's earliest slate the comforts and stability of a farmhouse. The poverty of design, the lack of finish, and withal, an uncertainty of outline, forced them into an unfavourable comparison with the more ambitious edifices. Between these two extremes, and marshalled among them, were to be seen tazeas of all degrees of size and beauty as the processional graveyard wended its way along.

There were no riderless horses led in this cortege as in that of the Arabs, which might be partly accounted for by the fact that a large proportion of the celebrants were gari-wallas, whose daily occupation of swearing at and thwacking such horses as they were accustomed to harness in their shafts had probably blunted their admiration for the noble quadruped, and led them to hold him in so poor repute as to render them incapable of believing that their honoured Hosein ever bestrode a horse. One ingenious designer indeed exhibited a partial exception to this feeling, for he sent forth on

the heads of his men a colossal silvered figure constructed as nearly into the shape of a horse as the
refractory nature of bamboo would allow, and on this
creature he mounted his tombstone like a howdah upon
the back of an elephant.

The necropolitan procession pursued it course with
becoming slowness. Beyond this there was nothing that
an Englishman would consider funereal about it. As
has been intimated, it was illuminated by torches, and
they were many and bright. Each consisted of a strong
staff, around the top of which had been wound with no
sparing hand a rich supply of cloths and rags till the
outline of a full foliaged tree was suggested, and one
could imagine Birnam Wood once more to be marching
on Dunsinane. Whence people whose sartorial necessities are so trivial and whose wardrobes are so meagre,
could provide themselves with so large a stock of cloths
remains a mystery. Suffice it to say that the provision
was made. These rags copiously anointed with oil and
set on fire made splendid torches, and, lest, during the
long hours of pilgrimage, there should be any slackening
of their lurid glory, bullock-hakris laden with further
supplies of rags and oil were admitted into the procession.

Certain athletes excited great admiration by their
performances with long poles having an overgrown rag-
mop flaming on each extremity. They twisted them
round and round in all planes until they appeared to
be dancing in a globe of gauzy light—a pleasant
spectacle to all but to those nearest, into whose eyes,

by the law of centrifugal forces, the constantly eman-
cipated fragments of burning rag directed themselves.
Nevertheless the worst stung did not dream of complaining. It was a holiday. There are, I believe,
natives of few lands who can submit to inconvenience
and pain more good-naturedly and philosophically
than these dusky folks when they choose. Let it
be a question of the executing of some wish of a
European master, and expressions of inability fill up
about one half of their dictionary. But when it is
a matter of pleasing themselves, nothing seems impossible, their energy and their good humour seem
alike exhaustless.

Beside the torches, and depending on them for effect,
were large semi-circular screens with a diameter of
about six feet. These were carried by men evidently
under orders not to stand still a minute, but to dance
up and down and to twirl their half-plates around as
far as their endurance justified. I though at first that
these screens were intended for peacock's tails spread
out into exaggerated fans. I saw afterwards that
they were intended as receptacles for the shields of
the mighty vilely cast away. To each were affixed a
number of shields, sometimes seven, sometimes eight,
and sometimes nine. Some of these were black, some
silvered, others gilt. The spaces between the shields
were mostly filled up with small steel plates like those
of a coat of mail. The circumference was edged with
fringe, and down the centre hung long tinselled tassels.
Their sheen as they were danced in the torch-light was

rather effective; but the motion was ridiculously suggestive of the jerky movements of the zoology of a Christmas pantomime.

The propriety of silence is another subject on which Mohammedan and European ideas concerning the right ordering of a funeral are found to be scarcely in accord. So far from silence being solemnly observed, this procession was unutterably noisy. One element in the noise was the ringing of bells, certain individuals being provided with what looked like clumsily made bows, in which the bow-string consisted of a chain of bells. Holding these things over their heads, with one hand on the bow and the other on the chain, the lucky possessors of these instruments exhilarated themselves by bending and shaking them, dancing the while in the most grotesque manner to the music they thus called forth. How riper experience enables us to smile at past agonies! I once lived in a village where some foolish man of philanthropic disposition presented every boy in the largest Sunday School in the place with a penny whistle. I remember the horror with which I took my walks abroad, knowing well the kind of song-bird to be found perched on every five-barred gate. But, after the Moharrem, methinks I could hear those strains and think less unkindly of the indiscreet philanthropist than, it must be confessed, I did then. There is some use in going to India if it be no other than to reconcile one to tin-whistles. But this is moralising. To return. The voice of the inevitable tom-tom was of course heard, "the vile squealing of

the wry-necked fife," and the supplementary efforts of
all manner of other musical monstrosities. The vocal
din, however, resounding from all parts well-nigh
drowned the instrumental. Sometimes the predomi-
nating sound would be that of a kind of funeral chant
consisting mainly in the repetition of the names of the
deceased, at other times there would be nothing dis-
tinguishable amidst the loud spontaneous shouting of
the crowd, more frequently the ear would be caught
by the sharp battle-cries that were uttered to the
accompaniment of the clashing of the swords of the
combatants. For each tazea was preceded by a number
of men armed with swords apparently of metal swathed
in cloths, and as often as the tazea stopped the torch-
bearers swinging round their torches cleared a space in
front of it in which the swordsmen executed some of
the most approved stage-fencing. With fierce countenances and complicated posturings they hammered
away at each other's weapons in a manner calculated
to reflect great credit on the manufacturers, for, as far
I saw, not one of them got broken. This was to recall
the bloody conflict in which Hosein fell,—poor Hasan
had previously fallen the victim of a wife's treachery.

In addition to this fancy fencing, there was another
kind of sword-exercise which did command an approach
to temporary silence. The weapon in this case would
almost have merited David's eulogium on the sword of
Goliath : "There is none like that." It was about six
feet long and made of bamboo. The handle was
formed by cutting away a portion for about a foot of its

length, leaving a half cylinder; the blade by cutting away all but a flat slice. This flat blade was silvered over, the fore-arm of the swordsman was tied into the half bamboo as into splints, and all was ready. Like a youngster playing the hero with his grandfather's stick, the valiant man gesticulated round the circle he had cleared for himself by the terror of his weapon, moving with a vibratory action of the limbs added to the general action of a horse with the springhalt, the bamboo blade pointing forward, quivering flashingly in the torch-light. After a little of this performance, tragic in the possibilities suggested by the savage mien and the threatening aspect, and which was watched with breathless interest; all at once the long blade was flashing and flying in all directions till its form was entirely lost in a glittering mist, he who wielded it meanwhile attitudinising in a way that would have called forth rapturous applause from the spectators, had any there conceived themselves as such. But all seemed to think that even the mere walking about constituted them joint-performers, so, though there was evident approval, no applause was expressed.

Thus with their tazeas and their flags, with their half-moon shield-racks, their tom-toms and their swords, do these Mussulmans invade the quiet hours of the Sunday night,

" Huzzin' an' maazin' the blessed [streets] wi' the divil's oan teäm."

But midnight brings relief; slow as is its course, the

L

procession at last draws after it its hindmost tail, the blaze of the last torch passes by, the din of the bells, the gongs, and the tom-toms dies away in the distance, until, in the words of the medical poet,

> " Silence, like a poultice, comes
> To heal the wounds of sound."

THE MAN OF HAN.

"There's no art
To find the mind's construction in the face."

SHAKSPERE. *Macbeth.*

"The greater number of nations, as of men, are only impressible in their youth; they become incorrigible as they grow old. When once customs have been established and prejudices have taken root it is both dangerous and futile to try to reform them; the people cannot endure even that their ills should be touched with a view of amendment, like those stupid and faint-hearted invalids who tremble at the sight of a doctor."—ROUSSEAU.

"A dog, an outcast kindly treat,
And so shalt thou be blest in turn."

Mahābhārata.

"'Your guest, Rabbi Zimri, must read the treatise of the learned Shimei of Damascus on "Effecting Impossibilities."'

"'That is a work!' exclaimed Zimri.

"'I never slept for three nights after reading that work,' said Rabbi Maimon. 'It contains twelve thousand five hundred and thirty-seven quotations from the Pentateuch, and not a single original observation.'

"'There were giants in those days,' said Zimri. 'We are children now.'

"'The first chapter makes equal sense read backward or forward,' continued Rabbi Maimon.

"'Ichabod!' exclaimed Rabbi Zimri.

"'And the initial letter of each section is a cabalistical type of a king of Judah!'

"'The temple will yet be built,' said Rabbi Zimri."

LORD BEACONSFIELD. *The Wondrous Tale of Alroy.*

CHAPTER I.

THE MUNDANE CELESTIAL.

THE Chinaman has been compelled to open his country to barbarians—as he calls us when, in politeness, he refrains from using the more natural term, foreign devils—but he has not opened to us his heart. He is ready to sell us his teas and his silks, but not to give us his confidence and his love, and we, so long as this is so, shall have to be content with guesses at the hidden workings of his mind, in which guesses it behoves us to guard against the suspicion, which this very reserve on his part tends to generate, that, like the antediluvians of old, "Every imagination of the thoughts of his heart is only evil continually." As Mr. Froude says, "One never knows exactly what is inside a Chinaman."

It is easy to credit the Celestial with goodness to which he can lay no claim or to suspect him of evil of which he is guiltless. We take note of him and observe certain facts from which, did the object of our observation belong to any other nationality, we should unhesitatingly infer certain other facts; we see certain characteristics which, in any one else, would justify us in assuming the absence of certain other characteristics. But inference and assumption are misplaced here. Amid all their unlikenesses, the diverse types of men who dwell in the "Celestial Empire," and own allegiance to the "Lord of all under Heaven" are uniformly and liberally endowed with a gift, peculiarly their own, of embracing, if not harmonising, the incongruous and the contradictory. Bunyan's Mr. Facing Both Ways is outdone. These sons of Han can not only face, they can go, both ways. They can swallow and maintain contradictory propositions, avow contradictory opinions and do contradictory deeds with a facility that is little less than miraculous. "The Three Religions," as they are called, have struggled together with excommunicating zeal and exterminating purpose. To the simple-minded foreigner, their teachings appear antagonistic and mutually destructive, but the Chinaman of to-day accepts them equally and is at once a Confucianist, a Taoist and a Buddhist—"three single gentlemen rolled into one." He prides himself on being a follower of "the Master," bows indiscriminately before Taoist and Buddhist idols, and fees with equal anxiety Taoist and Buddhist priests, rejoicing in the generally accepted formula, which no one has the hardihood to dispute : "The Three Religions are One." That this is a genuine capacity for incongruities, and not simply the easy-going indifference to all religions that allows a man to bow before every idol because he has faith in none, may be judged the more likely from the fact that it is not in theological creed, or even in religious worship alone that this gift is illustrated. Archdeacon Gray tells us, " The moral character of the Chinese is a book written in strange letters which are more complex and difficult for one of another race, religion and language to decipher than their singularly compounded word-symbols. In the same individual, virtues and vices apparently incompatible, are placed side by side. Meekness, gentleness, docility, industry, contentment, cheerfulness, obedience to superiors, dutifulness to parents, and reverence for the aged, are in one and the same person the companions of insincerity, lying, flattery, treachery, cruelty, ingratitude, avarice, and distrust of others."

It is not surprising that concerning such a people we should have had contradictory accounts given us by different writers whose opportunities of observation and whose desire to arrive at a just judgment have been equal. If honest men could, contradict each other regarding the colour of a shield which had only two sides, how much more may they be expected to do so regarding the heart and mind of a Chinaman ? This one cannot forget how he has been the victim of his lies and extortions; he condemns him accordingly. That one is rendered forgetful of the ways that are dark by the smile that is so child-like and bland, the manner that is so gracious and the honorific titles with which he so naturally and without the slightest appearance of artificiality addresses him ; and his praise accordingly is as loud as is the other's condemnation. This one sees the filthiness of his homes and his habits, perceives the pollution of even the country air, and suffers from the almost intolerable stench of his cities; he turns from him with disgust. That one recalls his early civilisation, his anticipation of the West in the art of printing, the invention of gunpowder and the discovery of the properties of the lode-stone; and he attributes to foreign bigotry all inability to recognise his worth. This one watches the procedure of his courts and the administration of his laws, notes the venality of the magistrate, the torture inflicted on the accused, and the barbarities to which the condemned are subjected; his indignation boils and he brands him as a savage. That one reads his wonderful literature, learns how high in honour he holds his sages and moralists, nay more, how reverently he regards even the pages on which are impressed their sentences written in those characters more "mystic, wonderful" than was the white samite of Sir Bedivere's vision, so that, as a work of merit, he sends men through the town to collect waste printed paper from the tradesmen, at whose hands it might otherwise suffer the indignity of the kitchen fire, and to gather from the streets all scraps which the still less scrupulous may have cast away, and on which perchance the priceless maxims of some sage are in danger of being trampled in the mire, that they may burn them in the sacred altar flames of the temple courts; and, learning all this, he is prepared to enter the lists forthwith as a champion of China—the land of a culture and civilisation as noble as ancient. This one sees the superstitious practices in the actual worship of

the common people, or learns about their fear of spirits
and their bondage to geomancers and priests who made
profit out of their ignorant terrors; he pities them with
a pity allied to contempt. That one reads about the
annual sacrifices of the emperor—the Huang-ti—to
the supreme and invisible god—Shang-ti—at the Altar
of Heaven and the Altar of Earth, where no idolatrous
accessories degrade the adoration paid by the sovereign
as the representative of his people; and he acknowledges a reverent awe which silences criticism in the
presence of a nation's worship. It may be assumed, I
think, that the judgment of the student who, not
having lived in China, has formed his opinion of
the country from English translations of its classical
literature will be likely to err on the side of excessive
praise. He has read, but he has not seen—or smelt.
On the other hand, it may be as readily granted that
the judgment of foreign residents in China is likely to
err on the side of excessive blame. For every one who
lives there is necessarily brought into contact with the
uncultured classes, only a few come to know also the
scholarly and the cultured, and, though not every one
who has to do with the educated Chinese will learn to
esteem them highly, as not every one who has to be
served by cooks and coachmen will come to despise
them, it may be taken for granted that the judgment of
the many who see the country chiefly as expressed in
the life and conduct of persons of a rank in life inferior
to their own, will be less favourable than that of the
few who can judge also by what they see in a social

rank equal or superior to that in which they themselves move.

One thing that ought to prepossess us with a kindly feeling towards the Chinaman is his love of nature. Whatever doubts may be entertained by the sceptical as to his claim to priority in the arts and sciences, in such matters as gunpowder and bells, there is little room to doubt that his eyes were opened to the charms of mountains, dales, forests, and lakes long before ours. We have had to wait till comparatively recent days for our poets of nature. He has boasted them for genera-tions. His appreciation of natural beauty often receives illustration as we climb among the hills or wander through the glens. In the secluded nook, in the spot which the artist would seize upon for his "bit," at the turn in the path where we instinctively stop to gaze upon the view, we shall have evidence that the native eye has seen and the native heart felt the charm before us. Just where the beauty or grandeur of the scene has stayed our feet, we shall probably find the ruins of a shrine or little temple that tell how in years long gone, Nature revealed her glory to the open eye and made the heart feel the place to be sacred.

Within the limits of his own garden, the Chinaman indulges this love of scenery, and builds up wonderful rockworks overhanging pools bright with gold-fish or lotus blooms. But it must be admitted that a certain taste for the unnatural and the grotesque seems always ready to discover itself. These rockeries are seldom kept within the limits of the merely picturesque.

They are supposed to represent mighty mountains, as the ponds beneath them the broad expanse of ocean-like lakes, but no mountains, under the weathering of our earthly atmosphere with its heats and frosts, could present such exaggerated crags and precipices as are here imaged forth. These are caricatures. In the fish below them, the same taste is seen. Though there will be perhaps a number of ordinary golden carp, the creatures in which chief delight is taken are the podgy little gold-fish with eyes protruding far out of their heads like telescopes, and with tails so amplified and so lengthened as to appear to be positive inconveniences to their possessors, useless incumbrances that have to be towed after them.

We in the West are not altogether free from this desire to improve upon nature, we breed pouters and fantails, clip our poodles, trim the ears of our terriers, and dock the tails of our spaniels; but the Celestial excels us all. In his national emblem he has given freedom to his imagination and has taught Nature the kind of animal she ought to have made; and when, in accordance with the custom of other nations, he devised a flag which his newly-launched fleet should bear, he caused his impossible but imperial dragon to struggle on a field of imperial yellow in ever unsuccessful endeavour to seize and devour a blood-red sun.

The shrubs too suffer from the same perversion of taste, which, while it does not run riot and distort everything, is seldom altogether absent. As you enter a garden you see green junks and pagodas, horses and cranes. The ingenuity and patience with which most unpromising plants have been twisted, stunted and clipped, " cabin'd, cribb'd, confin'd, bound in " to these several forms are worthy of praise and worthy also of a nobler enterprise.

To this his instinctive desire to perfect Nature's defective work may perhaps be attributed the extraordinary custom of foot-binding, which renders so large a proportion of his women more helpless than they need be. " Golden Lilies " he calls these mutilated feet, and he likens the awkward waddle of the crippled woman to the swaying of the willow in the wind—his fondness for plants asserting itself in his phrases and terms, though their application may occasionally seem to suggest an exceedingly imperfect sense of their true beauty and grace. Thus, while there can be no question as to the honour he pays in going to them for a designation to set forth the dignity of his native country, which he calls "The Flowery Land," the compliment seems more equivocal when he selects them also as a name for so loathsome a disease as the small-pox, which he calls "The Heavenly Flowers." This however may be a name given with the same thoughtful and propitiating anxiety as that with which the Greeks of old respectfully referred to the Furies as the Eumenides, in which case the compliment to the flowers may be considered sufficiently complete, for a Chinaman's flattery is not doled out in half measures and the terms and figures he uses will be those to which he attaches the highest value. He may cramp the flowers of his garden and the feet of his girls, but he will not cramp his own tongue. The freedom and the breadth of nature are in his words ; he regards it as a sign of our defective culture that we restrain ourselves in speech and say little, if anything, more or less than we mean. Like the Hindu, he has learned to wonder at and, in business, to see the convenience of, an Englishman's average accuracy and truthfulness. Nevertheless, as an artist, he is compelled to regard our speech as brutal in its directness. It is photographic and exact, but it offends by its lack of atmosphere. For example, "No admittance except on business," is simple and unambiguous. Perhaps "Trespassers will be prosecuted," is even simpler and more decided. To the Celestial these notices are unmannerly and much too absolute. He would post up such an intimation as "Persons of leisure are not invited to enter." But in the event of trespass, the offending person of leisure would probably prefer to be dealt with by the unmannerly European. The Celestial is polite in his phrase but he is savage in his penalties. He is grandiloquent and opens his mouth wide, but I doubt if magnanimity, largeness of soul, openness of spirit, can be claimed for him as his special virtue by even his most ardent admirers.

Not out of harmony with the flower-clipping and foot-binding is the method of mental discipline and culture which in China corresponds with education elsewhere. The mind too must be clipped and bound, made to grow in a certain direction and brought into the required fashion and limits. The educational system, as it is called, of China, has been loudly praised. Not only does the Chinaman regard it as perfect and point to it proudly as the crowning illustration of his country's superiority over every other land on the face of the earth, but foreigners have very largely joined the chorus of laudation and expatiated on the severity of the tests in the examination halls excluding rigidly all incapacity, on the open gates of eligibility through which the poorest may enter and win the distinction he merits, subject to no disadvantage on the ground of his poverty, and on the still more remarkable fact that the avenue to official life and the path of promotion under the Dragon-throne lie through these examination halls, so that, in theory at any rate—with the exception of the members of certain trades and callings which are disqualified—all are eligible, not only to compete at these examinations, but if proved competent by success, eligible also for the most responsible offices under government. It is a special feature, which has often been enlarged upon to the credit of the Celestial empire, that it regards tested personal ability rather than hereditary rank or inherited wealth as the ground on which appointments should be made and promotion granted. There is no other country in which the student and the scholar hold so relatively honourable a position and are so highly esteemed as here. Yet not a few regard it as a misapplication of the term to speak of "education" in connection with these studies and examinations. Our Western idea of education is the drawing out, exercising and developing whatever of natural aptitudes the student may possess, the stimulating of individuality and, if possible, of original effort; and so education is a means of progress. But the Chinese educationalist would deprecate originality, development, progress above all things. His system of mental discipline does not educate, it represses, turning the thought backward, running all minds into a common mould—and that of an ancient pattern. It is undoubtedly a serious matter for a girl to let her feet grow to their natural proportions. She must expect to be looked down upon with contempt and to hear the scornful feminine titter as the question is asked, "Do you see those two boats going by?" But even more serious would it be for a candidate in the examination to be suspected of letting his mind grow naturally. His prospect of passing would be ruined were he suspected of thinking for himself, having an opinion of his own, or writing anything that was not in the approved conventional form. The subject of the examinations, and therefore of the student's studies, is the national classical literature. The student's aim is to acquire a perfect mastery of this literature, to know every sentence that occurs anywhere in it so familiarly as to recognise any two or three consecutive characters that may be quoted, and to recall the context without requiring the quotation of the remainder of the passage. Volume after volume he has committed to memory in a manner practically inconceivable by us; he becomes so saturated with these old books as to have gained a facility in writing treatises and poems upon them, or upon any sentiment taken from them, in which each sentence shall be moulded on the model of, or contain a veiled reference to, some passage in them that any other scholar will at once recall, which passage will furnish him with a key to the meaning that is as much suggested as expressed, while the people that know not the classics, recognising no reference and reading simply the characters that are written, wonder at and admire its obvious unintelligibility. Thoughts beyond the teachings of the sages of old, expressions not warranted by their example and precedent are inadmissible. Therefore it is very largely the case that the more a Chinaman is "educated," the more he is turned backward to the study of a dead past, fettered and rendered incapable of participating in or sympathising with the life and progress of the present. The past is made the standard of utility and possibility the limits of which none need hope to exceed. Centuries ago a certain engineering scheme was urged on the emperor Wu-ti; his answer was that had the scheme been a feasible one it would have been carried out by their ancestors. Though I believe he was ultimately persuaded to undertake a work not executed by his predecessors, the spirit of his answer survives and will survive until the "educational system" of China is rendered educative.

There are indeed signs which suggest hope of even this. Perhaps the first direct evidence of much value was that afforded at the Provincial Examination at Wuchang in the year 1885, or 1886, I forget which.

Certain officials in that city had recognised the possibility of wisdom existing outside the ordinary studies of Chinese scholars. They had been especially impressed with the value of mathematics as taught in the West, and had established a monthly examination in this subject. A competent examiner was found in the person of a Nanking graduate, and examinees were induced to come forward by the offer of a prize of four taels to the candidate who headed the list. Notwithstanding the trifling value of this prize, it drew something like a hundred needy scholars to these monthly examinations to be tested in algebra, geometry and elementary mechanics. This in itself was a fact of value as an indication of awakening. But clearer indication was to follow. Wuchang is a provincial city, and when the next provincial examinations were held, to which only those who had taken the degree of siu-tsai were eligible, thirteen thousand candidates presented themselves to contend for the sixty-one chu-jen degrees that were to be given. In the third part of that examination in which the more general questions are set, the competing siu-tsai were asked to give a comparison between certain ancient and the modern mathematical methods. This was a question which scarcely any of them could answer, and the excitement which it aroused was not allayed when it was subsequently found that the examiners had evidently attached considerable value to it, since among the names of the sixty-one successful candidates appeared that of the student who had won the highest distinction in

M

the monthly mathematical examinations though it was generally understood that his literary essays were too weak to have justified any expectation of his passing through their merit. A friend, whose " teacher " was among the unsuccessful candidates, wrote me at the time that the said teacher was highly disgusted that pure and soul-elevating literature should have been to any degree set aside for studies so useless and puerile as mathematics. My friend offered to coach him up in the subject for the next examination, but he was too conservative to accept the offer. Courteously but firmly he declined. He would rather fail again as a student of his native literature, than win success by means of foreign innovations.

Corroborative testimony of China's awakening from sleep comes to us from the hospital in Tientsin under. the care of Dr. Mackenzie, of the London Mission. The facts are shortly these :—In the year 1881 a number of young Chinamen whom an Educational Commission had sent to America for the purpose of acquiring a general English education were suddenly recalled after residence in the States extending in some instances to a period of ten years. They were hurried home, not because they were wanted, but because rumours were rife that they were becoming denationalised, losing their affection for their own Flowery Land and learning to love too well the Land of the Flowery Flag.* Some little difficulty therefore was experienced on their return in deciding what was to be done with them.

* The Chinese interpret the stars in the American flag as flowers.

Dr. Mackenzie who enjoyed the friendship and confidence of His Excellency the Viceroy of Chihli—the famous Li Hung Chang—in whose family he had rendered valuable professional service, offered to undertake the medical training of some of these youths if His Excellency would place them entirely under his charge. The viceroy agreed to the doctor's proposal and a small medical school has since been an integral part of Dr. Mackenzie's hospital. The first class of students to enter on the course of training here consisted of eight of these young Chinamen from America. They began their studies in the end of 1881. In 1883 a second class, consisting of students who had been trained in English in Hong Kong, and in the next year a third class, also from the Southern British colony, were added to the school. The training is as far as possible assimilated to that of the medical schools in Great Britain. Dr. Mackenzie has received help in teaching from other medical missionaries and from the surgeons of the American and British navies who have been resident during the winter months in Tientsin. The examiners have been medical officers of these navies and of the Chinese Imperial Maritime Customs, or such medical missionaries as have been in the neighbourhood and available when examinations were due. Of the eight composing the first class, six completed their course and passed their examinations to the satisfaction of the board of examiners. They received diplomas in Chinese and English which were not only signed by the examiners but were stamped

M 2

with the government seal. Moreover, through the influence of the viceroy Li, these students received civil rank, and were enrolled in the ninth degree, the head student receiving a crystal button and honorary fifth rank, the other five receiving white buttons and honorary sixth rank. Thus this examination in a Western science and art, conducted by foreigners, has received a government recognition which classes it with the great examinations as a path to office and social position.

This is more than the most sanguine would have dreamed of a few years ago. But it is evidence of enlightenment and a readiness to accept reforms within a very narrow circle. The viceroy of Chihli is a great man, but he is not China. No amount of official recognition can give to these foreign-trained doctors the confidence of the sick and diseased in a purely native city or secure to them a remunerative private practice. The acupuncture and the monstrous and nauseous doses of the native practitioners will hold the favour of this conservative race for many years to come. Did not Mencius quote with evident approval from the Book of History, " If medicine do not distress the patient, it will not cure his sickness " ? and if Mencius was not a physician, what of that ? He was a sage, which is more. In the treaty ports, where there are a goodly number of Chinese who have lost their distrust of foreigners and learned to recognise the superiority of many things which foreigners have intorduced, there may be a chance of a foreign-trained native doctor getting a living, but his prospect as a private practitioner in China anywhere outside these few towns and settlements is not a cheerful one. His only hope is in the official appointment, which the power of the viceroy and the government seal on his diploma are sufficient to insure him.

But these can no more insure his being appreciated in the camp or on board a gunboat than in a country village. Dr. Mackenzie, in the *China Medical Missionary Journal* for September, 1887, shows how the real difficulties of the new scheme seriously commence when the school career is completed. Of these six young men who thus received diplomas and rank, the head of the class was appointed to the school and hospital and is, of course, in a congenial atmosphere in assisting his former tutor in the instruction of students or the treatment of patients. One of the others is appointed to a new military college in Tientsin, where he has the medical oversight of about two hundred students. His position is a good one, though it appears that his salary is not in proportion to it. A third is surgeon on board a cruiser but has the dissatisfaction of seeing officers and engineers, many of them formerly fellow-students with him in the United States, advanced in rank and pay while his own position is hopelessly without prospect of improvement. Two others were also in the navy—one having been previously sent into the army and transferred—but have obtained leave of absence from which they appear to have no intention of returning. Their relations with their commanding officers became strained as soon as their stock of drugs supplied on leaving the hospital was exhausted and application had to be made for a fresh supply. Both of these men, Dr. Mackenzie believes, would prefer to continue the practice of the art in which they have been trained, yet both for the present have felt compelled to relinquish it.

The career of the last of the six seems to have been somewhat more fortunate, since he has been able to continue at his post. He "was placed,"—I give the account in Dr. Mackenzie's own words—"at the service of General Chow, who has the command of a body of troops, said to number fifteen thousand, encamped some twenty miles from Tientsin. Soon after he had joined the general's staff an interesting though curious, and possibly unique experience awaited him. At the central camp, where the general's headquarters were located, there resided a native doctor who professed to treat upon foreign principles, but his practice fell sadly short of his profession, indeed it was of the most elementary kind, consisting in the administration of a few simple drugs backed up by much skill in rhetoric. He had the faculty of adapting his medicines to the theoretic notions of his patients, which is in China a great gift.

"The question arose, should the newly-arrived man be retained at headquarters, and the old occupant of the post be removed to another camp, or should the new-comer be placed elsewhere? A brilliant idea originated in the mind of the great man. He himself, aided by the other red-buttoned generals under his command, would sit as a sort of court of inquiry and investigate into the respective abilities of each. The order went forth, and on a fixed day, under a canvas pavilion erected for the occasion, the generals and colonels, attended by their respective staffs—and even a colonel requires a staff in China—assembled in full paraphernalia, and seated themselves in order of precedence. The two unfortunate medicos were then called in, and before this august assembly and in presence of each other, underwent an examination, the court putting the questions and deciding the verdict. Each candidate for the favour of the court was expected to show all he knew, but considering that one of the parties was an astute man of the world of fifty odd summers, equally conversant with Chinese etiquette and with Chinese ideas of anatomy and disease, while the other had not long entered upon man's estate, whose knowledge of human nature was drawn from the stand-point of the American youth of the nineteenth century, while his anatomical and medical learning, though agreeing with that of the Western schools, differed *in toto* from the innate knowledge of the examiners, the result may readily be imagined. The elder was adjudged the victor and was retained at his post, while the younger was placed at a small cavalry camp some distance away. The examiners, scarcely one of whom could read or write, as became men who have to wield the sword rather than the pen, returned to their quarters satisfied, no doubt, that they had upheld the dignity of their country. This surgeon is, however, comfortably situated, having better allowances than any of his fellow-students, and complaining chiefly that he has too little to do." In another paper on the same subject, Dr. Mackenzie sums up thus: "As for the army and navy, China needs fully trained surgeons, with such status and pay as will attract capable men into their ranks, but they should be formed into a district corps and not remain dependent upon the caprice of the commanding officer. It seems, however, as though many other reforms must come about before this one is ripe."

Those who are hopeful of seeing China one day free herself from her rusted fetters and enter upon the path of progress, may find encouragement in the officially recognised medical school at Tientsin and in so unexpected and unconventional a question as that put to the students at Wuchang, but they will do well to temper hope with patience. Every effort of the spirit of emancipation makes discovery of the strength of the bonds it would break. The most useless and injurious practices and customs, if they have been handed down from the past, will find advocates in a land where it is accounted akin to impiety to suggest that the usages of the fathers are susceptible of improvement. The Chinese reverence for old age invests even ancient abuses with a sacred character.

A natural result of the narrowing, cramping system of intellectual training is the arrogance that is born of learned ignorance, the pride with which the Celestial regards his own country, and the contempt for other nations which he scarcely deigns to disguise. His is the Celestial Empire, and his sovereign is the Son of Heaven. His modern geography locates Russia, France, Germany and England along with Japan and Corea, in a circle round his native land—the Empire of the Centre, the Middle Kingdom—like the rim round a plate. His older geography found no place for them at all. They are the lands of barbarians with whom it is little worth his while to acquaint himself, of whose very existence he would gladly still be as ignorant as were his fathers. It is true that Confucius said : "All within the Four Seas are brethren," a phrase which, without a very clear idea of what seas are meant, his followers to-day understand to be a rhetorical expression for the whole world. Still the saying has been robbed of its apparent catholicity by the inveterate habit of the Chinese mind of regarding the whole world as co-extensive with the Chinese empire. And though China can no longer seriously regard herself as the sole and only nation under heaven since other nations have, in unmannerly fashion truly, forced themselves on her attention, she still affects to despise if she cannot ignore them. Mencius has given a sentence which provides the modern scholar with an apt quotation : " I have heard," says he, "of men using the ways of our great land to reform barbarians, but I have not yet heard of any being reformed by barbarians." This utterance of the sage was supposed to receive a striking illustration when Dr. James Legge, the eminent sinologist, was appointed to the chair of Chinese in the university of Oxford. " Dr. Legge," said the gratified Celestials, " is a man of a great and impartial mind. He came out to China, under the auspices of the London Missionary Society, to teach us the doctrines of Christianity, but he studied our literature, and, becoming convinced by his study, he has now returned to his native land to teach English-men the doctrines of Confucius."

In the matter of mechanical arts, engineering skill or military discipline and power, there are indeed many individuals whose eyes have been opened to see their own inferiority. But these enlightened ones form a small proportion of China's millions by the great majority of whom the delusions of old are unfalteringly held to the nursing of self-satisfaction. They are not ready to believe even, certainly not to admit, that any nation can be superior to their own in any particular. In the days when foreigners, while allowed to build their factories in a certain prescribed spot in the suburbs of Canton, were forbidden to enter within the walls of the city proper, the wonders of that unseen region were the Chinaman's reply to whatever was told or shown him. Tell him of some European building of noble design ; with unmoved face he would reply : " Have got allee same inisidee citee." Show him some mechanism of intricate workmanship and ingenious device, some picture of bold conception and masterly execution—it mattered not what—the invariable reply, " Have got allee same inisidee citee," excused the tribute of admiration. Archdeacon Gray, if I remember rightly, tells how on the arrival at Canton of the first steamboat that reached that port, a Chinese gentleman was taken on board, was shown through her engine room, receiving explanation of the various parts of her machinery, and was told of her independence of favouring gales, her speed and in how short a time she had traversed the thousands of miles that lay between them and Europe. She was a wonder to the Europeans, but the Chinaman regarded all with a calm and unmoved countenance, and presently came the familiar words : " Have got allee same inisidee citee." That reply serves no longer ; since then, the gates of that city have been thrown open to the foreigner, its narrow streets profaned by his tread, and its wonders sought out by his untiring curiosity. But the arrogance and self-complacency remain, blinding the understanding to the most obvious evidence. Ministers and ambassadors, whom foreign governments have forced upon China at the point of the bayonet, are regarded as servants in the pay of the emperor; treaty rights, which foreigners have wrung from China by force of arms, are spoken of as the expression of the emperor's spontaneous pity, excited by their wretched and destitute condition, and every invading army is understood to be a humble embassage bearing tribute. Mindful of the way in which the officials direct the popular interpretation of events, the allied powers of France and England, when they took Peking in 1860, were not content to insist that the treaties they compelled China to sign should be inserted in the *Peking Gazette* which the unlearned people could not read ; they determined to leave behind

them evidence intelligible to all both of their having
been there, and of their having been there on a hostile
mission.   With this end in view, they burned down
the emperor's magnificent summer palace at Yuen
Ming Yuen, his favourite resort, full of the most costly
treasures of art.   But all has been in vain.   Though
the ruins of that paradise still lie at Yuen Ming Yuen,
it is commonly reported in China, I believe, to this
day that in the year 1860, a large and important
mission brought offerings and tribute from the distant
barbarian countries of France and England and was
allowed by the gracious condescension of the Lord of all
under Heaven to enter the city of Peking.

In speaking of the Chinese bearing towards the
foreigner, I have spoken of their national pride.   At
the same time, it may be doubted whether there is,
strictly speaking, any such thing as patriotism among
them.   The spirit that shuts off their sympathy from
subjects of other countries necessarily tends to paralyse
it even within their own borders.   For within the
boundaries of their empire are included a diversity of
men and manners, customs and dialects.   Foreigners,
more especially in former days, when means of com-
munication were fewer than now, often fell into errors
through failing to bear this in mind.   Thus the Rev.
W. C. Milne, who had travelled through the provinces
of Chehkiang, Kiangsi, and Kuangtung and seen not
a little of Chinese life during a lengthened residence
in the country, undertakes to disprove the charge of
infanticide, which is often brought against the Chinese,

and a strong point in his argument is this: It is said that in Peking carts are sent through the streets in the early morning to gather the dead bodies of the infants cast out during the night, which, he contends, must be false, because every one who has seen the streets of a Chinese city knows that they are too narrow for a cart to go along them. Now this seems conclusive, but Mr. Milne failed to remember that his acquaintance, say, with Canton, gave him no authority in speaking of Peking. The principal streets in the former are too narrow for a cart to traverse, but the streets of the latter would be accounted wide even in a European capital. Nor is it foreigners alone who make mistakes of this kind. The Chinamen themselves often know nothing beyond the customs of their own province, and yet assume that, knowing that one province, they know all China. Thus I remember hearing a Shanghai man inveighing loudly against the outrageous misrepresentations which foreigners are guilty of in speaking about his native land, and he cited, as a most flagrant instance of the injustice which had been done his countrymen, the fact that in more than one book he had found it stated that Chinamen ate rats! Could contemptuous and malicious fabrication further go? He challenged any one to bring forward a single case of a Chinaman doing anything of the kind. Here again is a forgetfulness of the fact that no one province is the whole of China. It is perfectly true that rats are not an article of diet in Kiangsu, but if our Shanghai man had gone to Canton he could have seen, as I have,

hundreds of these "small deer" exposed for sale in the
provision dealers' shops. Natives of the Kiangsu province and those of the Kuangtung province dress in the
same blue cotton and wear the same black queue, but
they are practically foreigners to each other, speaking
mutually unintelligible languages, and capable of the
most crass ignorance of each other possible. Speak to
a man of Shanghai concerning a man from the more
southern province as his fellow-countryman, and you
will not infrequently be met by a look of surprise and
the reply : "He no b'long Chinaman, he b'long foleign
man—b'long Canton man."

A larger illustration of the lack of sympathy between
the inhabitants of the different provinces which go to
make up the one empire of China, of the absence of any
common feeling of patriotism, was furnished during the
late troubles between France and China, by the apathy
of the Chinese in all districts not attacked or threatened
in regard to the movements of the French. Not only
were the ignorant agriculturists of the interior indifferent
to what was transpiring at the coast, but, owing probably
to a large extent to the system of independent vice-
royalties, the mandarins in one province seemed
scarcely to interest themselves in the struggles taking
place in another. While the Southern fleet was being
sunk in the river Min, the well-equipped Northern
fleet remained in masterly inactivity in the gulf of
Pechili, and that though the Frenchmen had put
themselves in the most convenient and tempting of
traps. What was happening at Foochow was, without

doubt, of gravest concern to the viceroy responsible for the well-being of the Fuhkien province, but the viceroy of Chihli could hardly be expected to concern himself with affairs so far off. The patriotism of a Chinaman is limited by his own province ; it is easy to narrow it still more and bound it by the limits of his own village. In fact, it is not difficult to complete the contracting process till all sign of patriotism is lost in an un-blushing selfishness. Selfishness is by no means confined to the Chinaman, nor does every Chinaman belong to the school of the philosopher Yang Choo, whose teaching of the principle, " Each one for himself," so roused the indignation of Mencius, as to compel him in one passage to exclaim : " Though by plucking out one hair he might have benefited all under heaven, he would not have done it." At the same time, considerations of self are allowed to control the conduct of the average Chinamen in about as candid a manner as may be observed anywhere. Though not a very religious person, he does engage in religious ceremonial. But it will never be found that he is stirred by the joy of worship ; he can always give a reason for his devotional exercise, sufficient to satisfy the most irreligiously selfish questioner, in the fear of some evil he wishes to ward off or in the hope of some advantage he wishes to gain. He has the credit of being charitable, and indeed the number of outstretched palms into which he drops a cash in the course of a day is very considerable, while foundling hospitals and the like in every city further attest the deservedness of this reputation. But almsgiving and benevolence are popular methods of "making merit." Every single cash that is given is a wise investment, and when the beggar gives the gentleman the opportunity of charity, and therefore of having so much merit put down to his account in the books from which his next birth will be determined, he is the gentleman's benefactor rather than the gentleman his by as much as merit is of more value than cash. To give to a Buddhist mendicant is even more meritorious, and, for this reason, when the said mendicant takes his begging bowl in hand and starts upon his rounds, the rule of his order forbids him to ask for anything, to look as though he wished for anything, or to thank any one for what is put into his bowl. He must accept it as one conferring rather than receiving a favour.

The freedom from simple promptings of benevolence in benevolent deeds, and the patent intention of making them serve the interest of the benefactor more than of the beneficiary, or, strictly speaking, of making the benefactor the beneficiary, may be seen most strikingly when the object of them belongs to the animal kingdom. The teaching of Gautama was as full of tender pity for birds and beasts, fishes and insects as for men. Sir Edwin Arnold tells how, when he returned to his royal home " to teach the law in hearing of his own," the whole universe hung upon his words.

> "The birds and beasts and creeping things'—tis writ—
> Had sense of Buddha's vast-embracing love,
> And took the promise of his piteous speech;

So that their lives—prisoned in shape of ape,
Tiger, or deer, shagged bear, jackal, or wolf,
Foul-feeding kite, pearled dove, or peacock gemmed,
Squat toad, or speckled serpent, lizard, bat ;
Yea, or of fish fanning the river waves—
Touched meekly at the skirts of brotherhood
With man, who hath less innocence than these,
And in mute gladness knew their bondage broke
Whilst Buddha spake these things before the king."

The master's living principles of unselfish sympathy
and compassion have come down to his disciples of the
present day in the form of rigid rules for the winning
of merit for one's personal advantage. The master's pity
for captive bird or beast would lead him to release it.
To-day there is quite a business going on at certain
festivals in the emancipation of sparrows which have
been specially caught for the sake of giving the benevolent an opportunity of letting them go again at so
much a head. Merit is laid up thus in rich store, but
the birds enjoy an equivocal advantage. One festival
day I saw a woman in the settlement of Shanghai
carrying a fish most carefully by a string that had
been so fastened to its dorsal fin, that it hung in
the horizontal position natural to it in the water.
Noticing her special care of it, I was led to follow and
see what she was going to do. She took it to the
cathedral compound, held it over a pond that is in the
grounds, cut the string and let it fall into the water.
Here was a fish that had apparently been netted out
of one piece of water that a woman might win merit by
setting it free in another, though it is just possible

N

in this case, since the pond was within the compound of a religious building, that the broad-minded
Buddhist woman supposed herself placing the fish in a
place of special safety, and even of special sanctity.

The most bare-faced making of spiritual capital out of
unnecessary and useless " kindness " to animals, that I
ever came upon was in Japan, but so Chinese an artifice
was it that it surely must have been introduced from
the mainland. At the end of a bridge an old woman
kept a number of pigeons in a large cage. Devout
Buddhists, pitying their sad captivity, bought their
freedom. The birds, received from the old lady, were
taken to the centre of the bridge and released, when
after a longer or shorter flight they, as pigeons do all
over the world, returned to the pigeon-house, some of
them flying thither direct from the hands of the pious
emancipators. Thus one pigeon might be bought and
freed over and over again, as fast, indeed, as compassionate zeal demanded, to the accumulating of merit
and, therefore, to the much future profit of those to
whom it afforded repeated opportunity of doing " a
good deed in a naughty world."

The methods which the Chinaman adopts to defend
himself against the cold of winter are not without a
certain value as aids to the reading of his mind. We
put wooden floors in the rooms of our houses for
others to walk on as well as ourselves, we even
carpet them to make walking on them more pleasant,
and in winter time we provide a fire which is intended
to warm the whole room and all who are in it. A

Chinaman renders himself independent of floors and carpets : he puts a two-inch sole on to his shoe, and thus makes sure of having a piece of floor under his own feet. In winter time he piles garment over garment upon his own back, slips little fur-lined cases over his ears, and envelopes his head and neck in a monstrous hood. If driven by the cold to the use of fuel, he does not light a fire for the sake of the family at large, but puts his red-hot charcoal balls into the metal vessel he uses as a footstool, and into the smaller one which he carries in his capacious sleeves for the warming of his hands. Of course, the rest of the family can do the same ; and perhaps, on the whole, the Chinese method is as effective against the cold as the English, though no one with our national restless activity could consent to be thus wrapped up into helplessness even for the sake of being kept warm. A Chinaman naturally portly is a sight in the cold season, while a little child clad in his winter clothes becomes a most comical object. He cannot get his arms down to his sides, they stick out horizontally, and should he fall, he is as incapable of getting up again as an overturned turtle or a mislaid sheep. However, he is Chinese, not English, so he wastes no strength in vain strugglings, he lies where he falls, calmly and contentedly, with his four limbs in mid-air, till some passer by thinks it worth while to pick him up. In the end, by the Chinese method in China, and by the English method in England, the comfort of the entire family is secured, yet it is surely not uninteresting to notice how in the latter case the object is attained by the common interest of the whole being arranged for from the beginning, while in the former case it is attained by each independently taking care of himself.

From the Chinese stand-point much is to be said for the Chinese method, but this very fact is instructive as to the stand-point, and the method is not without suggestiveness, not merely in regard to the Celestial's deliberateness, his freedom from hurry and undue activity, but also in regard to the personal centre of his thought.

"The flowers open, and lo! another year."

WEI YING-WUH. A.D. 702–795.

"The birth of a New Year is of an interest too wide to be preter-
mitted by king or cobbler."—C. LAMB.

"New Year is the universal holiday. There are other fête
days. ... But it is only on New Year's Day that the 350,000,000
of his Celestial Majesty's subjects give themselves up to. mutual
congratulations, unreserved festivity, and washing."

W. C. HUNTER. *Bits of Old China.*

CHAPTER II.

CHINESE NEW YEAR.

CHINESE New Year is a great time with the Chinaman, and the foreigner is not indifferent to it. A man, having been kept awake night after night for about a week by the noise of crackers let off in honour of the approaching day, will be likely to take an interest in it, though whether friendly or otherwise need not be explained.

A happy season is this for creditors, since it is a time for the general squaring up of accounts on earth and in heaven. A Chinaman will sacrifice a good deal rather than fail to set himself right with his earthly creditors at the New Year, and thus it becomes a time of debt-paying, a kind of Festival of St. Xmas Bills. And now also the " Kitchen god " of every house, who has for a whole year watched the domestic life of the family, has ascended to give in his record according to a most tenacious memory, not unaffected, as the poor earth-dwellers hope, by the special court and attention which he has received during the week or so before.

It is a season also for the interchange of courtesy and the exhibition of friendliness. On some cards—so to call them as indicating their purpose, they being, to describe them more exactly, slips of thin red paper—which I found on the table of the friend with whom I was staying during my first Chinese New Year, I noticed that there were some bold characters on the front, and some more modest characters on the back. The bolder characters were the name of a mandarin. The smaller characters on the other side corresponded to the printed matter one finds on the back of railway tickets explaining the conditions on which they are issued, and were to the effect that the card had been left by the great man as an act of New Year's condescension, but it was to be distinctly understood that it was not to be used as representing more than this annually blossoming courtesy. Whether this be a custom between Chinamen and Chinamen or whether it is a custom forced upon Chinamen in relation to foreigners, as a means of showing politeness and at the same time keeping the hated foreigner at a distance, I have not been able to learn.

At Soochow, on the testimony of a friend long resident there, this annual courtesy takes a stranger form, and one more inconvenient to the recipient of it. The magistrate sends round his servant with his card accompanied by a long list of the presents which he offers you in token of his high regard. The list enumerates choice wines, luscious fruits, and game in the richest profusion. But you would be foolish to look for the realities corresponding to the list. You express your thanks for the honour done in so highly rating your worth, and for the munificent gift : you hand a dollar to the coolie who has brought the card and is supposed to have brought the present, and return the catalogue to be used at the next house. Verily the heathen Chinee is peculiar.

The preparatory night explosions and the numerous tales about the New Year customs which I had heard made me anxious, when the day really dawned, to see something of it within the city walls where, rather than in the foreign concessions, I presumed the distinctively Chinese element would be most perfectly seen. Unfortunately for me the principal ceremonies take place in the forenoon and even early in the morning, and I was not able to get away till after tiffin. But then, under the able guidance of a missionary of between thirty and forty years' acquaintance with Shanghai, I set out. As a preliminary initiation into Chinese life, we went into an opium-den in the French concession. Such establishments were not in those days tolerated in the native city, and the Chinamen were wont to affect a keen sense of horror at the morals of foreigners who license and supervise opium, and other even more infamous, " dens," which they profess to forbid entirely. Facts seem rather against the Chinaman when he tries to claim for his brothers and sisters a high moral standard. None the less, it is true that disreputable people who want to carry on disreputable businesses flock from the various native cities into Shanghai, where they know the extent of the municipal taxes and licenses, while the amount of squeeze which is the price of official blindness to their doings in their own cities is more difficult to calculate.

To see the drowsy, stupid look on the faces of the opium-smokers—mostly men, though a few women were included in the number—no one would imagine that Chinamen were capable of making any noise at all. Evidence however had been already forthcoming to prove not only that they could make, but that they could enjoy it.

We entered the city by the New North Gate, a gate made by the French during the time they were in possession, or rather a gate made at the same place at which the French had made one ; for the French mode of constructing a city portal met with too little favour in Chinese minds for them to allow their work to remain. The French idea was to open out a wide space in the wall and approach it by a broad street. Not so the Chinese. Why, the veriest numskull among them could see that, with a wide street leading at once through an open gateway, especially on the north, all the good luck of the city would flow out into the adjourning foreign settlement. As soon, therefore, as the French had gone, the city fathers proceeded to reconstruct the gateway according to the orthodox method, and you now enter by a passage labyrinthine, narrow, filthy. The city's good luck will scarcely find its way out under the present arrangement.

Safely inside, we threaded our way along the narrow alley-ways, that are dignified by the name of streets because there were none wider, among our celestial fellow travellers, who did this day appear somewhat like troops of the shining ones. For it was New Year's Day, and silks and satins and furs which had slept peacefully for a whole year in the pawn-shops were enjoying their once-a-year airing. Gay, radiant and festive appeared cook and boy, compradore and coolie, arrayed in flowing robes with white-soled shoes and up-turned hats. The beggars too appeared to be honouring the day with special attention to personal appearance, being more carefully unwashed and pitiable looking than usual, as well as in fuller force. The " streets " were thronged, and where they ran along by the side of an indescribable creek—a kind of cloaca magna—it required one's wits to be awake to avoid being crowded into it, than which a more horrible fate can with difficulty be conceived.

In every available open space, especially at the "tea-gardens," dramatic legend spinners, and punch-and-judy establishments were attracting gaping audiences, while fortune-telling folks were plying a busy trade, deciding destinies for the coming year. Numerous stalls were improvised along the ways for the sale of sweetmeats, and blank walls were utilised by dealers in pictures which Polonius might have described as " tragedy, comedy, history, pastoral, pastoral-comical, historical-pastoral, tragical-historical, tragical-comical-historical-pastoral." The subjects of these works of art were mostly scenes of well-known dramas. My stopping to buy some of them was a matter of great interest. The crowd thickened around to see what th foreign devil wanted and to what extent the celestial picture dealer would be able to fleece him, for, however much the literary Chinaman affects the *nil admirari*, the average Chinamen of the streets behave like veritable children, ready to be amused with the merest trifle, and making no attempts to hide their curiosity, and the cheating of a foreigner by a Chinaman, though a diversion both frequent and old, never seems to lose its charm.

The pictures I purchased were worth study, but transcend my powers of description. If men whose physiology is normal are fearfully and wonderfully made, what shall we say of men—to whom must be added tigers and horses—concerning whose construction the most learned physiologist and the most skilled anatomist would have to admit that they stood on a level of ignorance with the little ragamuffins who mould mud-creatures in the gutters ?

We passed on to the temple of the guardian god of the city. It covers a good deal of ground, but it has nothing imposing about its architectural proportions. For its detail it might challenge admiration, were it not that this is largely obliterated by dirt. The softening, unifying haze that one finds in a forest of larch-firs, where the fine needles, too small to be seen separately, spread a gauzy veil of green over the whole, toning down and even wiping out distinctions, is reproduced, though in a less pleasing manner, in a Chinese temple. Clouds of dust and columns of in-cense-smoke, with grease of candle, have done their part; and over lamps and banners, tablets and gods there is one pervading grimy haze. You are reminded of the store of some dealer in useless rubbish, among whose stock no hand, prompted by the requirements of a customer, disturbs the accumulating dust. It matters not that the skin of the god was once of the brightest gilt: "How is the gold become dim, how is the most fine gold changed?" It matters not that the costume of his runners was once radiant in colour, the blue and the vermilion have long since given place to drabs and blacks.

In front of the temple is an open square in which stands a large upright stone-slab covered by inscriptions, and enclosed in a wooden framework supporting a tiled roof over it. There is also a large bronze altar for the burning of the mock-sycee or paper-money. On this New Year's Day it was covered with the ashes of burnt paper, representing untold wealth, though probably purchased for a paltry trifle. Fresh gifts were being thrown into this altar as we looked on. Passing from the square under the roof of the temple proper, one first enters into a kind of lobby, on either side of which stand four large and unhandsome figures. In front of each of these is a jar for incense sticks, and before each of them paper-money was being burnt as in the altar in the open court. For doorkeepers—and such these eight are supposed to be—are important persons in China. Whether or no one is to gain admission to the presence of the master of a house depends on the favour of the keeper of the door: and, admission being granted, the kind of reception one gets depends on the character that has been already given by that official. It would almost seem as though a magistrate leaves to his porters the duty of catechising any who come to him for redress of grievances, and, since the primary aim of a Chinese magistrate is not to dispense justice but to "squeeze," perhaps the porter is more competent to deal with the matter than would at first appear. He, at any rate, is less hampered than his master, whose dignity would be compromised by the bare-faced questioning and bargaining which the servant is at liberty to indulge in by way of discovering the squeezability of a visitor.

Now, since the temple of a god is the counterpart of the yamen of a magistrate, in the temple, as in the yamen, the man at the door has to be propitiated. The paper money, incense and candles burnt before these eight figures, between which one has to pass on entering the temple from the front, testify to the worshippers' sense of the necessity of bribery. Having propitiated the door-keepers, one can enter the temple proper; but, before getting into the immediate presence of the idol, one finds a place spread with mats, from which its face can be dimly seen through a forest of incense-holders, candlesticks, and other temple para- phernalia. Here the worshippers kneel down and go through a set form, including the knocking of the forehead nine times on the earth. Immediately before the idol is a smaller space devoted to similar exercises. I cannot say whether this is set apart for any special class or rank, or whether, as in English churches, native modesty retires to the more distant mats, and self-importance takes possession of the "highest rooms." I saw some repeat in the second the ritual performed in the first place, but whether all who bow at the first would be admitted to the second I could not discover. The necessary formularies having been gone through, the offerings placed before the deity, and the candles lighted on their iron "sticks," the priests indulge the suppliant with a little fortune-telling, to indicate the answer that the god is pleased to make. A box made of a section of a bamboo stem, containing a number of bamboo slips is placed in his hand. He shakes them up thoroughly, and then chooses one of them and draws it from the box. This slip has a mark or legend on it, which refers to some special passage in a book of answers. The idolater generally goes away happy, since if the answer be not a favourable one he refuses to accept it, and draws again, and yet again if the second be also unfavourable, until, by his importunity, he wearies the god to give a satisfactory reply. Whether he thus alters the inevitable is not so clear.

Behind this shrine are the courts in which the runners or messengers of the god—some fifty-six in all in this particular temple—stand ranged along the walls. One or two of these attendants were, at the time of our visit, recent substitutes for some who had decayed or fresh additions to the staff, for by their clean and bright appearance they made the rest look more than venerable. Over the heads of these runners near the ceiling were suspended two models of junks, presumably the votive offering of some successful trader.

Behind these courts again is a second shrine, containing an image of the consort or some female relative of the god. The arrangements of this second shrine were a repetition of those of the first, except that they were simpler.

Around this large temple cluster quite a number of smaller ones—parasitic temples as it were—where other gods are propitiated, though it is difficult for the uninitiated to appreciate the differences in their form, feature, or expression. The rough distinction between the smooth face of a Buddhist and the usually moustached and bearded visage of a Taoist deity is readily perceived; but there is nevertheless a monotony in the inane and expressionless faces which the occasional tendency to an idiotic simper hardly breaks. These gilt-faced deities bear witness to a conservatism in style among the artists worthy of an ancient, perhaps decrepit, country. Occasionally when several deities are to be placed side by side, the necessity of marking distinctions forces itself on the maker of them, and he effects his purpose by making one or two of their number monsters. It is so in a small shrine outside the court of this Shanghai City Temple. Here five gods board and lodge together, and over each one's head is written his name; but, to make assurance doubly sure, there is a dreadful distortion of features, a triumph of hideousness wrought in at least one of them. These five are the gods respectively of Injuries, Wealth, Serpents, Oaths and Dreams. The second of these is the popular god, his votaries are legion. Notwithstanding the "religious" observances of the Chinese, it has been often said by men who have known something of them that they are without a religious instinct. Their anxiety to propitiate the god of wealth is an illustration of their spirit. Of a religion the motive of which is love and which involves self-sacrifice and self-denial, they know little. Their religion is the giving paper money to a god from whom they hope to get a return in more solid currency. Their religious aims are the very reverse of those set before men in the Sermon on the Mount. At the same time, as often as we judge the heathen we have to admit, I fear, that there are men who think themselves Christians whose worship is not the spontaneous outburst of a heart s gladness or confidence in God independently of changing earthly conditions, but the calculated effort to gain some advantage—it may be to give to their lives an air of respectability, to buttress up their credit, to conform to custom, to please a friend, or, more seriously perhaps, to escape undesirable consequences in the next life by propitiating God in this. It is difficult to see wherein this kind of "Christianity" differs from the heathenism of the Chinese.

" Your railroad, when you have come to understand it, is only a device for making the world smaller; and as for being able to talk from place to place, that is, indeed, well and convenient; but suppose you have originally nothing to say."—RUSKIN.

" To employ an uninstructed people in war is what is called destroying the people. A destroyer of the people was not tolerated in the age of Yaou and Shun. Though by a single battle you should vanquish Ts'e and so get possession of Nan-yang, the thing ought not to be done."—MENCIUS.

"Build me straight, O worthy master!
  Staunch and strong, a goodly vessel
  That shall laugh at all disaster,
    And with wave and whirlwind wrestle."
        LONGFELLOW. *The Building of the Ship.*

CHAPTER III.

A LAUNCH AT KAO-CHANG-MIAOU.

CHINA is the Middle Kingdom. As to the Greeks of old all other nations were barbarians, so to the Chinese are the subjects of the outer kingdoms that are not under the immediate sway of the Son of Heaven who sits enthroned at Peking. Bitter is the hatred and contemptuous the pity of the Celestial for all foreigners. "Granted that you have your railways, that you can build steamships and gunboats, that your inventiveness is wonderful; you have no literature ! what is a nation without the Five Classics and the Four Books ? "

But notwithstanding this sense of superiority and her deep-seated hatred, there are matters in which China seems not only willing but anxious to follow the lead of other nations. *Fas est ab hoste doceri;* and even where the foes are inferiors, some lessons may be learned. Has it not been said that a wise man can learn more from a fool than a fool can learn from a wise man ? If the Central Kingdom can learn from the Circumferential, surely in that fact is evidence of her superiority and wisdom! But she is doing this wise thing in a way less wise than might have been

o 2

expected in a nation so exalted in privilege. She has long regarded with suspicion any attempt to develop the resources of the empire by railways,* or by applying the result of Western research in chemistry and experiment in engineering to her celestial agriculture, river-embankment and mining. The whirl of machinery in arsenals and the din of hammers in ship-yards have more attractions. There is more noise in these things and—which is of still more importance—more opportunity of official squeeze than there would be in quietly increasing the strength of the nation by adding to the prosperity and contentment of the people. To manufacture big guns, to collect a fleet of heavily-armed gun-boats, to supplement the rusty spears and tridents of her braves with modern breech-loaders— these are the ways in which China seems most ready to make the West her model, even though, in so doing, she beggars the country and fills her hands with costly war material enough to tempt the cupidity of any nation that itches to become possessed of a fine fleet without the delay and expense of building it. It is a pity that China does not develop herself first, and her fighting apparatus afterwards. A tiger's tooth is nothing without the mighty muscle that gives it grip.

With purity of government and local administration and other so much needed reforms, there might arise in the land a patriotism that should be the nation's strength, the ships being bravely manned, and the navy

* Since this was written something has been done in this direction.

an object of truly national pride, supported not merely by Imperial decrees, but by public enthusiasm. As it is, it is most likely that the estimate of a Chinese naval officer, with whom I was speaking in regard to the Northern Fleet, was correct when he said: "We have a very fine coat, but there is no man inside it." It cannot but "make the judicious grieve" to see the imperial dragon sprawling in his yellow triangle over the scare-crow of military and naval parade.

During the French invasion of Tongking and the carrying out of M. Jules Ferry's scheme of "intelligent destruction" of property and life on the coasts of China proper, the activity of this latter country in preparing warlike material was greatly stimulated. In the Kiangnan Arsenal at Kao-Chang-Miaou, near Shanghai, work in the heavy-ordnance department was for some time carried on day and night, and it was at that time that the first steel cruiser which the Chinese ever built, was launched. All the material had come out from Europe ready to be put together, I believe, which perhaps detracted somewhat from the credit due to the authorities at Kao-Chang-Miaou. The day of the launch was nevertheless a high day and as such nobly honoured. Having been invited to the ceremony, I went with one or two friends in a small steam-launch. We arrived off the arsenal about an hour before the time and found the whole river bank on either side of the building-shed already lined with eager Celestials whose almost universally indigo-dyed clothes formed a bright blue margin along the water's

edge. Fences were crowned with them, all kinds of
scaffoldings were covered, an old frigate lying in the
dock was crowded, while a watch-tower of open wood
work in several stories was so thoroughly filled that we
were reminded of the pictures of the wicker-work
figures stuffed with men from which we had been early
taught to imbibe appropriate horror of the cruelty
of the Druidical cult. Every point of vantage was
occupied, every available space thronged by blue-
clad Chinamen stirred to an unwonted enthusiasm, yet
maintaining their characteristic patience; smoking,
chatting and laughing, confident that now at last the
greatness of China would be recognised throughout the
West. It looked at first sight as though it would be
impossible for us to effect a landing, so thickly stood
the phalanx of spectators along the river bank. We
succeeded, however, in getting on shore, and forced our
way through into the open space behind, and made for
the gateway of the shed under which the vessel had
been built. Here a soldier was on guard to keep the
gate closed against the crowd outside, but to serve what
useful end we could not divine since inside there was
another crowd which seemed as numerous and as dirty
as that outside and was in every way indistinguishable
from it. But having been long enough in the East to
have got over the foolish occidental habit of expecting
to find reasons for things, we simply asked to have the
gate opened for us. The soldier promptly admitted us,
and the whole rabble seeking to make our entrance the
means of theirs, pressed in at the opened gate in a stream

which the poor soldier was powerless to shut out. As he had opened the gate for us, it seemed only fair that we should help him to shut it, however little reason we might see for the exclusion of the outside crowd from the privileges that the apparently similar crowd inside enjoyed. In a moment we were shoulder to shoulder, bearing back the celestial wave that was surging in, and almost succeeded in re-excluding ourselves, as our soldier, encouraged by our alliance, forced the gate to again. Receiving his thanks for our assistance we passed on through the multitude, almost stifled with the heat and the very appreciable adulteration of the fresh air inseparable from such a gathering of Chinamen.

As there was still plenty of time we did not take our places at once but strolled round among the people and —since some of our company were experts in ship-building—struck critical attitudes and made critical comments at the various points from which the " lines" of the vessel could be best seen. Due study having been given to, and comments passed on the vessel herself and the examination having been made of the arrangements for launching her, which I understood were more elaborate and expensive than would have been made at home for a vessel of much larger size, we sought the stage on which the arsenal officials were seated and supplied with tea. Having got through the ceremony of several introductions, we prepared to wait. Most of the company were standing, there being but one or two chairs upon the platform, but as we had a lady in our

party a chair was vacated and she was invited to be
seated. It was a little amusing to see the official,
whose chair was next to that offered to Mrs. ——, pre-
cipitately rise and retire to the rear with a look of
anxiety, if not terror, as he started and a look of relief
and re-assurance as he gained his refuge and began
volubly to converse with his brethren. Such close
proximity to a European lady was evidently a new
experience for him, and he doubtless congratulated
himself on being well out of a post of danger, if of
honour. Just where we were standing there was no
press. The crowd was held back at a distance of some
four or five yards by the august presence of the mandarins and the uniform of a single soldier who wore a
startling dress of deep blues and reds surmounted by a
huge hat with a diameter equal to that of a good sized
umbrella, but which must be useless as a protection
from the sun in front since, as the wearer of it walks,
the great flapping brim flies upward and backward in a
manner that is most picturesque but that leaves the
face completely exposed. The awe felt at the official
presence was imperceptible at any distance greater than
that mentioned. Encircling us was a group both dense
and motley. In the very fore-front of it, nearest, therefore, to the silks of the men of wealth and rank, were
some of the richest specimens of dirtiness and ragged-
ness that could well be imagined, unkempt, nondescript
figures whose clothes and persons were so over-laid
with what was unnecessary and probably inconvenient,
that the colour of their garments or the complexion of

their skins afforded material for speculation. Such juxtapositions strike new comers as strange but after a while one gets accustomed to them. The raggedest Chinese—outside the ranks of the professional beggars whose rags are their fortune—are generally to be found in the retinues of the mandarins. Such associations of dignity with impudence and rank with rags having become familiar to me, I doubt if I should have noticed it in this case had it not been pointed out by a more recent arrival in the Flowery Land.

Mr. ——, an Englishman, under whose superinten- dence the cruiser had been constructed, was to be seen here, there, and everywhere, as calm as the anxiety of the hour would permit. At last he came upon the stage where we were and, through his interpreter, spoke to the mandarin in charge. Then again he disappeared to take a last look at the preparations, and to give his final instructions. Returning, he took off his hat to the mandarin and by gesture intimated that the vessel was ready. The word was then given, and in forcible Chinese, all junks, sampans, and other craft on the river were suitably objurgated, and with a very babel of confusion, the workmen scrambled to their places. At another word the hammers fell, the ropes were drawn tight, and the huge mass of steel and wood began to move—slowly at first, but with a speed ever-increasing until, amid many cheers, it slid down into the water with a rush that carried it into the middle of the stream, where, bending round with the tide, it stood revealed, a vessel presenting her broadside to her builders, as if conscious that all eyes were upon her.

This was the moment of mutual congratulations, of Chinese kotowing and European hand-shaking. All trace of anxiety was gone from the face of the builder though he looked flushed with success and the hot weather. The countenances of the officials beamed with triumph, for there had been no hitch of any sort, and although probably another twelvemonth's work would be yet needed upon her before she would be fit for service, one more vessel could be counted as belonging to His Imperial Majesty's navy, and the Kiangnan Arsenal could pride itself on the first entirely steel-built vessel which it had launched.

The European visitors were now invited to adjourn to a neighbouring shed where a table had been covered with a cloth and surrounded by chairs for their use, the Chinese hosts either standing or sitting in an outer circle. There was tea on a little table in the corner but we saw none offered to the guests. The arsenal authorities seemed to have been taught that Europeans prefer champagne and in their hour of pride they scorned to appear mean. For my own part I took the liberty of asking for the unoffered beverage, not only for the lady member of our company but for myself, and while the toasts were being drunk and spoken to, we, at our side-table, duly honoured them in our tea, made, *à la Chinoise,* in the lidded cup that serves for both tea-cup and tea-pot, and guiltless alike of cream and sugar.

As we were sitting thus somewhat back from the rest of the visitors, we noticed that something about us had attracted the attention of the head-mandarin. Clearly he was particularly interested in something and most probably curious about it. So I rose to speak with him, and found that the object of his curiosity was my spectacles—ordinary slightly-made, gold-framed spectacles, but evidently extraordinary to him. He was anxious to try them on, and offered me his own immense circular Chinese-made instruments with large tortoise-shell rims, not unlike the port-holes of a steamer. I at once took off mine and handed them to him, accepting and putting his on my nose in their place. We were not able to appreciate the figure we cut as we could neither see ourselves nor, with each other's glasses on, could we see each other, but either the proceeding itself or the resulting appearance mightily tickled the Chinamen standing round who laughed heartily, and the mandarin returned my glasses and received back his own evidently highly gratified with the sensation he had made.

Soon after this we left cordially joining in the hope expressed in one of the toasts that this newly-launched cruiser might be a peace-maker, and, while armed to the teeth, might live long years of undisturbed indolence and finally decay in peace, having neither suffered nor inflicted injury in serious conflict ; hoping also that as little harm as possible would result from the Chinamen's deference to foreign prejudice in the matter of beverage, and regretting that more honour was not paid by them to their own national and home-grown tea. Our hopes in this matter, however, were not strong enough to compel us to disbelieve the report that afterwards reached us, that, before the company separated, many of them developed eccentricities of speech and movement that gave the sons of Han legitimate occasion for congratulating themselves that they were not as these barbarians.

"How sharper than a serpent's tooth it is
To have a thankless child!"

SHAKSPERE. *King Lear.*

"Filial piety and paternal submission—are they not the root of all benevolent actions?"—YEW THE PHILOSOPHER.

"In short, even Christians may learn from Hindus, as indeed from Oriental nations generally (notably from the Chinese, as well as from the Hindus), 'to love, honour, and succour their father and mother, to submit themselves to all their governors, teachers, spiritual pastors, and masters, and to order themselves lowly and reverently to all their betters.'"

SIR MONIER WILLIAMS. *Indian Wisdom.*

"... And so, twirling his mustachios, and flinging down his piastre, the young janissary strutted out of the coffee-house.

"'When we were young,' said the old Turk with the white beard to his companion, shaking his head—'when we were young——'

"'We conquered Anatolia, and never opened our mouths,' rejoined his companion.

"'I never offered an opinion till I was sixty,' said the old Turk, 'and then it was one which had been in our family for a century.'"

LORD BEACONSFIELD. *The Rise of Iskander.*

"Parents without exception demand that their children be filial, but the filial piety is not necessarily love."—CHUANG-TSI.

"Oh, my friend, cultivate the filial feelings, and let no one think himself relieved from the kind charities of relationship; these shall give him peace at the last; these are the best foundation for every species of benevolence."—C. LAMB. *Letter to S. T. Coleridge.*

CHAPTER IV.

THE FILIAL PIETY OF THE CHINESE.*

"WE in administering the Government uphold Filial Piety as the first of all the virtues." Thus says His Imperial Majesty the Emperor of China in the decree published in 1885, relating to the release and return to Corea of the Dai-In-Kun; and in so saying, H. I. M. is in full accord with the laws, traditions and customs of his empire.

Nothing is lacking in legal penalty or in "olo custom" to compel a reverential demeanour in young China in relation to parents. Disrespect or injury, even accidental, being visited with severe punishment in this world and with an introduction into the next where, according to the very favourite Buddhist tract, usually called *The Jade Register*, those who have failed in filial piety receive the special attention of the demons of the Eighth Hell, who crush them under heavy rollers. I suppose that there is scarcely a year in which the *Peking Gazette* does not contain the notice of at least one instance of the horrors of the ling-ch'ih,

* The substance of this chapter was read before the China branch of the Royal Asiatic Society at Shanghai, October 15th, 1885.

or lingering death, penalty having been inflicted on some poor lunatic, who, not knowing what he was doing, had taken a parent's life, or on some youth who had killed a parent by accident, or on some unfortunate girl who had been forced to murder in defending her honour from some debauched old father-in-law. The last volume published at the date of this writing recounts the horrible piecemeal-slicing of a lunatic who had killed his grandmother, the said grandmother having been previously warned of the dangerous nature of her grandson's lunacy and repeatedly urged to place him in safe keeping. On the other hand, the most outrageous barbarities and wilful cruelties are condoned when the elder generation is dealing with the younger. It is true that in the Penal Code there is a penalty of one hundred blows for the man who beats a disobedient son to death if he do it unintentionally, and of one hundred and sixty with a year's banishment if he do so designedly, but these penalties are seldom if ever inflicted. One is sickened by the horrors that every now and again crop up in the Shanghai papers. In the Hunan province it would appear that it is the custom for girls to be betrothed as mere infants, after which they are handed over by their mothers to their future mothers-in-law. Not long after I arrived at China I read of one of these mothers-in-law-to-be searing a child's face with a hot iron as a punishment for crying and then scalding her to death with boiling water, and of another seeking to save the doctor's bill by strangling her son's fiancée who had fallen sick. A little before this, the newspaper,. in which I read of these atrocities, had contained an account of a mother's burying a child alive without incurring a word of rebuke, and more recently the *Hua Pao*, an illustrated Chinese newspaper, gave its subscribers an illustration of a similar tragedy. The crime was represented as performed without haste or secrecy in the presence of a large and sympathetic crowd—sympathising however not with him who was to officiate as corpse, but with her who was officiating as chief mourner. Laws and customs that invest parents with practically irresponsible power, while they contain no hint of such injunctions as, "And ye fathers, provoke not your children to wrath," may be expected to rob the love of the parent of its rightful influence in the home; and though they may result in filial piety indeed it will be a piety in which love is likely to have little place, and reverence, lacking love, to become a hollow sham, punctiliously observed for reasons that may seem sufficient to the Celestial rather than commendable to us.

In truth, the filial piety on which the stability of the Chinese empire is supposed to depend, and to ensure which so many laws have been framed, so many ethical books written and tracts distributed, is a poor virtue after all. It is boldly asserted by those who know the people well, that it consists far less in loving service to the living than in religious formalities at the tombs of the dead. Even Bishop Moule, of Hangchow, who says he thinks the. outcome of the doctrine and practice of

P

filial piety in China to be on the whole good and
claims to agree with the moralists of the last century
in holding that the country owes her national longevity
very much to her national filial piety, admits that he
has heard of a son grudging his parent the "savoury
meat" he craved on his death-bed, as a futile expense,
yet, when the season arrived for the funeral feast,
beggaring himself to provide a costly banquet; while an
American missionary, who writes with the authority
attaching to a lifetime's residence in the Flowery Land,
hesitates not to say : "Of all the people of whom we
have any knowledge, the sons of the Chinese are most
unfilial, disobedient to parents, and pertinacious in
having their own way from the time they are able to
make known their wants." He then adds, "The filial
duties of a Chinese son are performed after the death
of his parents. A son is said to be filial if he is
faithful in doing all that custom requires for his
deceased ancestors." This is doubtless a rough judgment in both senses of the word, and is out of accord
with the impression left on the mind after the perusal
of Chinese filial piety as illustrated in the *Twenty-
four Examples.* There we see how the emperor Shun,
in his pre-imperial days, bemoans the evil in himself of
which he is unconscious, but which, since he is incapable of attributing wickedness to his parents or
injustice to Heaven, he infers from the, as he supposes,
Heaven-accorded cruelty of his unnatural father and
little less than devilish step-mother, and how he seeks
by all the means in his power to serve faithfully

and dutifully those who have more than once made attempts upon his life, until his virtue excites the admiration and compels the help of the very birds of the air and beasts of the field.   There we see the young Wu Mung lying on his parents' bed to allow the mosquitoes to take the edge off their appetites before the venerable severe one and the venerable compassionate one retire to rest.   There again may we see how the septuagenarian philosopher Lao Lai-tsz dresses himself in childish garments of the brightest colours and risks the breaking of his aged limbs and reverend neck in juvenile antics, to the end that he may keep from the minds of his still more aged parents the fact that they are tottering on the verge of the grave and may deceive them into thinking themselves a young couple happy in the frolics of their first-born.   But, notwithstanding all this, the words of my missionary friend above quoted are not without corroboration. The *Twenty-four Examples* may possibly represent the conduct of men at the date of its compilation, but we have fallen on degenerate days.   If Confucius had occasion to say in reference to virtues known in his early years: "Now, alas, there are no such things," how much more we ! Filial piety as taught by the maxims and examples of the ancients, does not live in the filial piety that is practised by their modern descendants which, notwithstanding the occasional cutting off of filial flesh to make medicinal broth for moribund parents, consists chiefly, we may suspect, as my friend asserts, in the observance of funeral rites and the worship at the tombs.　Dr. S. Wells Williams, in his *Middle Kingdom,* quotes from a Chinese tract, written against Christian missionaries, in which the writer unintentionally offers confirmation of our suspicion.　This Chinese apologist affirms that it is monstrous in barbarians to attempt to teach his countrymen, and among their many disqualifications which he enumerates, he includes their lack of this particular virtue.　He says: " Further, these would-be exhorters of the world are themselves deficient in filial piety, forgetting their parents as soon as dead, putting them off with deal coffins only an inch thick, and never so much as once sacrificing to their manes, or burning the smallest trifle of gilt paper for their support in the future world."　From this vigorous indictment we may infer the things which the zealous pamphleteer considers constitute filial piety, viz., providing one's parents with thick coffins of good wood, sacrificing to their manes and burning gilt paper for their support in the future world.　There is not a word about the filial attentions of which this world · affords the opportunity.　It will be noticed, moreover, that the absence of any accusation of neglecting living parents in this sweeping charge in which Christians are supposed to be proved unfilial, offers further evidence, if such be needed, that care for the living has but a small place, if any, in the Chinese idea of filial piety.　And even " the Master" in substantiating his exclamation: " How greatly filial was Shun ! " though he refers generally to his virtue and dignity, specifies but one act: "He offered his sacrifices in his ancestral temple." We have reason to believe that this is not an exhaustive account of the filial piety of the evidently worthy, if somewhat doubtfully historical, Shun; but when we have said: "He offers his ancestral worship," we have, I fear, exhausted the grounds on which many a living Celestial can claim to be "greatly filial."

If then it be a fact that the expression of the filial piety of the Chinese is postponed till after the death of their parents (and the evidence that this is at least largely the case seems to me to be conclusive), it is a fact calling for explanation. Nor is the explanation far to seek. The claims of the living parent are by no means to be neglected, as may be seen from what we have said of the savage barbarities that are condoned in a parent bent on enforcing them. But when a parent has joined the majority, the matter craves even more serious attention. There is need to brush up one's filial piety when one's parent is promoted to fiendship. And it is done. This is filial piety as taught and practised in China—propitiating a devil! a son's precaution against his father's dreaded demoniac rage! What would a child brought up in the careful nurture and tender affection of an English home, to whom his father and mother are the living embodiments of every virtue, think when told that, should a Chinaman get sick, one of the first things to be done is to present offerings at the ancestral tablets on the assumption that the sickness is the work of some inadvertently neglected, and therefore dissatisfied, father or grandfather? Yet, misled by the phrase, our instructors not infrequently hold up the Chinese to us as worthy examples.. Such filial piety as they exemplify may be found but too abundantly in the back slums of all our large cities, but it is not held up for admiration here. It may be seen where children crouch and tremble before the home-return of fathers, heavy-booted and maddened with drink, able and not unwilling to thrash, kick, curse, and even murder them. When we take away the foreign flavour and look at this Chinese filial piety in an English dress the inclination to admire and imitate is lost. There are many who mourn in England over the decay of filial respect, and wonder to what we are drifting when they see so much more pains taken to train up the parent in the way he should go than to train up the child; but the homes of England have still their sanctities, and woe be to her should the day ever come when such back slum scenes furnish the examples of our home-life, and the fearful forebodings and pitiful pleadings of helpless children, the examples of our filial piety.

It need scarcely be pointed out that this filial-pious worship will often be paid as grudgingly as scrupulously. The man who most fully appreciates the necessity of rendering it may as keenly regret that it is a necessity and may recognise that it would be better to remove the risk than to pay the cost of insurance against it. Now a Chinaman seems to combine with his fear of spirits a marvellous faith in their stupidity, as is witnessed by the expedients he adopts with a view to circumventing and deceiving them. He apparently attributes to them, among other things, a curious incapacity for recognising their claims upon their own people if only they can be got to enter upon their spiritual existence on the premises of others. In such a case the penalty of any neglect will most probably be visited on these latter unfortunate persons. It is they who had better provide the funeral and pay the expenses of it, lest the spirit, starved or piqued, should return to the place whence he had set out to wreak his vengeance. On this account no innkeeper will knowingly receive into his house of rest and entertainment an obviously moribund traveller. He can safely refuse him admittance and allow him to die on the road outside. If he admit him to the comforts of his establishment, he can refuse him neither coffin, funeral rites nor worship with safety. An incident that occurred in the experience of a Shanghai missionary, somewhat amusingly illustrates a bold attempt to remove altogether the risk that men ordinarily provide against by their ancestor-worship. The missionary was sitting one cold winter evening at his study table. A servant came and informed his master that a dead man had been found in the garden. The missionary went out to look into the matter. Sure enough, under the wall of the garden lay a human body, loosely covered over with straw. An economical family had evidently brought the dying man and laid him there that they might save themselves the expenses of the funeral by throwing them on the foreign missionary, and the ruling passion of thrift had further dictated the substitution of a covering of straw for his personal clothing. The missionary felt the body all over and found it already cold, but, on the chance of there being life left, he had it carried indoors where he poured down its throat a dose of a patent medicine in which he had great faith, at the same time ordering more straw to be thrown upon it. He then returned to his study. Sometime later he thought he would go and see how his corpse-patient was getting on. On this second examination he fancied he detected a faint sign of life in the region of the heart. More of the patent medicine was given and more straw. To make a long story short, the dead man came to life again and stood up in all the naked dignity of his manhood. Well, the missionary, who was a particularly tall and large man, rigged out the little Chinaman as best he could in clothes from his own wardrobe, and, as soon as he was well enough, sent him back to his loving wife and filial sons. As he approached the house some of the latter saw and recognised him, notwithstanding the strangeness of his garb, and, being sincere believers in the doctrine of transmigration, rushed to their mother, crying aloud that their father had come back again to earth and that this time he had been born a foreigner. Many a friendly interview in after days did the missionary and his patient have, the latter always profuse in gratitude, declaring that his daily prayer to Foh was that when his next change came he might be foaled a donkey for the special riding of his foreign friend who had added to his life so many years in which to eat rice. No meagre gratitude this considering the weight of his benefactor.

Our estimate of this much vaunted virtue will not be raised if turning from the consideration of it as the result of laws that environ living parents with protection in the exercise of the most savage passion, and of teachings that render possible the conception of one's deceased parents as vicious demons, we now seek to judge it from the results of which it has become itself the cause. It is probably the most potent of the influences that have moulded the Chinese character. That what is meant by the term has not always been what is meant now may be readily admitted, but the present perversion is not of yesterday and has had time to do its work. The Chinaman of to-day is pretty much what his filial piety has made him. I am not unmindful of what is said in the *Mahabharata :*

> "An evil-minded man is quick to see
> His neighbour's faults, though small as mustard-seed;
> But when he turns his eyes towards his own,
> Though large as vilva-fruit, he none descries."

It is with no evil mind that I would judge the Chinese, nor with any blindness to our own faults. The good temper and patience of their poorer classes may well challenge the admiration of the irascible, impatient and impetuous European, and be reckoned among the sweet uses of the adversity of the mandarin's squeeze and oppression ; but even for these long-suffering ones our admiration is not unqualified, while, when we look at the conceit and ignorance of their "gentry" and literati, and the well-nigh universal corruption of their officials, we almost forgive the mild pharisaism of the verse :

> "I thank the goodness and the grace
> That on my birth have smiled,
> And made me in these Christian days
> A happy English child."

Nor is it to be forgotten that unlike some horrible doctrines which, while they cannot but taint the heart of him who believes them, are comparatively innocuous from their believers' impotence to give them practical expression, the Chinese theory of Filial Piety, not only corrupts the individual heart but dominates the life and conduct of the entire nation, making its effect felt from the! centre of every family to the circumference of the whole empire. It controls every institution. Marriages are consummated earlier than would be the case but for the feverish anxiety to ensure the perpetuation of the worship at the tombs, threatening to introduce a system of child-marriage approaching that which is acknowledged to be so great an evil in India. A criminal whose parent has recently died, is either acquitted or receives a more lenient sentence than justice demands in order that his duties at the grave may not be interfered with. A prominent instance of the requirements of justice being made to stand aside for those of filial piety occurs in the decree regarding the restitution of the Dai-In-Kun to which reference is made at

the beginning of this chapter. In that decree His
Imperial Majesty states that it is by a special act of
grace that Li Kan-ying (the Dai-In-Kun) is liberated
"to satisfy the filial longings" of his son, the king of
Corea, and that "the Board of Rites is to let the Corean
king understand that in this act we are benevolent
even beyond the law." The teaching of Mencius on
this point is clear. He distinctly taught that an
emperor ought to set the claims of filial piety above the
demands of justice. A disciple asked what would have
been done if when Shun was emperor and Kaou-Yaou
chief minister of justice, Koo-Sow—Shun's father, the
inhuman old wretch spoken of on p. 210, and whose
name, composed of two characters both meaning "blind,"
is said to have been given him on account of his mental
and moral blindness—had committed murder. The
sage replied that Kaou-Yaou would have had Koo-
Sow arrested. "But would not Shun have forbidden
any such proceeding?" inquired the other. "No," said
Mencius, "how could he, Kaou-Yaou having received
his authority from Heaven?" The disciple then wanted
to know what Shun, the great example of filial piety,
would have done, and Mencius replied, "Shun would
have regarded abandoning all under heaven as throwing
away a worn-out sandal. He would privately have
taken his father on his back, and withdrawn into con-
cealment, living somewhere on the sea-board. There
he would have been all his life, cheerful and happy,
forgetting the empire." Thus filial piety would not only
have required him to shield a murderer from justice.

but would have compelled him, for the purpose of doing it, to withdraw himself, the ideal monarch, and to deprive his empire of the peace and security it was enjoying under his rule.   The succession to the Dragon throne is no less under the despotism of filial piety's requirements.   The statesmen of China may acknowledge the truth of the words: "Woe to thee, O land, when thy king is a child," but, since filial piety must find expression in ancestor worship, no one of them dare question the necessity of each emperor being the junior of his predecessor, at however tender an age that predecessor may have died.   The emperor of to-day must be accounted the son of the emperor of yesterday, that there be no failure in funeral rite or ceremony.

And not only must the administration of the law and the succession to the throne conform thus to necessities created by this theory of filial piety, the direction of the imperial policy must yield also.   The affairs of the empire may be in a most critical condition and there may be only one man possessing the ability to steer the ship of state at such a juncture, but should that man's father or mother die, he must relinquish all into the hands of less competent statesmen and go into the regulation period of mourning retirement lest his deceased parent not only visit him with his displeasure but bring calamity on the empire, attention to the affairs of which had been the occasion of the unfilial neglect.*   This tyranny is felt of course in all depart-

* The Chinese law allows a man two wives, and public opinion approves the law when a man's first wife has no children; but the

ments and through all ranks. At a meeting of the China Branch of the Royal Asiatic Society, Mr. C. F. R. Allen, of Her Majesty's Consular Service, gave the following instance that had come under his notice. A native of Peking having been appointed to an official post in Yunnan, had to borrow money to defray the expenses of so long a journey. When he had gone the greater part of the way, the news of his mother's death overtook him. The necessary result was the man's bankruptcy and the state's loss of his services. Mr. Allen added that he thought the Chinese themselves must have an uneasy feeling that there is a certain amount of humbug in the law about the three years' mourning, as occasional exceptions to it are permitted.

This feeling unquestionably possessed at least one Chinaman as long ago as the days of Confucius, since it is recorded in the *Analects*, that one of the sage's disciples, by name Tsae Wo, had the temerity to say that he considered the three years' mourning ordained for sons on the death of their parents to be unnecessarily long, and that one year would be amply sufficient —with which sentiment, if the mourning be simply that ordained by law, my readers will probably agree. Said Tsae Wo to Confucius: "If the superior man

---

second wife is always regarded as the representative of the first, on whose death her children have to assume mourning. It may therefore happen that the services of a valuable officer in the state have to be lost by his compulsory mourning for a woman to whom his relation is fictitious and for whom he may never have felt the slightest affection.

abstains for three years from the observances of propriety, those observances will be quite lost. If for three years he abstains from music, music will be ruined." "The Master" asked if he would be at ease in eating good rice and wearing embroidered clothes after a single year of mourning. On Tsae Wo's replying that he would, Confucius severely said that if he could feel at ease in so doing it would be legitimate for him to do so; but that the superior man would not feel at ease unless he denied himself palatable food, comfortable lodgings and the pleasures of music for the full period. "Tsae Wo," we read, "then went out."

"O wad some power the giftie gie us,
To see oursels as others see us!
It wad frae monie a blunder free us,
And foolish notion."—BURNS.

"He cannot flatter, he,
An honest mind and plain, he must speak truth!
An they will take it, so; if not, he's plain."
SHAKSPERE. *King Lear.*

CHAPTER V.

In the spring of 1884, a Mr. Sing San published an Illustrated Guide to Shanghai. The aim of the author was to give to his fellow-countrymen a description of life in the foreign settlements, depicting not only the customs of the foreigners themselves, but those also of their Chinese fellow-residents as affected by them. These two volumes contain forty-two illustrations in red ink, accompanied by letter-press in black, and are exceedingly interesting, affording to the foreigner in Shanghai a favourable opportunity of seeing himself as others see him.

The first picture is of a Bowling Alley in a Chinese tea and opium shop, clearly enough a foreign importation the second is a landscape of paddy-fields, with the Lung-hua pagoda set well in the middle—the only picture in the work in which the foreign element is hard to detect. The fourth is the first picture distinctively foreign. It is intended to disfigure or to present, as Peter Quince would say, the Central Police Station, and though it is not an accurate picture, it, at least, gives a fair cata-logue of the contents of the place. There is a bell-tower in the drawing, with a house, an electric-light

Q

standard, a small, leafless magnolia in bloom and a fence. All these things in the spring of 1884 were to be found in the station compound, but any stranger to the neighbourhood, designing a picture and introducing these items according to taste, would be as likely to be as successful as Mr. Sing San in producing a representation of the Central Police Station.

Following this, is a sketch of an auction, in which the Chinese idea of a foreigner's personal appearance is first seen. It is to be doubted if there be an auctioneer in Shanghai who would feel flattered by it. But the figure here delineated is not special to the auctioneer. It is one of a large family. Throughout this Guide, wherever a foreigner is represented, he will be found to be a reproduction of this far from flattering picture. The face is, roughly speaking, a circle, with a diameter about equal to the width of the body at the hips, or a little less than the width across the shoulders. The hat has a crown in size proportionate to what the head ought to be, but since the head is so excessively developed, the sides of the hat have to be made to slope from the crown outward as well as downward, to be of sufficient size to encircle it. In one picture representing some sailors making merry in a grog shop, a hat is seen upon the table and, being out of use, its sides are allowed to descend vertically, giving it a more usual shape but a most ridiculous size as compared with the bulbous head of the owner who could clearly swallow it with more ease than he could wear it. The lower half of this circular face is usually surrounded by a fringe of unsteady flourishes or a semi-circle of short rays of tolerably uniform length, while a little shaky shading crosses the face in a horizontal bar. The facial hair of Europeans is a mystery to the smooth-faced Celestials. They are not supposed to indulge in moustaches till they reach the mature age of forty or thereabouts, or in beards till they reach the happy dignity of grandfatherhood, and the beards and moustaches that are then allowed to grow are of the scantiest. It confuses all their ideas of relative age to see the variety of style in which foreigners wear their beards, whiskers, and moustaches. When I arrived in Shanghai, I was thought to be more than sixty on the strength of about six inches of beard, while, when travelling in a house-boat at some distance in the country, I was once carefully scrutinised by an old lady who ultimately inquired as to my age—a question which in China is an act of politeness and not of impertinence as with us—and went away with the satisfied look of a person whose judgment has been confirmed when my companion told her that I was two hundred years of age.

About once a year one sees short hair on the Chinese. With constant shaving of the fore part of the head, the razor naturally encroaches little by little on the circular region from which the hair that forms the queue is grown. This area is therefore periodically enlarged, by the barber leaving a border round it, when hair at once begins to stand up all round the man's head, forming a halo, the image of which had perhaps dominated the mind of the artist, alike in studying and portraying the whiskers of his foreign subjects. It has been remarked by some housekeepers that their servants are specially stupid during the halo period— the stage between the hair beginning to grow and becoming long enough to work into the queue. If this be a fact, it may not be without bearing on the generous way in which the Chinese artist supplies nearly every foreigner with luxuriant whiskers of the halo pattern.

Our Recreations seem to have been taken less notice of than would have been expected, since in scarcely anything is the difference between the Chinaman and the foreigner more obvious and striking than in them. A Chinaman derives his idea of a man's worth or otherwise from his equatorial circle. He localises the intelligence in a lower region than we, and estimates men by their corpulence. Where we, to indicate mental deficiency, say of a man that "he has no brains," the Celestial would say in pidjin English, "He no b'long clever inside." And so he regards with amazement the narrow lines within which a foreigner may live and yet command respect among his countrymen, and looks with a wondering pity at the slim and wiry forms of men playing at cricket, foot-ball and other athletic sports, and marvels that they do not hire coolies to do the work for them, while they, as would better befit their position, sit still and grow fat. It is surprising therefore that in Mr. Sing San's gallery of illustration, the race-course and the regatta should alone represent the foreigners' holiday-making. The picture of the former is calculated to delight the heart of all who would pour contempt on horse-racing, and to send a thrill of pleasure through those who denounce the conventional attitudes of horses in pictures. The attitudes in this representation are in no wise like those into which the mind interprets the perceptions of the eye, and which therefore previous artists have attempted to depict on their canvas. They are as strange, stiff and ludicrous as the attitudes caught by Mr. Muybridge's cameras in his interesting experiments. One cannot but wonder how horses with such action are going to finish the race, but this wonder is balanced by the other, as to how they began it. The representation of the regatta in the Soochow Creek is as wonderful as that of the horse-race, and implies varied accomplishments on the part of the oarsmen, for they could never have got themselves as mixed up as they seem there to have done and at the same time have preserved the equilibrium of the boats without acrobatic talents of a high order. Perhaps in the Chinaman's view, the grog-shop belongs to the same category, and the picture of Jack ashore is intended further to illustrate foreign recreations. Poor Jack is the victim of land-sharks in every port at which he makes a call, and the ports of China are no exception. But it must be admitted that Jack is too often an exceedingly willing victim. The Chinaman who wants to represent the Britisher in an unfavourable light has the material ready at hand. A sailor, staggering along, brandishing a bottle in each hand, is the picture he draws.

The Volunteers and the Fire-Brigade are subjects of two notable illustrations. Our volunteer force is divided into companies and possesses a flag, the honour of holding which is given for the year to that company which, at the annual inspection, is accounted to have acquitted itself most to the satisfaction of the inspecting officer. Mr. Sing San has chosen this " fight for the standard " as his special subject, but his understanding of the competition is evidently at fault. He depicts the captains of two of the companies engaged in a hand-to-hand conflict with naked swords, while the companies stand ranged in the background. One of the combatants holds the coveted banner at the moment chosen by the artist, but seems heavily handicapped by its possession, as it obliges him to wield his sword in the left hand, and the eyes of all are turned sympathetically upon him, with the exception of those of the three horses, two of which exhibit a cold indifference to the whole proceeding, while the third is taking a sleepy interest in his rival. The illustration of the Fire Brigade is quite a spirited one. The fire is represented as raging furiously and the Chinamen are busy rescuing their goods from the burning houses. Three foreigners in something like the brigade helmets are seen in charge of a fire-engine and hose, while a member of the Hook-and-Ladder Company is performing prodigious feats aloft.

The Missionary world finds recognition in two pictures. In one of them a gentleman of long residence in Shanghai suffers much at the hand of the artist, but

ample amends for the injustice done to the face are
made by the extravagant eulogy of the character given
in the letter-press—unless, indeed, it be thought that
the injustice is repeated by the extravagance over-
stepping the boundary that divides eulogy from ridicule.
The other missionary picture, which, by-the-bye, Mr.
Sing San thought it appropriate to put next to the race-
course, is very amusing though naturally its subject is
serious. Here are two missionaries preaching to an
audience of two women and a child on one side of them,
and two men on the other side. They are moon-faced
and haloed, as we have noticed are most foreigners in
these volumes, and are dressed in a costume which is
neither Chinese nor Western, but a curious combination
of both. Whether our artist is acquainted with the
narrative of the Book of Exodus I cannot say, but
since the gentleman who is not speaking, is burdened
with an oblong object which, judging from the straight-
ness of the arm that supports it, appears to be very
heavy, it looks a little as though he was intended for
Moses laden with the stone tables, while the speaker
may be assumed to be Aaron, who was to be to Moses
"instead of a mouth." One of the women is turning
her head in a coy sort of way as though affecting to
disapprove of what she is apparently interpreting as
personal flattery. The other woman looks as though
bewildered and meditating flight. One of the men has
a very solemn look, and with uplifted little finger,
appears to be telling the other missionary—the Moses
—that he knows he ought not to be doing so, and

Moses appears to be dangerously near responding with a wink.

The picture representing a sitting of the Mixed Court, a tribunal where a Chinese magistrate sits with a foreign assessor to try cases in which Chinese are defendants, and foreign interests are involved, adds nothing to one's sense of the majesty of the law. Nor is one's sense of the sublimity of architecture deepened by the picture of the French Municipal Buildings with the statue of Admiral Protet—a picture into which two Chinamen are introduced striking attitudes of astonishment which would not be unnatural were the buildings as here portrayed.

Of all the pictures the one that is perhaps most true to life is that of a Chinaman in a jinriksha passing an electric light. The tired, creeping manner of the riksha coolie is admirably depicted. His passenger has made his bargain with him, and the number of cash he has promised to pay does not call for speed. The poor coolie, free from stipulations as to the time to be taken, is crawling along at a pace suited to his opium-shaken constitution. The passenger, not being a "great man," is at liberty to manifest his curiosity, and is pushing aside the screen at the back and looking at the light with undisguised interest.

The Public Gardens, the one place in the settlement where one can go without being crowded by the Chinese, are made the scene of the meditations of a foreigner who, from his expression, may be judged to be desperately in love.

In many of the illustrations the foreigner does not appear at all, though his influence may be apparent enough. Thus there are pictures dealing with the wine and tea-shops, the theatres, the opium-dens and places and doings of even more questionable character con-- cerning which Chinese writers are not so accustomed as are we to use circumlocution and paraphrase. Even in these things which are patronised exclusively by the Chinese, the foreign element is not absent, for the foreigner is generally the landlord, and it is the foreign control that seems conducive to their multiplication and publicity. The foreign settlements of Shanghai bear a bad name among the Chinese. They regard them as the refuge and hunting-ground of the worst characters among their fellow-countrymen. Very rough and ready are Chinese methods, and justice does not seem to be the chief end aimed at in the proceedings of the mandarins; still there is little doubt that, amidst the indiscriminate penalties inflicted, evil-doers often meet with their deserts. Coming into these settlements, however, the evil-doer in common with others enjoys a considerable freedom and is able to evade the power of squeeze to a very large degree. Things which are not allowed openly in the native cities and which have therefore to exist under assumed names and by the sufferance of heavily bribed magistrates, flourish un- blushingly within the municipal limits.

In the year 1883 a gentleman, who was in a position to know, told me that some time previous to that the authorities at Nanking had made a raid on all the houses of ill-fame in that city, whereupon the keepers of them had migrated in a body to Shanghai, where the abominable trade is licensed and undisturbed, and had been readily absorbed. Facts such as these justify the Chinaman, as he thinks, in regarding foreigners as less careful in moral matters than himself. As for his fellow-countrymen, he knows how many of the most depraved of them have come into the settlements, and since he does not for a moment suppose that their character has or will be improved by intercourse with foreigners, he has no hesitation in placing the moral average of the Shanghai Chinese below that of the population of any other city in the empire.

"A man I am cross'd with adversity."

> SHAKSPERE. *Two Gentlemèn of Verona.*

". . . one Pinch, a hungry, lean-faced villain,
A mere anatomy.
      *   *   *   *
A needy, hollow-eyed, sharp-looking wretch,
A living-dead man."

> SHAKSPERE. *Comedy of Errors.*

"The happy man's without a shirt."

> JOHN HEYWOOD.

"O life! thou art a galling load
  Along a rough and weary road,
    To wretches such as I!"—BURNS.

" . . . least of all can aught—that ever owned
The heaven-regarding eye and front sublime
Which man is born to—sink, howe'er depressed,
So low as to be scorned without a sin."

> WORDSWORTH.

CHAPTER VI.

GO HANG, THE 'RIKSHA COOLIE.

Go HANG was a jinriksha coolie. The jinriksha—by simple abbreviation, and usually, riksha; by abbreviation, touched with a slight suspicion of affection, rikky; and by abbreviation, dominated to re-enlargement by a spirit of descriptiveness, rickety—is a small two-wheeled carriage, a miniature buggy drawn by a man who takes the place of the horse between the shafts, from which is derived its name made up of the three words: man, power, cart; leading to its being playfully and most accurately, though at the same time, most misleadingly, called a Pullman car. It was imported into China from Japan where it is said to have originated in the fertile brain of an American resident and where it is a respectable carriage drawn by a wiry muscular fellow who laughs at his work. But into China it has come with an abject and apologetic air, and so far has failed to inveigle into its shafts many but those who have fallen on melancholy days. Men who had been all their lives living as beasts of burden in the capacity of · chair-carriers, and men who had staggered through their years between the handles of unmanageably over-weighted wheel-barrows looked with scorn upon the jinriksha and felt that it would be derogatory to their human dignity to put their hands upon its shafts. They would not thus demean themselves. No man would enter the profession who could possibly get anything else to do, and its ranks were largely recruited from the list of poverty-stricken opium smokers against whom most other avenues of deriving an honest living were shut.

There are some in China—and medical men are among them—who affirm that opium smoking does no harm, or at least, but little. There are others—including all the medical missionaries, I believe—who as firmly maintain that it is the ruin of the people. Perhaps both are right. It seems to be pretty generally admitted that a well-fed man of firm will can smoke opium for years, smoking it regularly but in very small quantities, without receiving any perceptible harm. It has to be admitted however that a man cannot smoke opium moderately who cannot afford to " live well." With him whose frame is ill-nourished, whose stomach is empty, the craving becomes more and more imperative ; he is compelled to sacrifice everything to his pipe, he must return to it again and again, it must be kept filled at whatever costs : furniture and house, children and wife must be sold to supply it. In such a case the drug does a terrible and short work.*

* I purchased a picture by a native artist in Peking, representing a poor shrivelled, skin-covered skeleton with an opium pipe in his hand beseeching a tiger to devour him. The tiger was turning

Go Hang belonged to the emptier and sadder class. He knew nothing of those rich repletions and super-abundant satisfyings with which the more favoured defy the opium. For him were none' of those comfortable post-prandial thunders with which in China the guest courteously acknowledges the affluence of his host's entertainment, nor did his abdominal measurement approach the figure that indicates respectability. He was long and lank and brown as is the ribbed sea-sand, though perhaps his memory could take him back to days when he was inclined to *embonpoint*, when his table was sumptuously provided and his chopsticks dallied daily with shark's fin, sea-slug and other delicacies, when a whole district stood in awe of him as the mandarin who had a right of squeeze over his fellows. Such a case was portrayed not very long ago in the *Hua Pao*. A Chinaman coming out of a shop calls for a riksha; a number of coolies rush forward and offer their vehicles. The one who is first on the spot and who would naturally have the first chance, suddenly hides his head and turns away his wheels.— Mutual recognition has taken place. The riksha coolie was once a petty mandarin and the would-be passenger had been his servant.

Go Hang is miserable but not witless. He draws a jinriksha duly licensed by the municipality, for has not

---

away his head and with his right paw waving aside the miserable suppliant. The expression on the great beast's countenance said, as plainly as the artist could make it, that he disdained so un-promising a dish.

a policeman observing a certain looseness about the
machine, demanded his authority for dragging after
him so crazy a chaos of boards and wheel-spokes, and
has he not shown his license and the council's stamp on
the jinriksha itself ?   He has been to the periodical
inspection with a friend's sound jinriksha and obtained
all necessary credentials, and has carefully taken from
the stamped and approved machine the board that
bears the stamp and placed it in his own rickety
contrivance, his friend's sounder vehicle, meantime
repaired, going up to be passed and stamped anew.

And now Go Hang forms one of a dismal funeral
procession.   Certain cheerful-looking and eminently
ragged and unreverend coolies by forced marches and
frequent rests are hurrying along a coffin under
bamboos to the intoned grunts with which all residents
in China are familiar.   Following them in a string of
rikshas are the mourners in their dirty white rags,
endeavouring by their inordinate lamentations to
impress the magistrate of the spiritual yamen, before
which the deceased is now supposed to be, with a sense
of his great worth, and scattering paper sycee for the
benefit, and to the appeasing, of vagrant spirits who
might otherwise take advantage of a new comer and
cause him unnecessary inconvenience.   When the
coffin-bearers rest, the whole procession stops and the
mourners cease their wailings and their grimaces and
look a little more like ordinary beings.   As soon as the
march is resumed, the yellings and howlings are
resumed also.   Go Hang and his brethren of the shafts

are under no obligation to identify themselves with the solemnities of the occasion. Anything beyond the conveyance of the mourners "no b'long their pidjin." They therefore pass the time in the cracking of such jokes as misery can deceive herself with, finding themselves a little more cheerful than usual perhaps, as the sight of alien griefs takes their thoughts from their own.

By-and-by, the hard earned cash having been counted one by one into his hand, he finds himself once more within the municipal limits, and, having quenched his thirst at one of the great street-side tubs of tea provided by the charitable for public use and as a work of merit, he sets down his jinriksha in the shade of a wall, loosens his jacket, rubs himself down with a filthy rag which he carefully puts back under the cushion of the seat, and draws out his fan to cool himself as best he may.

Presently he seizes his jinriksha and rushes forward. He has seen a sailor who appears to be looking for the services of such as he. There is no fare for whom Go Hang is so eager as a sailor. In taking him about there is an element of uncertainty which is dear to the gambling-loving Chinaman. Go Hang has not yet learned how greatly the morals of the present race of seamen have been changed for the better as compared with those of their predecessors. Occasionally one may have engaged him who knew where he wanted to go, and, to his surprise, steered him straight for the Temperance Hall. Generally speaking, the sailor does not know where he wants to go; he gets into a jinriksha and bids the coolie go ahead; and the coolie assumes that he must take him to those regions where the Municipal Council draws its revenues from grog shops and worse. Of course Jack gets drunk while his carriage waits, and it is an even chance whether, by the time he wants to pay off his coolie, he will have any money or no. And again, if he have, it is another even chance whether he will have got into a good-humoured stage in which he will turn his pocket inside out and gladden the coolie's heart with all his loose change, or whether he will have got into a stage in which a suggestion about payment will call forth a savage oath and yet more savage blow. Go Hang is ready to take his chance. If he gets paid at all he will probably be paid liberally, and if he gets nothing it will not be much less than he would get from a Chinese passenger in the ordinary course of travel. So he secures Jack and trundles him off to the nearest public-house in which for a while he is lost. When he comes out Go Hang regards him critically to see how he is influenced—whether towards good-humour, stupidity, or savagery. His hopes rise a little as Jack jumps into the riksha, throws himself back in it, and, with a lordly wave of the hand, bids him go on. At other houses of call his fare stays longer, and at last comes out of one wondering where he is. Presently he becomes conscious of the riksha and gets into it. "Drive on," he manages to hiccough out, emphasising the order with a stamp of the foot. Go Hang takes him at a slow pace along the

Bund, and the more open streets, in the hope that the air will sober him a little. He lies contentedly and helplessly, making no sign as long as there is motion. Very little evidence is there of returning sobriety and Go Hang is getting worn out. He stops, doubtful as to what he had best do. Evidently he may wheel his fare about as long as he likes, but to what profit? Jack stirs a little uneasily at any cessation of movement and mutters, " Drive on."

At last Go Hang stops short. "Drive on," growls Jack. Go Hang turns round in the shafts and looks at him. "Drive on," again says Jack, this time with a little more force. " What side wantchee walkee ? " asks almost piteously the bewildered Go Hang. " Drive me to——" and Jack names a place not mentioned usually in ears polite. Go Hang has probably already done his best to anticipate this instruction, and his uncertainty is still unresolved. But light at last dawns on his indecision and a fierce imagination fills his dull soul. His labour shall not be for nought; he has learned very heartily to hate his burdensome old man of the sea and now he knows what he will do with him. The fields to which he had gone earlier in the day pass before his vision. He will go there again. Even in his growing desperation he would not venture to tackle a foreign seaman capable of defending himself, but this man is stupid with drink, and it is now dusk and will soon be dark. He will wheel him out of the settlement and into the country where he may leave him to the sobering humours of a ditch after wreaking his vengeance on him and paying himself from his pockets and, if need be, from his clothes. Buoyed up by this resolve, the wearied and worn-out coolie puts on a spurt, is soon out of the busy streets, has passed the race-course, and is making his way along the Bubbling Well Road.

But stimulus is not strength. He is going ploddingly, like a man in his sleep, and his chariot drives heavily as erst did Pharaoh's at the Red Sea, howbeit the road is better. Just as he is passing the gateway of one of the villas, a bright light dazzles him; it is the lamp of a carriage coming out into the road. He had not heard the wheels as they rolled down the gravel path and the horse is already upon him. He makes a sharp turn to clear it—too sharp a turn, for his somnolent and unconscious passenger is lying over the side, and his weight together with the little momentum of the jinriksha proves sufficient to overturn it. Jack is thrown out in front of the horse's hoofs, a little hurt but more sobered, and thinks he has fallen from the maintop. But what of Go Hang? Poor fellow, the shock is too great for his opium-undermined constitution. He has fallen in his harness, and other hands draw home the fragments of his jinriksha.

"Wearisome nights are appointed to me."—Job.

> "For see, the morn,
> All unconcerned with our unrest, begins
> Her rosy progress, smiling."
>
> Milton. *Paradise Lost.*

> "But yonder comes the powerful king of day,
> Rejoicing in the east."—Thomson. *Seasons.*

> "The country cocks do crow, the clocks do toll,
> And the third hour of drowsy morning name."
>
> Shakspere. *Henry V.*

> "Sweet is the breath of morn, her rising sweet,
> With charm of earliest birds; pleasant the sun,
> When first on this delightful land he spreads
> His orient beams, on herb, tree, fruit, and flower,
> Glistening with dew."—Milton. *Paradise Lost.*

CHAPTER VII.

SUNRISE.

SUNRISE is a subject of much rhapsody and many persons doubtless—including officers of ships whose watch covers its hour—have seen a good deal of it. For my own part I have once or twice been induced to get up to see it, but this is not my habit, and these exceptional enterprises have not been marked with exceptional success. However, the climate does make fools of us all, and often what we would not do from choice we do from compulsion. The other night I found my bedroom far too close to hope to have much sleep in it. I therefore had my canvas stretcher set up in a room that had a better aspect and in which there seemed a little movement of air. This room faced the east. There, tossing uneasily, I managed to sleep more or less through the night till a rosy streak stretched along the horizon. Here was a threat—for so I judged it, rather than a promise—of another day. Few men are optimists in the height of a Shanghai summer. I did not care to try to sleep again with the risk of sleeping on till the sun should have risen in strength, and be pouring his rays fiercely on my unprotected head, so, between sleeping and waking, I rolled off my stretcher and on to a bamboo lounge in the verandah to watch the sky. As low down as the roofs of some distant intervening houses would allow me to see was a band of light every moment deepening in colour; above this a band of dark cloud; above this again, another band of light but without colour; and then the dark edge of the universal blackness that stretched upwards to the zenith. Brighter grew the rosy streak until, instead of looking like something on or through which light was shining, it dazzled my blinking eyes as though itself the source of light, and from it there radiated upon the whole of the eastern sky a glow of colour defining the edges of the more distant clouds with a brickdust red and the edges of the nearer ones with a bright crimson, while the horizon itself became a glorious orange and the band that had been colourless now revealed a depth of most delicate green and blue.

The growing beauty of the scene completely woke me up. It was gorgeous as a sunset, but its effect totally different as all the conditions were different. The streets were quiet, the air was fresh and sweet as it could never be at evening after absorbing the business and smells of a town in China and after being baked for a whole day by the summer sun. Doubtless I too was more thoroughly a different man from myself after a day's work than I realised.

A bulbul in a mulberry-tree just in front began to sing his little song, at first with a quiet apologetic note, but gradually he reached his full compass and sang gaily, welcoming the advent of the sun as though forgetful that when the object of his praise really rose, he and his fellow-songsters would have to seek the shadiest coverts they could find. One unblushing cicada for a moment startled me with his shrill pipes, but, realising that he would have it all his own way presently when the sun at noon would be scorching everything but him and his.chitinous race into silence, even he had not the conscience to go on and modestly desisted.

The bats still filled the air but seemed hurried. I knew that they would soon hang themselves out of the way in dark corners of the houses in the immediate neighbourhood, some perhaps in the very verandah where I was lying, but I could not resist the imagination, as they flew on leathern wings across the glowing sky, that they were evil spirits hasting conscience-stricken before the dawn of light and colour to some far off and deep abyss. One was flying directly eastward down my line of vision to the very brightest point in the horizon where the sky seemed glowing with an almost white heat. Owing to its direction its position remained unchanged, and no motion could be seen but the fluttering of its wings as its size gradually decreased till in the brightness it was lost from sight. Blame me not if I thought I was watching, in a parable, an evil spirit bathing in light and, to paraphrase Milton, purging and unscaling her long abused soul at the fountain itself of heavenly radiance, while the doves were beginning to coo of mutual love.

Just then, our neighbour's baby—since the beginning of the hot weather, a sad sufferer from boils and prickly-heat—awoke and expressed its sense of the inconvenience of the same in the manner usual to an infant crying in the night, but with perhaps unusual vehemence. A white-necked crow on a roof hard by with distinct enunciation called out most opportunely, "Hark! hark!" but instead of silence there broke forth a sudden and noisy remonstrance from a hitherto quiescent colony of sparrows. I had not seen the sun rise but the glamour was gone. The baby, the crow, and the sparrows were too prosaic, and I determined to desert the verandah and try if in the bedroom I might possibly yet doze, or even by good fortune sleep, an hour or two longer.

"With money you may move the gods, without it you cannot move a man."—*Chinese Proverb.*

"When Confucius was crossing the T'ai Mountain, he overheard a woman weeping and wailing beside a grave. He thereupon sent one of his disciples to ask what was the matter; and the latter addressed the woman, saying, 'Some great sorrow must have come upon you that you give way to grief like this?' 'Indeed, it is so,' replied she. 'My father-in-law was killed here by a tiger; after that, my husband; and now, my son has perished by the same death.' 'But why, then,' enquired Confucius, 'do you not go away?' 'The government is not harsh,' answered the woman. 'There,' cried the master, turning to his disciples, 'remember that. Bad government is worse than a tiger.'"—T'AN KUNG.

"A goodly, portly man, i' faith, and a corpulent; of a cheerful look, a pleasing eye, and a most noble carriage; and, as I think, his age some fifty, or by'r lady, inclining to three score."
SHAKSPERE. 1. Hen. IV.

" . . . Hissed the locust-fiends that crawled
And glittered in corruption's slimy track."
S. T. COLERIDGE. The Destiny of Nations.

"Let me have men about me that are fat."
SHAKSPERE. Julius Cæsar.

CHAPTER VIII.

CHINESE OFFICIALDOM.

SANCHO PANZA could not read or write but he doubted not his ability to govern the island which the prowess of Don Quixote was to win for him. It may even be that—the personal element in the testimony excepted—he was not very far from the mark when he told the duchess that he had seen more asses than one go to a government. Nevertheless the illiterate is not the ideal ruler of men even when blessed with as much sagacity and proverb-born wisdom as the squire of La Mancha's knight. In their rulers men look for not only mother-wit but culture, not only shrewdness and natural ability but ability disciplined to the possession and exercise of its full possibilities. Rusticity may be decked with ribbons by poets and painters, and ignorance may be of large comfort to him who enjoys it, but in mercy withhold power from his hands, or it will prove of but small comfort to those under his sway. It was when the queen of Sheba saw the wisdom of Solomon, she exclaimed how happy were the people over whom he was king to do judgment and justice.

But if Israel was to be congratulated on the control
of one wise man, China must merit a chorus of congratulation, governed as she is by scores of wise men—
having in all the offices of her eighteen provinces
mandarins who have ascended the steps of power from
the avenues of learning, who have been proved by
questions as difficult as any that the queen of Sheba
put to Solomon, and who have stood the test of writing
poems and essays on morals and government. The red
umbrellas, the sonorous gongs, the processional tablets,
the pheasants' tails and sugar-loaf hats, nay, the very
rags of the retinues, the personal rags beneath and the
official rags, which, for the nonce and somewhat scantily,
cover them above, all, in their several ways, proclaim
the praise of learning.

The uncivilised West is not unacquainted with the
manner in which filthy lucre buys power and foolishness
inherits it; in defiance rather than in conviction she
speaks of the honour paid to Wisdom, and tells of its
worth sadly as mindful of how little it is accounted.
What the author of Ecclesiastes wrote in Western Asia
is read sympathetically in Western Europe. The " poor
wise man " saved the little city from the great king
that besieged it and " by his wisdom delivered the
city ; yet no man remembered that same poor man."
How our eyes ought to glisten with the dews of admiration as we hear of and see a mighty empire in which
learning is not despised, in which the highest offices and
the most honourable places are before the feet of him
who walks in wisdom's ways. It is no matter of sur-

prise that this wondrous land has been held up as an example for all nations. What men more incorrupt, more competent to hold the reins of power than those whose minds have been regulated by the severe study of the ancient moralists and sages? What people more secure than those who live under such a philosophy-chastened rule? The emperor is the son of heaven and father of the empire, and every viceroy is the father of his province. Peace, plenty, patriotism—these are the natural consequences of such a system of government. Blessed among nations must be the Middle Kingdom.

But the awkward fact remains that it is not. There is probably no other country as thoroughly honey-combed with caves of Adullam, as full of sedition, as seething with discontent, for there is no other country in which official life is so corrupt. "The big fishes eat the little fishes, and the little fishes eat the shrimps," says the not unobservant proverb of this happy people, adding with a sad bitterness, "and the shrimps eat mud." Squeeze pidjin is the life of China. And this is not merely the cynical testimony of "mercenary merchants," who come to the land to make money out of the people, and live at Treaty Ports knowing almost nothing of China proper; nor is it the biassed testimony of "fanatical missionaries," who have come with preconceived ideas of heathen depravity, and are too blind to see any good in customs and morals which they hope to change. No; it is the witness of the Chinese themselves. The proverb just quoted is a

Chinese proverb,* and for the severest criticisms on the manners of the mandarins, one must look to what the censorate says to the emperor as published in the *Peking Gazette.* Official after official, who has qualified for his office by writing essays in the purest and most polished classical style on the necessity of a ruler studying the welfare of the ruled at any cost and self-sacrifice, is accused of making his office the means of grinding the faces of the poor. It is true that on investigation a large proportion of these charges are declared to be without foundation. But this is a fact of easy explanation. The censors are themselves Chinese officials and doubtless something has to be allowed for possible personal grudges, accusations that have been duly paid for, and the like. The investigators also are Chinese officials, from which it follows that the accused will find it quite worth while, and not always hopeless, to devote one part of his ill-gotten gains to the saving of his credit and the other part of them. There is little occasion for surprise at the verdict of not guilty pronounced in so many of these cases, but, with all deductions, the number of accusations that either receive or are susceptible of confirmation is simply appalling.

Further than this the accusations actually made are

---

* It finds indeed a wondrously close parallel in the wisdom of Shakspere learned by the study of Englishmen of his day :

Third Fisherman.—Master, I marvel how the fishes live in the sea.
First Fisherman.—Why, as men do a-land ; the great ones eat up the little ones."—*Per. II.* 1.

but samples of what are possible. The imperial frown is supposed to be dark on every form of bribery and extortion, yet, since the salaries which the officials receive are ridiculously inadequate to cover the legitimate expenses of their offices, it is perfectly well understood that they must pay themselves from other sources. Confucius said it was shameful when officials thought only about their salaries, in which remark, though not in his sense of it, they heartily concur. Their salaries are the smallest part of their income and the least worth thinking about. Courtesy demands that they accept what the government pays them, but the exigencies of their position demand that they pay themselves. The only thing that is really required of them is that they pay themselves discreetly; that they set a tolerable limit to their squeeze. As long as they do this every one is satisfied; the people below submit cheerfully, and the greater men above in their turn squeeze comfortably and proportionately. But where a mandarin squeezes so inconsiderately and recklessly as to provoke discontent, he is imperilling the peace of the empire, and it will go hard with him. An official extortion that drives the populace to united action is an unpardonable sin, even though it be an extortion to which the poor official considers himself driven by some imperial demand. The people may rise in a body against such an officer, mob him, and even put him to death, and their conduct will be condoned and his condemned. It seems to be assumed that whatever arouses general and organised resistance must be blameworthy. It should be borne in mind that China is governed by the emperor by grace of the people. The emperor is the son of heaven, and, as such, the people obey him and invest him with an air of sanctity, regarding him with an almost idolatrous reverence. He claims their loyalty as the earthly representative of heaven. But if he do anything unworthy of such filial relation to heaven, he, by such an act, dethrones himself, proves himself to be no son of heaven but an impostor, and his people are thereby absolved from allegiance, and perfectly justified in rising against his power. Long years ago, Mencius was bold enough to say in one of his books, "The people are the most important element in a country; the spirits of the land and grain are the next; the ruler is the lightest." And further, "When the prince of a state endangers the altars of the land and grain, he is changed, and another appointed." In another book he deals with the question of heaven appointing the emperors, and, being asked by his disciples for explanation, speaks of the people and heaven as equally accepting the candidate for the throne, adding, "This view is in accordance with what is said in the Great Declaration, 'Heaven sees as my people see, heaven hears as my people hear.'" Doubtless if in these days the people endeavoured to change the occupant of the throne on the ground of the unworthy character of some imperial act, the emperor would seek to prove that the act was not unworthy, and among the arguments he would use would be the Manchu soldiery, but if the people succeeded in confuting these somewhat solid arguments, there would be no question of treason or guilt. Their view would have been confirmed and therefore their action justified. Now if the people have an acknowledged right to rise against an emperor shown to be unworthy, how much more right have they to rise against a viceroy or less official !

Squeeze within limits, then, is tacitly assumed to be legitimate and necessary. But the man who has learned the art for the sake of practising it within limits will be sorely tempted to experiment beyond. It requires more moral courage than Chinese training is calculated to call forth to stop firmly in such a matter at an uncertain and indeterminate border-line, marked by no definite law but only by one's own discretion and sense of the fitness of things. Most feel that they are lacking in justice to their dependents and themselves if they stop short of the limit of what is allowable ; up to that they must surely go. And that limit is seldom found except by the act of passing it. Who can tell beforehand at which straw the camel's back will break ? Yet all short of that is permissible, all beyond extortionate.

A resident in Peking some time ago got hold of the following figures, which he gave to the foreign public through the press. The condition of things which they illustrate is well known, but it is not always that one can lay the hand on the exact figures as in this case. In 1876 the Peking lekin on foreign opium was forty taels a chest, and in that year two thousand three hundred chests were taken into Peking, of which five hundred were smuggled and eighteen hundred paid duty. This should, at forty taels a chest, have amounted to seventy-two thousand taels, whereas the Superintendent of Customs acknowledged the receipt of only eleven thousand two hundred and ninety-nine, leaving sixty thousand seven hundred and one taels unaccounted for! The proportion reminds one of the sack and the bread in Falstaff's tavern score. Although it grates harshly against the national pride, the government has seen the expediency of retaining the Imperial Maritime Customs under foreign management. The head of the service is an Englishman, and all the servants on whom the least responsibility rests are Europeans or Americans, and, roughly speaking, it has been said that in these Maritime Customs ten per cent. goes in salaries, and ninety per cent. goes to Peking; while in the inland Customs, which are under native management, the figures are reversed, only ten per cent. ever reaching the capital. This balanced arrangement of figures may have been affected somewhat by considerations of simplicity and effect, moreover they may possibly be susceptible of partial explanation on account of just provincial claims, but they will require a good deal of manipulation to make them other than an illustration that the literary officials in China are, of all officials that fatten in any land, the most guilty of malversation, and this notwithstanding the much-lauded practice of raising to office only those whose virtue and culture have been tested by examinations in the classics and the writing of moral essays.

That this should be so is not strange. In a previous

chapter I have tried to show that what is called education in this favoured land is something altogether
different from what is meant by education among us,
that the two things indeed have little in common.
Culture in China is skill in playing with quotations and
veiled literary references, legerdemain in words and
phrases, with a pious conservative horror of innovations ;
in which is a development of cleverness, but no purifying of the heart or preparation for the governing of
men. To maim the mind rather than to expand it, is the
effect of Chinese study even at its best, when carried on
for study's sake, for the love of the learning itself. But
the average candidate is little likely to seek the simple
advantage of disinterested culture. The very commendable notion that prompted the decision that every
aspirant to office should be required to become familiar
with Confucian ethics has somewhat defeated itself, and
the said Confucian ethics are far less likely to be
studied and valued for their inherent worth by reason
of their manifest value as the ladder from the earth of
the oppressed to the heaven of the oppressor. Literary
attainment is with him a means of political advancement. The ancient writings are not studied for the
love of them, but with a view to esteem and influence,
power and office. And so it comes to pass that a man
learns to write elaborate panegyrics on impartial justice
as magic charms to open the gates of the hall where he
may shamelessly fill both hands with bribes, and justify
the common proverb, " The yamen-doors are open wide
to him with money on his side." Having no interest in

study except as a passport to office, he will even—as testified by the censors and published in the *Peking Gazette*—hire a poor scholar to personate him in the examination and to write for him the required platitudes on Integrity and Uprightness.

The educational system that has not freed Chinese officialdom from the avarice and like vices, against which it was supposed to be specially the safeguard, is not likely to have freed it from superstition. And so we find the *Gazette* enlivened by all manner of memorials presented by these literary and cultured mandarins to the emperor for tablets and other signs of imperial favour to be shown to canonised saints, and river gods, and tutelary deities of hills and forests for all sorts of supernatural assistance rendered by them. There is possibly a good deal of the knave mixed with a proportion of the fool in some matters of this kind, as when, a memorial being threatened against some mining project on the ground that the intended operations will disturb the peace of the Earth Dragon, it is soon discovered that a sufficient favour bestowed on the person proposing to memorialise will still all anxiety in regard to the Earth Dragon's discomfort. But it is most probable that the literary graduate, while he would undoubtedly be ready to make use of the popular superstitions for the purpose of managing the people, even if he did not believe in them at all, has, as a matter of fact, almost as firm a faith in them as the veriest rustic. The following notice of a memorial concerning a gifted dragon that lives in a well, and from its murky depths answers the people's prayers for rain, I copy in full from the *Gazette.*

"A Postscript Memorial of P'an Yu requests that an additional title of rank and a tablet written by His Majesty's own hand may be conferred on a Dragon Spirit, who has manifested himself and answered the prayers made to him.

"In the Ang-Shan mountain, a hundred li from the town of Kuei-hsi, there are three wells, of which one is on the mountain top in a spot seldom visited. It has long been handed down that a dragon inhabits this well. If pieces of metal are thrown into the well they float; but light things, as silk or paper, will sink. If the offerings are accepted, fruits come floating up in exchange. Anything not perfectly pure and clean is rejected and sent whirling up again. The Spirit dwells in the blackest depths of the water, in form like a strange fish with golden scales and four paws, red eyes, and long body. He ordinarily remains deep in the water without stirring. But in times of great drought, if the local authorities purify themselves and sincerely worship him, he rises to the top. He is then solemnly conveyed to the city, and prayers for rain are offered to him, which are immediately answered. His temple is in the district city on the Ts'ang-hsi Ling. The provincial and local histories record that tablets to him have been erected from the Mongol and the Ming dynasties. During the present dynasty, on several occasions, as for instance in the years 1845 and 1863, he has been carried into the city and rain has fallen immediately. Last year a dreadful drought occurred, in which the ponds and tanks dried up to the great terror of the people. On the 15th day of the 8th month the magistrate conducted the Spirit into the city, and with the assembled multitude prayed to him fervently. Thereupon a gentle rain falling throughout the country, brought plenty in the place of scarcity and gladdened the hearts of all. At about the same time the people of a district in the vicinity, called Chin-yu, also had recourse to the Spirit with equally favourable result. These are well-known events, which have happened quite recently.

"It is the desire of the people of the district that some mark of distinction should be conferred on the Spirit ; and the memoralist finds such a proceeding to be sanctioned both by law and precedent. He therefore humbly lays the wishes of the people before His Majesty, who perhaps will be pleased to confer a title and an autograph tablet as above suggested."

" A very ancient and fish-like smell."

SHAKSPERE. *The Tempest.*

" The people here live in alleys two yards wide, which have a smell about them which is peculiar but not entertaining. It is well the alleys are not wider because they hold as much smell now as a person can stand, and of course if they were wider they would hold more, and then the people would die. These alleys are paved with stone and carpeted with deceased cats and decayed rags and decomposed vegetable tops and remnants of old boots, all soaked in dish-water, and the people sit around on stools and enjoy it."

MARK TWAIN, *on Civita Vecchia.*

CHAPTER IX.

ACROSS THE HEAVENLY FORD.

TROUBLES that gather round one's head in the very hour of congratulation that they have been escaped, are hard to bear. Such troubles are not unheard of, however. Travelling northward from Shanghai, on one occasion, we had a remarkably pleasant trip through the Yellow Sea, the water being as placid as though it never had harboured ill-designs on man's comfort: getting into the Gulf of Pechili, we were conscious of just a sus- picion of ·a ground swell—it was no more than a suspicion, yet it called to mind seasons of sea-sickness which the motion of the more open sea had failed to awaken—so that it was with a feeling of relief that we heard we should make Taku Bar about six o'clock in the evening. The swell became no more agreeable on further acquaintance but we thought we could hold out against it till then. Alas, we did make Taku Bar at six, and we found all manner of craft lying at anchor outside pitching mercilessly and straining mightily at their anchor-chains, for a storm of wind and rain had arisen, and it was with a shudder that we admitted the thought that the reasons which caused them to lie outside, might detain us also. The horror of the thought was

our comfort, we judged it too horrible to be possible. It
could not be.   But it came to pass.   The air was too
thick with the rain to admit of our seeing the signals
which tell the depth of the water on the bank.   There
was nothing for it but to drop our anchors—one would
not hold us—till it should clear up, of which there was
no likelihood during the little daylight remaining.
So we lay all that night at the mercy of the waves,
tantalised by the knowledge that just across the bar and
within the river's mouth the waters were still.   Here
was the point at which we had hoped to bid farewell to
all our fears; here in our sanguine anticipations the
ground swell would cease from troubling and we should
be at rest; and here it was that our troubles really
began.   As long as the steamer was ploughing her way
through the waters, her own uniform movement did
something to neutralise their vagaries and to correct
their irregularities.   But as soon as the fatal order,
" Stop her," was rung to the engine-room, she lay a toy
for the waves to play with as they listed.   Here, where
we had hoped to gain a steady motion or a quiet
anchorage, we had to steel our hearts to the prospect of
a night's wild tossing.   Here, where we had expected to
be able to laugh at forebodings of sea-sickness, we had
to succumb to its power, and watch for the morning.
It seemed a long watch but the morning dawned at
length and, as soon as the tide allowed, we crossed the
bar and steamed into the river.   The crossing was not
without difficulty since the water was scarcely sufficient for us.   At last evening-tide, as we now learned,

the water was two feet higher, the storm from which we were then suffering driving the water landwards and piling it up at the river's mouth, though it obscured from our eyes the signals which would have told us how free a course it had provided for our keel. By this morning the wind had shifted and tended to drive the water out of the river's bed, so that we were in danger of being detained yet another tide. Fortunately we managed to drag across.

Though the price of it was greater than we would have paid voluntarily, we enjoyed a sight this fine morning which would have been stripped of its impressiveness had we steamed into the Peiho in the darkening twilight and the drizzling rain. Among our passengers was the General Chow, mentioned on page 166 as holding an examination in medicine and surgery. He had been down to Nganking, or some other city or town in Nganhwui, to fulfil the decreed days of mourning retirement for the death of his mother. He was now returning to his command. A young Chinaman among our saloon passengers informed us that the general was in charge of the whole of the Tientsin Army—whatever that might be—and that he was under orders to march thirty thousand men from Taku to Tientsin,* to be inspected by the Seventh Prince—Prince Chun—the father of the reigning emperor, who was breaking through the imperial

---

* This was probably a natural Chinese exaggeration. Dr. Mackenzie, as quoted on p. 166, gives fifteen thousand, and that in a somewhat qualified phrase, as the number of his entire command.

customs and traditions, and starting on a tour of in-spection of the army, the navy and the fortifications at Taku, Port Arthur and Wei-hai-wei. As we passed into the river, between the forts, we found troops drawn up upon the ramparts, and banners were un-furled and cannon fired in honour of General Chow, to the dazzling of our eyes and the deafening of our ears. One of the steamer's officers had asked the gallant soldier for his flag to hoist at the mast-head, but he had preferred to put it on a small launch and send it ahead. Of course the steamer soon left the launch behind, and the general was flagless. But, though no longer advertised by the introductory banner, he was known to be on board and was blazed at with blank charges and honoured from every point of vantage where men could be drawn up on gunboat or on shore. There was a sinister whisper through the ship about our being kept for some twenty-four hours here on this old gentleman's account, and it is astonishing how low he sank at once in his fellow-passengers' estimation, so low, indeed, that we were all perfectly satisfied and pleased to say good-bye, when, after keeping us waiting awhile for his steam launch to overtake us, he was persuaded to go on board of it. There was great ko-towing of his subordinates, who were be-silked, be-satined and be-feathered to a degree which contrasted strangely with his not only plain but shabby and dirty costume. A member of one of the foreign legations, who was well versed in Chinese etiquette, expressed himself strongly, as he watched the proceedings from our deck, in regard to the old general's discourtesy in not landing in more becoming and suitable dress. But these military mandarins will not bear comparison with the civil. They are often rough and ill-mannered men who have obtained promotion for some act of personal courage, or for skill in archery, or for great physical strength—uncouth bears, whom no taming or training can teach to dance other than clumsily.

After we had got rid of our general, we started afresh and at the next camp we passed, the garrison, not knowing how empty of worth our vessel now was, turned out duly, the men in ranks with their banners outspread, the cannon blazing, while one of the feathered officials, in a most prominent position, first knelt, and then prostrated himself, reverently holding forth toward us a large red paper. When a Chinaman on board shouted out that the great man was no longer honouring us with his presence, the expression of disgust that spread over the faces of those troops was a sight which we would gladly have studied at a less distance. The prostrate official tumbled up indignantly with none of the educated grace which had marked the processes of descent, and the men threw their flags down or began to twist them up with an emphasis indicating that Chinamen are human and do not like to be sold.

The passage of the river was restful—to the passengers. To the captain it must have been a somewhat anxious one, demanding incessant attention. He was on the bridge the whole time and the engine-room signals and the wheel were scarcely ever still. The

river is as devious as a river can be, so devious in fact
that it is wonderful how the water finds its way down
and out of it; the bottom of it seems getting very near
the top; and it is crowded with junks, which always
seem thickest where the channel is narrowest—which
may be accounted for by the channel being narrowest
all the way. The annual freshets do something to
deepen and widen the bed, but, whether it be from increasing draining off of the waters for irrigation and
canals, or from other causes, there seems to be a
growing difficulty, where the difficulty need not grow
very much to make the river altogether unnavigable
by such steamers as are now on the Chinese coast.
But the responsibilities of the captain did not prevent
the irresponsible from enjoying the quiet surface after
the tossing of outside Taku, and the bright spring green
of the crops after the grey horizon of the rain-storm at
sea; we had leisure to lie back in lounge chairs and to
follow the swinging wing-stroke of the terns and the
more gay skimming of the swallows, which, though
they never by any chance allow themselves to lapse
into intentional frivolity, too seldom gain the credit
they deserve for serious attention to business. We
listened with a kind of lazy indifference to the successive orders and signals from the bridge, till we heard
the order, "Let go the anchor," about eight or nine
miles short of the Tientsin wharves. That touched us
more nearly, but since it was the farthest we could get
in the then condition of the river, we had to make the
best of it and do the remaining miles in a small boat,

for which, of course, the boatmen, feeling that they had us in their power, demanded exorbitant fares.

Tientsin, the Heavenly Ford, was all agog about the Seventh Prince, of whom we got as heartily tired as the brave Geraint did of the sparrow-hawk in Earl Yniol's town. But the doings of lesser personages soon became of more pressing moment to us, affording quite unnecessary illustration to our already initiated understandings of that spirit of obstructiveness by which, in important matters and in unimportant, the Celestial endeavours, and not seldom successfully, to thwart the stranger that is within his gates, nullifying the stipulations of treaties with nations and the promises to individuals. The "No-can" of a Chinaman, blandly smiling regret at inability, while making no attempt to hide the most palpable evidences of ability, is an earth rampart into which the fiery shot of a foreigner's go-aheadness, buries itself helplessly. Not long ago, I wanted to go into an empty house and asked the gate-keeper for the key. He at first affected not to understand me, and then, when he found that that would not do, he told me that he had not got the key, that Mr. —— had got it. I pointed to a key hanging on the wall, which I felt sure was the key I wanted, but he said, "No, that was not the key," and refused to give it to me. Not caring to take it from him by force, I wrote a chit to Mr. ——, asking for the key of the house which the gatekeeper said he had. Mr. —— wrote back that the gatekeeper had it. I now attacked that functionary with Mr. ——'s letter in my hand,

T

and calmly and without hesitation he took down the key, to which I had before pointed, and gave it me. As far as I know, he had no other reason for keeping me out than that I wanted to get in, and all the advantage he could derive from it was the pleasure of putting me to as much inconvenience and subjecting me to as much delay as possible. And now in the North, I found the same spirit as in Mid China. Our amah came to us the evening of the day we landed, saying that she had had nothing to eat all day, and was feeling very faint. The servants had refused to give her any food. On being questioned, they admitted the facts as stated by our famished woman. It was so, and of course, it would have to be so: the amah was a Shanghai woman, and therefore could not eat Tientsin chow, and they were Tientsin people, and therefore could not cook Shanghai chow, and so—the amah would have to go without; there was no help for it. Our good hostess remonstrated with her servants, and asked if the amah was to have nothing to eat while she stayed in Tientsin. They replied by saying that they did not see how it could be done—they could not get the proper food—they could not cook it—they could not, &c., &c. So our good friend accepted the situation and made an appeal on other grounds. She pointed out that if the amah got no food, she would certainly die; and further if she died there, they would as certainly be held responsible, and that the least evil that they would suffer would be the bearing the expense of the coffin and full funeral rites. This was not put as a joke but as a serious argument, and it had the effect of bending a little the previously inflexible. By-and-by it was apparent that the impossible was becoming possible and that an effort would be made to see if, for a suitable and sufficient consideration, Shanghai chow could be got and cooked for the intruder. The motive here was probably two-fold : first, to inflict as much bother upon us foreigners as possible and thereby incidently squeeze us a trifle extra for our servant's food; and second, to gratify their feeling of dislike to the servant herself. For China is rich in provincial jealousy. Cantonese amahs are the occasion of a like trouble in Shanghai; in fact, as pointed out on an earlier page, many of the Shanghai inhabitants deny to Cantonese the credit of being natives of the Middle Kingdom at all. At last it was decided that the cook should prepare the amah's food, and he undertook to do so, but the very next morning he failed her, stating that she could have nothing that day as he had not time. Being remonstrated with mildly, he found relief for his hurt feelings in thrashing his wife, after which he felt better and the poor Shanghai woman got something to eat.

Tientsin is built on a plain as flat as that on which Shanghai stands, but it rejoices in a drier air. Certain fertiliser - manufactures, of processes altogether too simple, serve to indicate more effectually than pleasantly when the wind is in certain quarters, though in spite of their extensive business, the soil, charged with soda or some such substance inimical to vegetation, refuses to adorn itself for the advent of Spring. The landscape, as far as the eye can see, is one miserable stretch of brown earth relieved only by brown grave-mounds. The native city is surrounded by a moat for which some have ventured to claim the palm for fragrant filthiness among all the city-moats of China. It may even merit it, though others will run it close for the honour. Such a moat is naturally an object of pride to the inhabitants, and it is popularly understood that whenever a stranger, unacquainted with the language and with the topography of the place and therefore more or less helpless, is committed to a jinriksha coolie, to whom instructions are given as to destination, discretion being allowed him as to the route, that coolie will take that stranger along the city moat, if there be any possibility of getting to his destination by that way, however indirect it may be. It is one of the lions of the place, and however unappreciative or ultra-appreciative the stranger may be, he has got to be trundled along it.

The city itself lieth four-square, having walls fronting the four cardinal points of the compass, and in the centre of each wall a gate. From the North Gate to the South, and from the East Gate to the West, run the main streets in the intersection of which, in the middle of the city, stands the Drum Tower, from which the signal is sounded in case of fire. From this tower a capital view may be got of all there is to be seen: the shell of the Roman Catholic church destroyed in 1870, the Mohammedan mosques, the temples, the watch-towers on the walls and the junk masts in the river.

Here, as elsewhere, the ineradicable gambling spirit of the Chinese is seen on every hand. The streets are full of dealers in trifles, a man's entire stock-in-trade being worth, perhaps, half-a-dollar, but among their appurtenances, are inevitably the bamboo tube and the bamboo slips marked at the lower end with dots like that in use in the temples to indicate the answer of the god. As I was told, if a man wishes to purchase something—say the half of a walnut—he draws two of these slips from the shaken tube, and, according to whether the number of dots on his slips exceed or fall short of a given number, he gets his half walnut without paying anything, or pays its value without getting it. But as I observed for myself, the tradesman always saved himself from loss, at least partially, by the preliminary charge of one cash for the privilege of drawing the slips. Wherever you go you hear the monotonous rattle of these things as the hawkers thus advertise their whereabouts in the intervals of business. In Shanghai the same thing is done by the use of dice in a cup, the bamboo tube and slips being there reserved for the use of priests deciding for suppliants the answers which the gods are pleased to give to their petitions.

Peking is distant from Tientsin two days for those who are prepared to travel all the way by mule-cart. Those who are not in a hurry will devote longer time to the journey going as far as Tung-chou by water. We concluded not to be in a hurry, and engaged boats, sending them off from the Bund overnight, that they might get through the bridges of boats, and other obstructions, before we went on board. My friend sent his cook and boy with them, instructing the former to come to us next morning, after the boats were moored, to act as our guide to the place. At breakfast-time he arrived duly, and a procession of some half-dozen jinrikshas forthwith started and were soon buried in the narrow, crowded, crooked, uneven and far from sweetly perfumed lanes of suburban Tientsin. Our men shouted at others, and others shouted at them to the little aiding, that we could see, of their or our progress, and whenever we came to a block—which was at every corner, and generally about twice between the corners—we were jammed up helplessly against some most unsavoury and redolent specimen of beggardom giving himself a finger-nail shampoo on his liberally unclothed surfaces. This was sufficiently disagreeable to make it a pleasant change when we crossed, at the cost of some jolting, a bridge of boats very defectively joined together, and entered a more open country. But here we noticed that our riksha coolies were making remarks, more or less sarcastic, to the cook. We were certainly travelling in a rather circuitous fashion and the men who had the pulling to do seemed to doubt the profitableness of such indirect procedure. At one point they all stopped to call the cook an old grandfather with more effect, and to argue the matter out. They were eventually persuaded to go on again; but presently a more distinctly retrograde

turn exploded altogether their faith in the guide; they
struck, and putting down the shafts of the rikshas,
refused to proceed further. This was at a village
the name of which we found to be, translated into
English, Brick Kiln Hollow, a name accurately suggestive of unshaded heat. The cook cleared off at once to
see if he could find out where he was, and also, it may
be supposed, to escape the lively and withering sarcasm
of the irate coolies and the more sober, but not less
deep, displeasure of his master. For about an hour we
waited for him there in the sun, the whole village
turning out to do us honour and to inspect. Chinamen
are creatures of large leisure. Let it once get wind
among them that a foreigner is about, and that he is
going to do something, or that he does not know what
to do, or that he is going to remain still long enough to
be looked at, and all the available population will
attend at once, and stand placidly staring for a half-
hour, or an hour if necessary, the front row, perhaps,
squatting on their heels to allow the second row a
better view. During the hour we were waiting for our
lost cook, all domestic, household, and other duties in
Brick Kiln Hollow were deferred. With folded arms,
and solemn intentness, mostly in silence but with an
occasional interchange of comment, the patient villagers
ranked themselves before us like an audience at a
public entertainment. It was a great relief to us when
a man pushed his way through this decorous assembly
and announced himself as one of the boatmen. The
cook after an exhausting exploration, had at length

found the boats, and had sent him to us as our guide. A few minutes took us back to the Bridge of Boats, which we recrossed, and found our craft and our cook at a point close by which we had been a long time before.

Though the native house-boat is not fitted up like a mail steamer, it is not by any means an uncomfortable mode of conveyance, and when we got our bedding laid out on the kangs, or raised platforms, which in native houses and house-boats serve as bedsteads, we lay in peace and coolness that compared favourably with the sun-scorched and Chinaman-criticised rest which we had been involuntarily compelled to take at Brick Kiln Hollow. The Peiho had seemed devious below Tientsin, we had not then seen its reaches above it. At times our boats would be passing up the stream in a line of sails, and across the bank we would see close by another line of sails on the right, perfectly parallel to our line, and across the left bank, yet another parallel line. These were not on other streams, they simply marked our own course that had been, and that was to be. At other times we would see close before us, and at right angles to our course, a line of sails, apparently continuous and yet, though we could with difficulty see where the break occurred, one half of that line was following, and the other half preceding us.

There was little to take note of by the way. The country between Tientsin and Tung-chou is quite flat and the river, notwithstanding its windings, monotonous. An occasional turtle might be seen on the bank; crows, magpies and swallows almost summed up the fauna. Except a colony of herons at one point on the river, where the trees were somewhat larger and served them for a roosting-place, these were nearly all that we saw in the way of animal life. One pair of crows attracted our special notice. They had built among the ornamentation of the mast of a junk, and as the junk was sailing on, one bird sat proudly on her itinerating nest, while the other kept the look-out from a decorative iron arm close by. A dignified self-possession, a sense of proprietorship marked their every movement; they most evidently regarded themselves as in charge and familiar with all that pertains to the management of junks. They therefore showed no surprise when, just as we passed by, their sail was let down with a great rattling of the bamboo ribs. The clatter would have scared any other birds, but if these felt nervous, they were bound not to show it, they had to maintain their dignity as captain and mate—how could it be supposed that they should be startled by the execution of their own order ?

The chief feature of this part of the Peiho, at the season we were upon it, is the multitude of imperial rice junks with square bows, full on the front of which are painted wondrous eyes, the pupil black, the cornea yellow, surmounted by fiery red eyebrows, the rest of the square space liberally treated with blue and green, and red and white according to taste. Of these we were told that there are some two thousand five hundred on the river manned by slaves, and travelling in strings of about fifty, the leading junk bearing a distinctive flag and being preceded by a petty official in a small house-boat. When the trackers pulling the leading junk stop and its anchor is laid out on the bank, the trackers of the next junk draw her up close against the first, the third is drawn up against the second, and so on till the whole of the series have their noses on the bank and a busy village is improvised on shore as in a moment. A cabbage market begins at once, the barbers are busy plying their trade, while the children and puppy-dogs stroll across the plank to enjoy a game with that oriental deliberateness, which is a reliable safeguard against recreation degenerating into labour. The progress of these junks is most leisurely. When they are being pulled, they are pulled slowly enough, and their stoppages are long and frequent, and independent of any apparent cause in wind, current or meteorological condition. Most probably they are purposely delayed on the journey, on account of defective arrangements for unloading at their destination.

The lot of these slaves is pretty easy if ignoble. They have their wives and children on board and generally a couple of pups, with a lark or siskin in a cage, a rooster for a clock, and some little bit of green stuff growing in a flower-pot. Their opportunities of escape are many, in proportion as may be judged to their unwillingness, for probably they consider themselves better off than many of their free brethren. There are, indeed, in China, slaves who are wealthier than their owners. It comes about in this wise. A man finds among his slaves a man of exceptional ability and smartness, of capacity far beyond what is needed for ordinary slave occupations. He will allow such a slave to go into business, stipulating that a determined proportion of his profit comes to him. The slave may thus grow wealthy himself, and at the same time be greatly profitable to his owner. He can buy his liberty of course, but then the price of his liberty would be exceptionally high, corresponding to his exceptional value, so he is content to go on with his owner as partner in a thriving business. The great hardship of slavery in China is the law that no slave can compete in the examinations, nor indeed any free man who cannot show a free parentage for three generations. But this is a disability not confined to slaves. It attaches to others, butchers, prostitutes, and yamen-runners falling, I believe, into the category of those to whose line the anxieties and honours of examination are forbidden till the fourth generation.

At Tung-chou, though perfect strangers, we were hospitably entertained by the missionaries of the American Board of Commissioners for Foreign Missions. They were holding their annual meetings, to which many had come from other stations, and their houses were pretty thoroughly furnished with guests. Nevertheless they would not hear of our proceeding at once to Peking and insisted in putting us up for the night. We were easily persuaded, and it proved a great pleasure to us both to make their acquaintance and to attend the meeting that was held that evening though I, at least, have long since forgotten most that was said in the various speeches made. One statement, far from being the most important, has, however, remained entangled in the meshes of memory. Speaking of the inability which the Chinese seem to have in accepting the idea of a personal and supreme God and Creator, and of their belief in the supremacy of a law originating everything, one of the speakers said : "I had a Confucian teacher a little while ago, and talking with him on this subject, I said, 'Now, if I were to go into the garden and pile up a heap of stones, and then when I had piled them up, were to begin to pour water on them, and you were to come and to ask me what I was doing, and I were to reply that I was looking for a living man to come forth as a result of the action of water on matter, would you not say it could not be so ? ' And the teacher unhesitatingly said, 'But it must have been so in the beginning.'" The willingness of the Confucian teacher to accept such a version of the Chinese cosmogony as a fair one and to abide by it was too striking to be forgotten.

"Thy voice is a complaint, O crownèd city,
The blue sky covering thee like God's great pity."
E. B. Browning.   *The Soul's Travelling.*

"Leaving [Tung-chou] in the afternoon we went alongside, and sometimes upon that famous causeway—famed once for its grandeur and ease, but now a species of terrestrial purgatory, over which ambassadors and tributaries pass on their way to audience with his Celestial Majesty."—Dr. A. Williamson.

"It [Peking] is a city worthy of note on many accounts. Its ancient history as the capital of the *Yeu Kwoh* (the 'Land of Swallows') during the feudal times, and its later position as the metropolis of the empire for many centuries, give it historical importance; while its imperial buildings, its broad avenues with their imposing gates and towers, its regular arrangement, extent, and populousness, and diversity of costume and equipage, combine to render it to a traveller the most interesting and unique city in Asia. It is now ruinous and poor, but the remains of its former grandeur under Kienlung's prosperous reign indicate the justness of the comparisons made by the Catholic writers with Western cities one hundred and eighty years ago."
Dr. S. Wells Williams.   *Middle Kingdom.*

CHAPTER X.

THE CITY OF THE GREAT DUST.

THE block in the traffic at the East Gate at Tung-chou, the gate by which we entered, is chronic. On each of the three or four times that we had occasion to pass through it, we found · it and the street for some little distance on either side filled with carts and barrows, while the carters contentedly—as to the manner born— sat gambling or lay sleeping on the shady side of the street as though they had given up all thought of ever being able to move on. In order to get through we had to thread our way round, and among, and over these vehicles as best we could. Whether they were always the same carts and carters that we saw I dare not affirm. Perhaps not, but they looked the same. As we had impedimenta necessitating our taking mule-carts for the journey to Peking, it was fortunate for us that our route lay in the opposite direction. The Western quarter of Tung-chou offers a contrast to the Eastern. Business is dull ; there seems to be scarcely any traffic in the streets, and quiet inns take the place of thickly-crowded shops. The West Gate is in a picturesque condition of decay, and on the walls the genius of dilapidation holds revel : the once horizontal lines of the bricks run at all angles, and in many places large sheets of masonry are sliding bodily along and away from the earth mass that constitutes the bulk of the wall. Our carts passed through without hindrance, and a little beyond the gate we ventured to get into them.

To our great comfort the weather for some little time had been fine and we were therefore able to travel by what is called the Mud Road, which is not available in wet weather since it then too well deserves its name to be passable. At such times passengers have to follow the Stone Road, which has a more promising name, and is indeed a road of considerable pretensions, but which is never taken by any one who can possibly go by the other, except high mandarins and ambassadors—" thrones, dominations, princedoms, virtues, powers "—in whose case *noblesse oblige.* We had to take it for a short distance, and the sample was sufficient to dispel any desire to test it further. It must have been a magnificent causeway once; this, however, is small comfort to travellers of to-day. Think of an embankment, on the top of which great blocks of stone, from four to fourteen feet long, and about two feet across, are laid in the fashion of the logs on a corduroy road. When these were first laid there they were evidently fitted close together. But constant traffic has worn the stone at the joints that run in the direction of the road, in some cases half way and in other cases the whole way through, until the stones are mostly divided by ditches about a foot deep, and six to nine inches wide. The transverse joints have also been worn but in less degree. In addition to this the stones on the edge of the embankment are disappearing down the slope, some have gone, others lift up one end in sorrowful farewell while the other end points downwards, and every now and again, even in the middle of the road, a vacant and considerable hole now knows its stone no more. It is enough to break the heart of any but a Chinaman to see the poor wretched ponies, mules and donkeys tugging the luggage-carts through all the irregularities of this pavement. The loads are generally such as require three or four beasts to draw them, and, since the road, as I have described it, involves a constant succession of fresh starts, and since the beasts are not usually of equal strength* and do not all start at once, the strain upon them, as the drivers shout and crack their whips at them, is severe beyond the knowledge of any but the beasts themselves.

The condition of the road may perhaps be best realised from the fact that the drivers of the passenger carts, such as we travelled in, will, to avoid a very short distance over the stones, consider it worth while to go down the steep slope of the embankment and travel over the rough field at the side, scrambling up the embankment again when compelled to return to the stones. This relief, however, hardly purchased as it is in any case, is impossible for the loaded luggage-carts, for their centre of gravity is much higher and they cannot venture on inclines. In fact, in the capital itself, where, as in some other towns in the north, flagstones for some inscrutable reason are placed, set on edge, across

---

* I once noticed an ox, a horse, an ass, and a mule attached together to one cart.

the opening of a narrow street into a broad one, and
even across a main street should any narrowing of the
passage afford a favourable opportunity, I saw one of these
top-heavy carts overturned in the middle of the road.
It was too heavy for the mules to drag over the stony
ridge in a straight course, so the driver crossed diagon-
ally, getting first one wheel over and then the other.
By the time the second wheel was on the top of the
stone barrier the balance was lost and the cart capsized.
The shaft mule was kicking in mid-air, and two men,
passengers on the top of the luggage, were flung half-a-
dozen yards into a group of idlers, who suspended their
conversation and turned lazily round to see what
would happen next and how the carter would get
things righted. Not one of them volunteered to help
him. But they were all open to come to any suitable
arrangement whereby, for a consideration, their assistance would be at his service. It will readily be
understood that carts of such unstable equilibrium that
they cannot safely get across what may be called the
legitimate obstacles to be met in the ordinary street
must not risk experiments on steep embankments,
These, therefore, have to keep upon the stone road.
Not only for the alleviation of our own discomfort, but
almost as much perhaps for the avoidance of the sight
of the wretched strugglings of which it is the scene, we
were glad enough when we left it a little outside the
gate of Tung-chou, close by the Palikao Bridge.

But even on the mud road, a passenger unaccustomed
to the luxury of mule-cart riding is not soothed to

sleep. A mule-cart is a notable vehicle. Being a passenger conveyance it is nicely polished, its windows are of silk gauze, and its wheels are decorated with metal bosses. But it is strong enough to go upon the roads of the country and has no springs. The accommodation it affords is all above the axle and (unless the passenger sits outside on the shaft, as carters do in England, a mode which is not considered the thing, and which has inconveniences beside that of sacrificing one's dignity) he has to sit tailor-fashion inside. This puts the uninitiated in a more helpless condition than would be imagined by those who have not tried it, making the two sides of the cart into battledores and the passenger's head a shuttlecock, and a pretty lively game is played. Practice may doubtless enable a man to ride upon the storm that prevails inside a mule-cart on a rough road. I speak only of the unpractised for whom I would advocate the padding of the cart's sides, not forgetting the top. Some foreigners in Tientsin, I noticed, had private carts made with a little well into which to drop the feet. This adds wonderfully to the strength of one's defence. May the fashion take !

The massive wall of Peking was a welcome sight, though as we neared it the roads became worse and worse. I remember just the turn in the road where it came into view. The spot was fixed upon mind and memory by a severe jolt, in the course of which both sides of my head got into collision with the cart and I settled at last, to its no small detriment, on the top of my pith helmet, which was wandering aimlessly about.

By a comparatively insignificant gate we entered the Chinese, or Outer City, and found a broad border of open ground running along inside the wall—a political precaution, I was led to understand, to secure the wall from harm. Along this open space we jolted our spring-less way until we came to the Ha-ta-men, a double gateway through the main and enceinte walls of the Tartar or Inner City. The walls of this city are much higher and more massive than those of the other, and the gateways which pierce them are quite respectable tunnels. When we got here we realised that we were in the city of the great dust. We had found something of this as we came along the open space under the wall of the outer city. The numerous carts going and coming were rather indicated by travelling clouds than clearly seen. But when we got to the Ha-ta-men, a gust of wind rushed through, fortunately for us from behind, and, in a moment, a dense black cloud completely blotted from sight men, mules, carts and camels, of which a mingled crowd were entering from the other side. It was neither a vicious nor an unusual storm, it was simply a frolic of the wind such as we soon saw repeated, but it was our first introduction—our reception at the Tartar city's gate, and therefore unlikely to lose its specially appropriated niche in the memory. The dust is a thing of mark in Peking—a palpable nuisance to the new arrival who experiences from it undoubted inconvenience and knows no more, but, according to some who are better versed in the mysteries, the salvation of the city's life and health. Except

during the wet season, when all is mud and the carts
that go about the streets charge double fares, the city is
enswathed in dust. It covers everything and everybody, within and without, epidermis and epithelium.
The rule that the streets in a Chinese city should be
narrow is so almost universal that the exceptions are
the more striking and noticeable. Nearly every one
must have heard that the streets in Peking are wide, an
undoubted fact, but one to which attention would not
have been so repeatedly called were it not the case that,
with this exception and that of Moukden in Manchuria
and I believe another city somewhere in the west, all
the cities of the empire are content with streets across
which opposite neighbours could shake hands were
handshaking a custom of the land. The road proper is
not wide even in Peking. It consists of a raised portion
running down the middle about wide enough to allow
of two mule-carts passing. The open lower space of
either side of this is also used for traffic in the less busy
parts, but in the principal streets it is taken up by
booths and stalls of trinket-sellers and dealers in eels
and snails, of story-reciters and cloth-merchants, who,
under ordinary circumstances, do a thriving business un-
molested, although they are liable to a summary notice
to quit should the emperor announce that in some
weeks time he will pass down the street. Carts stand
for hire here, while at convenient intervals are openings
into the great stagnant sewers, with the liquid contents
of which the enlightened authorities water the raised
roads, while with what dries and hardens they macad-

amise them. That dust should abound and be black
follows as a matter of course. Disgusting as this dust
is, the practices of the people are so much more so that
they turn the curse into a blessing. A medical friend,
resident in the place long enough to have observed and
not too long to be open to impressions, assured me that
were it not for the dust always in the air ready to settle
on, cover up, and in a measure disinfect the abomina-
tions of the place, the whole population would be
carried off by some epidemic in about a month. As it
is, the place has the credit for being healthy. An older
resident adduced its health as a reason for accepting
very cautiously the dogmas of doctrinaire hygienists.
He argued that, if what they are always so loudly
insisting on about personal cleanliness and drainage and
sanitary precautions in household arrangements were
true, Peking would be an impossibility; and came to
the sage conclusion: " We "—by which he meant they—
" do not know everything yet."

The architecture of the capital is disappointing.
There is indeed much delicacy of detail in the wood-
work, and considerable taste in the colouring and gilding
which many of the tradesmen lavish on their shop-
fronts, but this loses a good deal of its effect in a very
short time from the action of the ubiquitous dust. In
general design the Chinese do not seem to have got
beyond their early nomadic ancestry. The great temple
of Confucius, the lamasary near it at the north-east
corner of the city, an establishment in which are over
a thousand monks, even the series of imperial buildings

are little more than various reproductions of the tent. The consequence is a great sameness and monotony in the view as one looks over the city from the top of the high walls that surround it. The gateways are the most prominent features, but they share the same design and beside them, the Bell and Drum towers, a pagoda, and the blue roofs of the Temple of Prayer for the Year, which stands to the north of the Altar of Heaven, there are few things that rise above the level of the tree-tops. The views obtained in the streets are often picturesque enough. There is a rich profusion of contrasts, not to say incongruities. The raggedest booths hide the wealthiest shops. Some of the pailos, or archways, rejoice in the freshest of paint, others are venerable to a degree in which they have lost all trace of colour and so large a proportion of what goes to make them pailos that they are little else than a collection of forlorn poles. Before the shops are all manners of signs in all conditions, new posts and rotten ones, bright flaming rags, and rags whose original tint is problematic, while on the shop-fronts themselves are to be seen carvings elaborate, and of intricate and changeful patterns, with varying degrees of colour, from the brightest vermilion and blue and gold on the newly decorated, to the dingy greys on those which it is time to embellish again. From the Marble Bridge broader views may be obtained, which are really pretty without depending for their interest, as do the street-scenes, on quaint and grotesque detail, views in which figure the walls, gateways and guard-houses of the palace, its moat of shallow water, where graceful herons wade among the water plants, and the Tibetan dagoba crowning the neighbouring hill.

The Confucian temple is of its sort a fine building. It consists of a large oblong hall, forty or fifty feet high, shrouded in dust from top to bottom. Between the timbers of the roof are painted canvases, many of which, at the time of our visit, were hanging suspended by a few persistent threads while some were already on the floor. The lacquer covering of the huge pillars that support the roof gave evidence of the many changing seasons it had seen ; in fact there was a mild flavour of decay about the whole place which harmonised well with the aspect of the venerable old cypresses in the courtyard, under which we had walked to reach it.

In the central place of honour stands the tablet of the great sage, inscribed in Chinese and Manchu characters : "The Tablet of the Soul of the Most Holy Ancestral Teacher, Confucius." Round the walls overhead are nine or ten larger inscriptions telling forth his praise ; one, for instance, affirms him to be the fulness of all sagely excellence, and another that since the birth of mankind there has never been his equal. A third reads : "The truth is here"; while yet another ventures the bold assertion : "His virtue fills the whole earth." On either side of the tablet of Confucius are those of Tseng-tsi, Mencius, Yen-hwuy and Tze-sze—four of his chief disciples—and, in more reverent and distant attendance in the background, are those of a dozen more.

Under the gateway of the courtyard of this temple

stand the ten granite drums, said by some to be two thousand five hundred years old, covered with inscriptions cut in the seal character where the decay of the surface has not removed them. Strictly speaking, there are only nine drums and a half, and for many years there were only nine, one having been lost by some mischance, until, in a farmstead at Kai-fung-fu in Honan, a large stone horse-trough was found, bearing a number of characters, by which it was identified as the hollowed out half of the long-lost stone drum. It was brought back to its place and stands with its fellows to this day. Ten new marble drums of a most approved modern pattern, were placed on the south side of this same gateway by the order of the emperor, Kien-lung, to preserve on their sides the memory of the inscriptions which the old drums are shedding. As however they have little age and no historic interest, and cannot be used for the purposes which their name and shape indicate, it is a little difficult to stir up much enthusiasm concerning them.

Close by the temple of Confucius is the National College, or Hall of the Classics, a small building surrounded by a pond, across which, from each of its four sides, radiates a bridge. The sides of the pond and the bridges being all of white marble, the effect is very pleasing. There are indications that this edifice once blazed in gold and colour, but the glory has departed. Inside it, in the centre, is a raised seat, and hither the emperor is supposed to come periodically and, from this throne, to expound the classics to his officers standing reverently round him. Of late years this imperial exposition has been dispensed with, owing, among other things, to the minority of the emperors. Surrounding the courtyard, in which this Hall of the Classics stands, are cloisters or sheds, under which are two or three hundred huge stone slabs like the headstones of graves, rank behind rank. On these was engraved the whole of the classics to provide an authoritative edition, but the weathering of the stone is largely removing the characters and, if an authorised version be still accounted a necessity, some other method of providing and preserving it will have to be adopted. Wherever in China an inscription becomes celebrated, devotees and enthusiasts come and take rubbings of it. As a consequence, nearly all the famous engraved stones and tablets in the land are disfigured and blackened. The granite drums, referred to just now, have been made to look like ebony. Some enterprising publisher, awake to the necessity of advertising, has put a notice in the Hall of the Classics to the effect that it is unnecessary for scholars to take rubbings of these stones since complete copies can be obtained at his publishing house.

In the same yard, just opposite the Hall, is a rather handsome pailo, the arches being bordered with white marble and the rest of the face being chiefly worked in green and yellow porcelain tiles, though a blank space in the most prominent part is of plain stucco. Dr. S. Wells Williams, in his *Middle Kingdom*, speaks of this as " one of the most artistic objects in China."

Not on account of its architectural merits but on account of its history, I found a little church of the London Missionary Society one of the most interesting of the buildings of the city. It was originally a temple of the god of fire, and, though the idol and altar have been of course removed, no changes have been wrought in the arrangement of the building—even the twin poles that mark the entrance to a temple still stand—so that, as you go from the street through the tablet hall, where once those who thought their prayers to the fire-god answered hung their tablets of commemoration, and through the little courtyard into the main building, you naturally expect to be confronted by a hideous idol, instead of which there stands before you an unpretending pulpit or desk, while, along the walls, where attendants had been imaged, hang copies in Chinese of the Beatitudes, the Lord's Prayer, the Apostles' Creed, and the Ten Commandments. The natives refer to the change tersely in four characters: "Gods out, devils in." Such a transfer would probably be impossible to-day. The feeling of the Chinese towards the foreigner has not changed for the better lately, and now if any one in time of adversity felt inclined to sell to foreigners a temple built in palmier days he would find heavy pressure put upon him by the officials. It is quite easy for these gentry to forbid and prevent perfectly legitimate acts, the legitimacy and even desirability of which they are loud in affirming. For example, a man at Hang-chow was bold enough to sell a piece of ground to a foreign missionary against the wish of the local mandarin. He very soon found himself in prison—of course without any reference to the sale of the land— and he did not get out till he had been squeezed of more than he had realised by the sale of his property. That man concluded that it might be lawful but was not expedient to sell to foreigners in the face of official displeasure.

The unused Observatory is a monument of the past. A solid tower, about fifty feet high, and so somewhat overlooking the city-wall against which it is built, dates back to the year 1296, when the Mongol Kublai Khan ruled in Peking, or Khan-baligh as it was called in those days. This tower was first occupied by the bronze instruments which are now in the courtyard at the foot of it, their place above being taken in the seventeenth century by the instruments still to be seen there, which were made by the Jesuit, Ferdinando Verbiest, at the order of the emperor Kang-hi. Of such excellent workmanship are they that they have lost little of the keenness of edge and definiteness of design either in the instruments proper or in the ornamental supports, and it seems impossible to believe that they are the handiwork of a man who died so long ago as 1688. But the same is true even of the older pieces now down below, to which Byron might have said, as to the ocean :

"Time writes no wrinkle on thine azure brow."

In a building just behind these is a clepsydra, con- sisting of five copper cisterns arranged one over the other, which, notwithstanding the invention of clocks and watches, is still used to mark the time. It has an advantage over that I saw at Canton in the number of the cisterns, the Southern one having only four, and also, I believe, in the matter of capacity, the water having to be returned to the upper cistern twice in every twenty-four hours in the Canton clepsydra, and only once, as I understood, in that at Peking.

From copper cisterns the transition is natural to copper cash. It is impossible to speak of all the objects in and about Peking that are worthy of notice. The city is full of much that is interesting if of little that is admirable. But my pen would fail in the task, more-over, are they not all written in the books of the travellers? But the efforts I had to put forth to master the mysteries of the Northern coinage and currency—I never having been good at arithmetic—compel me to put on record what I think I found out about it before closing this chapter. It had always seemed to me that we were sufficiently confused in Shanghai by our taels and Mexican dollars, and Japanese cents and Chinese cash, with their ever-varying relations. But we did at least call things as we professed to find them. There were no obviously fictitious values. When we got to Tientsin, however, we found a change. Returning from a riksha ride in the settlement, I said to my friend, " Would you kindly tell the boy to pay the coolie three hundred cash "—for where one has to do with the clumsy, multitudinous and dirty cash one naturally makes the boy paymaster.

My friend said he thought from the time I had been out that the coolie deserved a little more. "All right, let him have more." Some time after when I met my friend again, he asked, "When you said three hundred cash this morning, how many did you mean?" "Why three hundred of course, how many should I mean?" It then came out that in Tientsin they have a large way of saying double of what they mean, and that my order of three hundred meant the poor coolie's receiving one hundred and fifty. No wonder my friend had suggested an increase. So I discovered that one hundred meant fifty, and two hundred meant one hundred, twenty meant ten, and forty twenty. These copper cash are strung together on a string running through the square hole in the centre of them. Each string is called a tiao, which means a thousand, and has on it five hundred coins divided into hundreds by knots in the string; that is, it would have on it five hundred but for the further complication of the string itself being counted, and so between each knot are ninety-nine coins, plus a piece of string. Therefore a tiao, or thousand, really comprises four hundred and ninety-five coins and a piece of knotted string. By the time I was ready to start for Peking, I was getting familiar with this exaggerative mode of reckoning four hundred and ninety-five as a thousand, and proposed before setting out, to get some dollars changed to provide myself with cash for the payment of small sums. Then I was told that in Peking they used a different coin altogether. These little perforated coins which are used in the South where twenty are twenty, and are used in Tientsin where ten are twenty, are not used at all in the capital, howbeit they are the legal tender of the empire. There we found cash of monstrous size. The town cash are of much greater weight than their poor relations and country cousins; and their greater importance justifies them in dealing yet more recklessly with a poor stranger's ideas of arithmetical nomenclature. Outside Peking you have learned to call a string of four hundred and ninety-five cash a tiao—a thousand. You pass within the walls, the cash are more than double the size, and a string of them is six tiao—six thousand—a tiao between each knot in the string. You count a tiao, but, instead of finding one thousand, or even five hundred, i.e., four hundred and ninety-nine plus the string, you find fifty or rather forty-nine, for the string still figures. I was wanting to go up on the city wall one afternoon, so at tiffin I told my host, whom I knew to be too busy to go with me, what I intended and asked the best way up. Among his instructions was: "Take five hundred cash to tip the gateman at the bottom of the slope." I thought of the huge Peking cash, and, knowing that I had no stitching about me that would stand the strain of five hundred of them, felt that I had not yet grasped the instruction. It could not be five hundred, that I knew, but how many was it? To elicit explanation I asked my friend if he would lend me his coolie to carry it along for me. He looked at me with astonishment, and I found at last that five hundred meant twenty-five. Each cash bears the number, Ten, upon it, and presumably represents ten of some now disûsed iron coins. This ten being multiplied by two, as in Tientsin, gives the twenty, by which in Peking it is necessary to multiply the actual to arrive at the nominal value. Should a person wish it to be understood that he means what he says, he uses the word equivalent to "big," or "great." This, as it were, puts him on his oath and compels accuracy. "Twenty big cash," would mean twenty; and, to simplify the nomenclature, it seems that this mode of speaking is adopted for low numbers. One is spoken of as one big (cash); two as two big; three as three big; and four as four big; but five is spoken of as one hundred; six as one hundred and twenty, and so on. Whatever other exceptions a•longer stay might have revealed I know not. Just as I had learned to divide by twenty with a fair amount of freedom, I left the only place, as I trust, where the art is of any service.

x

> "Priests, tapers, temples, swim before my sight."
>
> POPE. *Eloïsa and Abelard.*

>   "At such a time,
> Between the hot walls of a nullah, stretched
> On naked stones, our lord spied, as he passed,
> A starving tigress. Hunger in her orbs
> Glared with green flame; her dry tongue lolled a span
> Beyond the gasping jaws and shrivelled jowl;
> Her painted hide hung wrinkled on her ribs,
> As when between the rafters sinks the thatch
> Rotten with rains; and at the poor lean dugs
> Two cubs, whining with famine, tugged and sucked,
> Mumbling those milkless teats that rendered nought,
> While she, their gaunt dam, licked full motherly
> The clamorous twins, yielding her flank to them
> With moaning throat, and love stronger than want
> Softening the first of that wild cry wherewith
> She laid her famished muzzle to the sand
> And roared a savage thunder-peal of woe.
> Seeing which bitter strait, and heeding nought
> Save the immense compassion of a Buddh,
> Our lord bethought, 'There is no other way
> To help this murderess of the woods but one.
> By sunset these will die having no meat;
> There is no living heart will pity her,
> Bloody with ravin, lean for lack of blood.
> Lo! if I feed her, who shall lose but I,
> And how can love lose—doing of its kind
> Even to the uttermost?'"

> SIR E. ARNOLD. *Light of Asia.*

Clown. What is the opinion of Pythagoras concerning wild fowl?

Malvolio. That the soul of our grandam might haply inhabit a ' bird.

Clown. What thinkest thou of his opinion?

Malvolio. I think nobly of the soul, and no way approve his opinion.—SHAKSPERE. *Twelfth Night.*

CHAPTER XI.

THE CITY OF THE WHITE ELEPHANT.

BANGKOK is somewhat out of the world. Though it stands on the banks of a deep river—the Meinam—no vessels save those of the lightest draught are seen alongside its wharves. All others are prevented from entering the river by a deposit at its mouth.

This, of course, could be easily dredged were the Siamese government inclined to dredge it, which it is not. It has taken to heart what it has seen of the dealings of European nations with its neighbours, and has learned suspicion. It cherishes towards this bar feelings akin to those with which the Chinese authorities regard the "heaven-sent barrier" at Wusung. It relies for protection from hostile invasion on this fluvial deposit and, to make assurance doubly sure, has sunk some stone-laden junks in the channel behind it. In former days its confidence in this obstruction was perhaps as just as it was natural. Now, however, the conditions are changed. France has annexed Tongking and become neighbour to Siam on the one side, and Britain has annexed Burmah and become her neighbour on the other, so that the kingdom of the White Elephant has probably more occasion to anticipate evil from the mutual suspicions of these two powerful friends than from aught else. A bar therefore at the entrance of the river in the south—even if supported by a couple of gunless forts—is a somewhat inadequate safeguard against the march of powers which, if they come at all, will probably enter from the north-east or the north-west.

Still the refusal to dredge the bar outside, the maintenance of forts and the sinking of junks at the mouth of the river, the building of the fort and erection of the watchstaff at Paknam within—all have conduced to the people's sense of security and to their confidence in the forethought and ability of the royal house and the government, which, even if misplaced, are in the meantime worth something. That a channel will some day be opened so that vessels of deep draught may enter the port is not to be doubted, but this is not likely to be speedily realised. Now that the vested interests of a number of European merchants are involved in the present condition of things, these will be found more difficult to deal with than the original Siamese idea of the political value of the bar. For example, because steamers have to lie outside to receive either the whole or part of their freight, a goodly fleet of large and strong lighters, capable not only of coming down the river but of crossing twenty miles of open sea to Koh-Si-Chang, which is the steamers' anchorage during a good portion of the year, has been launched at considerable outlay ; all of which lighters would be worth their weight in firewood on the day when the bar is removed. In the owners of these, Siam has disinterested foreign advisers, who are not to be expected very earnestly to urge such a step, and for a long time, therefore, the trade of Bangkok—capital city of a kingdom though it be—may have to be developed by coasting steamers of the smallest class.

These, however, are considerations of more interest to the mariner and merchant than to the ordinary traveller. To him Koh-Si-Chang is one of a picturesque group of islands. Even when the anchor is rattling down, he thinks less of the fathoms of water beneath the keel than of the trees that crown the heights and grasp with firm roots the precipitous sides of the hills, and of the huts that here and there peep out from among the foliage along the shore, from which the primitive inhabitants venture forth in their equally primitive canoes. And as for the distance from the city and all its consequences of delay and expense in the landing of the steamers, he would not, at any rate for himself and on his first trip, wish it less. He leaves his vessel to the din of the steam-winches and starts off in some smaller and slower craft. First Koh-Si-Chang is left behind, and by-and-by the lighthouse at the bar standing knee-deep in an expanse of shallow water, and at last he enters the river. As his eye rests on the deep rich green that shuts it in on either hand, he feels that he would not care if he had twice as far to glide between such banks ere he should reach his journey's end at

Bangkok. It is true that there is nothing to be seen beyond the immediate shore, the distance is shut out by the foreground; but the cocoanut and atap palms, together with all manner of other trees and shrubs, which constitute this foreground, satisfy the eye so fully that it seeks for no beyond. These stemless ataps springing up thickly side by side completely hide the ground with their spreading leaves. The natives use these for thatching, not however without labour, for, although nature seems to have provided them in a form almost identical with that in which they are at last used, the pinnæ are first stripped off the stalk and then sewn together again in short comb-like lengths, which are laid on the roofs overlapping each other, as we place tiles or slates.

They are said to form very strong roofs, effective alike against sun and rain. Standing out in front of the dark green of their still living and growing kindred, covering the huts that are built upon piles over the water, or that are floating on rafts upon it, and still more when partially revealed among the foliage, they add much to the charm and brightness of the scene, as do also the numerous little canoes gliding swiftly along the water, breaking for a moment the reflected inversion of huts and trees with a cheery ripple. At one particular point, just when we passed to leeward of the spot to which deceased elephants are towed down from the city for the greater convenience of the vultures, we felt in a little greater hurry and propounded to ourselves a problem in proportion, asking if " dead flies cause the ointment of the apothecary to send forth a stinking savour," as the writer of Ecclesiastes affirmed, what will dead elephants do? But this was a passing experience merely. It was pungent but it was brief, and, with this exception, the whole of the winding length of the Meinam below Bangkok—thirty miles—was pleasantly and, as it seemed to us, almost too quickly passed. Long before we were tired we found ourselves passing the rice-mills and salt-sheds, and, steaming in among the shipping, we anchored at the " Venice of the East."

Our visit was short, shorter than we could have wished and therefore necessarily hurried, but, thanks to the friendly guidance of a gentleman familiar with the place, we saw, probably, as much as could be seen in the time, certainly sufficient to amply repay us for our toil. To do this, however, although almost every point of interest may be reached by boat, we had to take a gari, as being a somewhat quicker if rougher and more tiring mode of getting about. The roads were fairly good—for an eastern city, very good—but the particular Jehu, of whose services we availed ourselves in our first expedition, spared neither his ponies nor his passengers, and the tops of our heads were every now and again testing the roof of the gari. The Venetian character of the place involves the necessity of carrying the roads over the canals by a multitude of bridges which are short and sharp. Up one steep incline and down the other our coachman would make his little ponies tear in the most reckless way, while along the level stretches between he evidently considered that the safety of the foot passengers that swarm the roads would be far better studied if each cared for himself, than if he were to assume the responsibility of caring for them. He, therefore, rattled on unconcernedly, and got us from place to place safely, swiftly and, happily, without injury to our fellow-men.

While we were waiting for this gari to be got ready, our eyes being open to new sights and our minds sensitive to new impressions, we preferred strolling along the road to sitting within the house. As we thus loitered and talked with each other, we heard a distant sound of shouting, and presently saw the approach of a dense cloud of dust, out of which soon emerged a loudly clamorous throng evidently in a high state of excitement. Under an ornate but very tinselly and shaky canopy, placed upon a sledge which was being dragged along the road, stood, thanks to the support of cords and kindly hands, a gilded Buddha, not of the comfortable portliness of the Future or Laughing Buddha as he is conventionally represented with exaggerated and untrammelled abdominal development, nor of the serene gravity and meditative expression, also familiar to frequenters of Buddhist temples, nor graceful—only lank and expressionless. Two ropes were attached to the sledge and grasped eagerly by a mixed multitude of men, women and children, while a venerable-looking old gentleman, standing beside his godship, gave them instructions when to go on and when to stop. The enthusiasm was great and the expression of it pro-

portionately loud, not unassisted by gongs and drums
and other instruments of noise. It proved to be a
newly-made image which was thus being escorted with
great rejoicing to its temple, and all who had contributed
anything towards the making were entitled to share in
the privilege of dragging it along. Our thoughts went
back to Serampore. It was, on a small scale indeed, a
reminiscence of Jagannath. Nor is this surprising
when we remember that many whose right to have an
opinion is unquestioned, see in the Jagannath festivals
a survival of the Buddhist. cult. So interested did we
become in this procession that, long before it had
passed by, the gari for which we·had waited was waiting
for us.

The best place at which to begin sight-seeing in
Bangkok is doubtless Wat-Si-Ket, and thither we drove
first. A wat is a temple or religious-house, and
generally in the compound of such a wat, beside the
large building containing the idol before which the
devotees worship, are a number of other buildings
terminating in graceful spires, in form not unlike the
pagodas of Burmah or the dagobas of Ceylon, many of
them covered with a rough mosaic of coloured glazed
tiling, giving them an exceedingly beautiful appearance. In the palace grounds stands one which is richly
covered with gold leaf sent from England. One of the
buildings of Wat-Si-Ket is set on a little conical hill,
so that from it a general introduction to the whole city
may be obtained before the places of special interest
are visited and studied in detail. It is built four-

square, and has windows on all sides. North and south, east and west, you may look and, if the day be fine, may get a splendid view of the city lying at your feet, and of the country stretching far beyond. The scene is charming. The sombre thatched roofs are set in the varied green of the gardens and laced with the sheen of the river and innumerable canals, while the royal palaces and public offices, the graceful spires and lofty roofs of the wats glittering in the sun, give a beauty to the prospect which is all the more striking if, as was the case with us, you come to it fresh from familiarity with the monotonous level of the architecture of Chinese cities.

We stood and gazed with delight, and while we gazed there passed over our heads a line of vultures on outspread wings. One of them left his place, and, sweeping through ever-narrowing circles, descended earthward, passing almost, as it seemed, within reach of us, drawing our eyes after him to a small dome just below on which and on an adjacent tree some dozen or more of his kind were congregated. What is the attraction of this place that, among other apparently as available roofs, it alone is chosen for this sleepy parliament of carrion birds? So we queried, and our friend said "I will take you there and show you when we go down;" and he took us.

We passed through a narrow doorway just inside of which sat and begged an old man—I was going to say, on the verge of the grave, but what we saw just after would suggest a doubt as to the appropriateness of the phrase. Under a roof beyond him was a boy-priest reciting Buddhist scriptures to a number of men and women patiently listening though what he was reciting was in a language unintelligible alike to them and to him. Near by under another roof was a raised platform on which the bodies of deceased persons of wealth and consideration were burned with becoming ceremony. But the vulture cared for none of these things. Passing through another door, however, we apprehended the explanation by more than one sense. Here was the yard on which the bird's eye rested or of which he dreamed as he slept. On a shelf on one side were a number of clean-picked human skulls stacked in something like orderly array, while on the ground in front were skeletons and bones piled up in a horribly promiscuous heap. On the other side of the yard were thrown together all the rough boxes in which the dead bodies had been brought. These were the relics of the poor who could not afford the luxury of cremation. The only rites here witnessed are the casting of the corpses to the attendant vultures to whose efficient undertakership the matter is trustfully left. Each bird tears away his share and adjourns with it to a neigh-bouring tree or roof, and before all have participated in the sepultural ceremony the bones have been picked clean enough to satisfy the most exacting requirements of Bangkok's sanitary officials.

Putting the protest of sentiment aside and having regard merely to the interest of survivors, it must be admitted that the digestion of a corpse in the body of a living organism is a process safer for the said survivors than its decay in the earth on which they still walk. But the method strikes a stranger, well—as summary. It is doubtless otherwise with those to the manner born. Siamese sentiment does not in this matter sympathise with ours, and good Buddhists, believing in the sacredness of all life, and further, in the possibility of their grandfathers and grandmothers, their uncles and aunts, being incarnate in these hungry vultures, not unfrequently leave it in their wills that on their decease their bodies, for which they will then have no further use, shall be devoted to these fallen kindred, these poor relations. And so with all ceremony and respect, sorrowing friends bear their bodies to this spot and reverently watch the useful toil of the carrion bird; or, since in this case the disposal of the body is esteemed a work of merit, they assist in it themselves meritoriously taking a knife and slicing off tit-bits for any weaker vulture that may seem in danger of being crowded out of the solemn ceremony, or for the dogs which are also in hungry and hopeful attendance. When the casting to the birds is determined by piety rather than poverty, the dry bones are collected after the vultures have finished with them and are burned instead of being allowed to rot on the common heap.

From this place we went to the king's palace, not far from which a temporary pramene or crematorium was being erected for the burning of a deceased member of the royal house. When a king or queen, a royal prince or princess dies, a great wooden temple-

like building, called a pramene, is erected, the wood of
which is provided from all the provinces of the kingdom.
In the centre is a raised platform on which the royal
corpse is burned. These buildings are made glorious
with gildings and illuminations, and are used but once,
each member of the royal house being honoured with a
new one. Nor may the timber, on its being pulled
down, be utilised for any secular or mean object; it is
generally devoted to the construction of a wat or to
some similarly sacred service. And thus in our minds
the poor age-stricken beggar whom we had left with
his prospective undertakers dozing over his head and
His Supreme Majesty the King were associated together
in the frailty and fate of their common humanity. The
royal and special pramene was doubtless as imposing as
the public one was filthy and disgusting, but the uses
were the same, and we thought of Hamlet's words:—
"Your fat king and your lean beggar is but variable
service, two dishes, but to one table : that's the end."

Near the palace are the royal stables and the
elephant sheds, where the common herd stand in a
row under a common roof and the white elephants, as
becomes their sacred character and royal title, enjoy
separate apartments. At the time of our visit there
were two of these exalted pachyderms. One of them
was certainly as fine an animal as a man need wish
to see—an immense creature, in good condition, with
a noble head and bearing. He had mighty tusks
curved upward with a bold and graceful sweep. As to
his whiteness, he was white but relatively. The other,

also of a whiteness relative rather than absolute, was evidently an aged animal and, though not without a certain dignity, bore the responsibility of state with a careworn look. His tusks were simply enormous but were without grace of curve—mere prolongations of ivory. Like the other, he stood on a small platform raised some nine inches or a foot, and his tusks reached to the ground in front of this platform. How much farther their natural termination would have been I do not know, for the ends were truncated, the taper points having been either intentionally sawn off for the animal's convenience, or worn down by friction at the level of the ground.

From the elephant sheds we went to several wats, in one of which, much to our astonishment and amusement we found among the attendant disciples of Buddha a couple of painted plaster casts of the first Napoleon. These had most likely been purchased at the auction of a foreign merchant by some devout Siamese, who, by placing the European soldier in the train of the Asiatic teacher, thought to make the West pay homage to the East. In another wat, Wat-Poh, is an image of Buddha in the recumbent attitude which represents him dying and attaining Nirvana. This is one hundred and sixty-five feet long, and is said to be the largest image under cover in the world. It is made of brickwork, coated first with cement and then with a finer plaster to receive the lacquer and gold-leaf with which it is, or once was, completely covered. Upon the soles of the bare feet, which are perfectly flat, are inlaid beautiful little pictures in mother of pearl, which one admires, at the same time wondering how the sage could have remained quiet under the necessary tickling by the artist's toil. In this compound, a rather extensive one, we were about to pass through a gateway when our priestly guide was courteously asked by some one coming from the opposite direction whether we would not wait a moment. Though not knowing the reason of the request, we of course yielded the way, and forthwith there passed through a number of Siamese ladies followed by men carrying children and a string of young men and maidens each carrying some small article—a fan, a spittoon, or an umbrella. These proved to be some of the king's wives, children and attendants taking an afternoon stroll. The present king makes it his boast that he contents himself with a less number of wives than any of his predecessors. Sometime ago, when he had only about thirty, he was reported to have said that he really did not care to take any more. But occasionally reasons must be found of force sufficient to compel the admission of others, for, as I understand, the number is gradually increasing. Considering the style in which each member of the royal family is expected to live, the maintenance of so large a luxury must be a considerable burden on the poor Siamese taxpayer.

Leaving our gari we took a boat to the opposite side of the river to visit Wat-Chang the highest of the wats of Bangkok. This, instead of terminating in the ordinary graceful needle-like form, has a blunted finger-shaped

spire, which though not without grace, compares unfavourably with the more usual type. By a flight of
steep steps one may climb nearly half-way up the face
of it, whence a good view of the country is to be obtained,
though less extensive than that from the hill-throned
Wat-Si-Ket. The whole surface is covered with varied
designs and patterns, wrought in many-coloured glazed
tiles, most of which are not larger than a finger-nail:
and to the multitudinous detail of colour corresponds
an equally multitudinous detail of outline. In both
perhaps the detail has been somewhat overdone to the
loss of effects that would have been attained by a
bolder and broader style. Nevertheless, the effect is
very pleasing, and when on high days and holidays
every point which it is possible to reach by steps or
ladders bears its little lamp, the sight must be beautiful
indeed. We were told that to increase this beauty,
prisoners under sentence of death were graciously
allowed the chance of redeeming their lives by climbing
and placing lamps upon points which ordinary people
considered inaccessible. As one looked at the places
indicated it seemed a barbarously cruel clemency that
offered pardon on such conditions.

Taking our boat from Wat-Chang we bade our
venerable oarswoman steer down the stream, past the
floating houses moored along the banks, many of which
were quite imposing stores filled with European goods,
to another wat that is owned and largely patronised by
the Chinese who, in this capital of the kingdom, rival
if they do not exceed in number the Siamese them-

selves. Here is a huge Buddha, the largest sitting image under cover in the country. We found it an interesting place; still we were conscious of getting just a little tired of wats which, though they have some distinctive features, seem to have much more in common. But a little incident that occurred as we were drawing up to the river steps of this temple struck us forcibly and pleasingly as an illustration of the natural courtesy and the desire to put others at their ease, even when one is placed in an awkward predicament, that we would gladly see yet more of. I may be judging too favourably, but I hope and think not. Just in front of us as we were heading for the steps was a young woman paddling a canoe. All at once, in an apparently most uncalled for manner, she upset her little craft and precipitated herself into the water. We asked her why she did it? She replied that she wanted to take a bath. As her mats and other goods that would scarcely be improved by a soaking, were floating in the water beside her, we ventured to express scepticism as to her intention, on which she admitted that she had been a little startled at suddenly catching sight of foreigners and had lost her balance—a proceeding not calculated for in the construction of Bangkok canoes. "But it does not matter at all," said she, in response to our expressions and looks of regret, "since I am in the water, I will take a bath and so all will be well."

It was graciously said, and proclaimed her one of Nature's true gentlewomen, who—fair be they or tawny—sweeten the life and soften the manners of our humanity, preserving for high and worthy use that very term, which else might be in danger of degradation into a synonym for selfish thought and base behaviour. Long since hast thou righted thy canoe, my Siamese sister, and pursued thy journey, forgetting, it may be, in the daily routine of a toilsome life, the pale-faced foreigners' intrusion among thy native streams, but the pleasant memory of thee has crossed the weary waste of the "black water" and lives on these Western shores of which perchance thou hast never heard.

> "God's benison go with you; and with those
> That would make good of bad, and friends of foes."

LONDON: PRINTED BY WM. CLOWES AND SONS, LIMITED,
STAMFORD STREET AND CHARING CROSS.